"The Towers of Power"

A supernatural thriller based on the biblical war between Good and Evil!

Tome one: The Antichrist's Scrolls 1-8

The team...

Edited by Keidi Keating
Front Cover — M. Waqas
Illustrations — Bobbi-Lee Hunt
      Joseph Mueller
      Michael Smith
      Charles W. Staunton
Formatting / Design - Charles W. Staunton
Website — Charleswstaunton.com
Edition — Fifth
Story Creation Date - 1980
Copyright © 2009 by Charles W. Staunton
Library of Congress Number -TXu001780994

The Towers of Power is a hybrid, written
as a novel...with a graphic novel spiciness.
All resemblance to any persons, living or
alive is entirely coincidental.
No part of this book or any of its contents
may be copied, reproduced, modified, or
adapted to any means without the written
consent from the author.
All rights reserved.

The Towers of Power is available in...

Paperback

Hardcover

eBook / color

Audio

The narrated audio was created inside a professional studio. It features, epic soundtracks and amazing special effects.

This book is available in many countries, and on thousands of popular, online platforms.

Please visit us at – **CHARLESWSTAUNTON.COM**

"Red Dragon Series"

1st Scroll
SCOTT MILLER

2nd Scroll
ROCKIT

3rd Scroll
WATCHED

4th Scroll
BROTHER'S DEATH

5th Scroll
STEEL BRIDGE

6th Scroll
DARK WORLD

7th Scroll
LIPTON

8th Scroll
SCROLLS OF LUCIFER

"I AM THAT I AM"

In the beginning, God walked upon the vast oceans of darkness, and he traveled through the endless spheres of time. But, he walked alone. As sadness touched his heart, he placed his right hand inside his body and withdrew it; the blood from his heart trickling through his mighty fingers to fall upon the universe. *Life was created!*

Seeing this to be good, our heavenly father once more placed his hand into his body; however this time, he removed one of his ribs. Blowing gently upon it, he birthed his very first angel: Metatron, the guardian of life. This Seraphim stands at the gates of heaven, and reads the names of the dead from the book of life. Metatron is charged with the placement of souls, whether it be in Heaven or Hell.

Once again, our heavenly father reached into his body, this time taking not just one rib, but two—holding one in his right hand, and the other in his left. Blowing gently on the rib in his right hand, he birthed his second angel: Michael. This powerful Cherubim is not only the guardian of light, but the champion of the guard. Blowing gently on the rib in his left hand, our heavenly father birthed his third angel; Samuel. This powerful Cherubim is the guardian of night, and protector of the stars.

Gabriel, Rafael, Ariel, Uriel, and Abaddon were the first of the Archangels. Endowed with both beauty, and strength, they were placed high in God's court. Upon their celestial births the lesser angels, also known as 'Sentinels' were sent to the worlds where God's precious blood had fallen. They were sent to nurture the seeds of life with his unbreakable love. In the fullness of time, the worlds became populated with his children, who gave birth to their children, and their children. God was joyful!

Thence he came...an extraordinarily powerful immortal present since the very beginning.

He...who dwells inside the abyss!

He...who is the evil within the darkness!

He...who is the jackal to all that is holy took from God a son, and fashioned an instrument of terror, one he would use to destroy all that was created!

On top of an anvil it was shaped.
In the fires of Hell it was forged!

Following the days of Adam, and prior to the death of Moses, the epic battle against all that is sacred began.

It is written that one day war will come upon us, and the lands will be stained in our blood...for he who occupies the 'Ninth Hell' has sought long to murder the children of God. And, if he is successful...

The Christ will be destroyed!

"I stood upon the sands of the sea, and I saw a beast rise, having seven heads and ten horns, and upon his horns ten crowns, and upon his heads was the name blasphemy" – **John 7.2**

"They worshipped the dragon that giveth power unto the beast: and they worshipped the beast, saying who is like unto the beast, who is able to make war with him" – **Revelation 13:3-18**

"Children, it is the last hour; and just as you heard that the Antichrist are coming, for even now many Antichrists have already risen; from this we know that it is the last hour" – **John 2:18-19**

"Understand oh, son of man, for at the time of the end shall be the vision" – **Daniel 8:17**

From the coldest depths of space,
a voice thunders forward...
IT IS TIME, MY

He thinks, he is dead!

Blackness encloses him, wrapping him like a blanket on a bitter winter's night. And though his eyes are open, there is only the cold cruel darkness, such darkness that it makes him believe he is slipping into madness. Inching his way to the threshold of insanity, the frightened young man touches his body and feels the firmness of it—believing he is en route to that heavenly place souls travel to after death. But, as he ponders this notion, while dangling like a puppet inside the abyss, an unimaginable horror plays out before him, one that instantly terrifies his soul:

IMAGES OF BUTCHERY AND SLAUGHTER!

An unseen explosion rumbles within this cosmic vacuum, followed by a penetrating crimson light that momentarily devours the darkness. Overcome by this mysteriousness, the young man closes his eyes. But, he swiftly reopens them upon suffering an intense burning sensation on his legs; he finds himself nailed to a wooden cross, dull copper spikes impaling his hands and feet. Looking down toward the base of the cross, tears escape his eyes, for it is submerged in an infinite lake of pure...

LIQUID FIRE!

Scorching flames gnaw his unshod feet, and upon lifting his miserable gaze, the young man spots a structure, archaic in nature, where none stood before. An ancient bridge made from primitive stone has appeared...with scores of children staggering across it, amidst threats of pain and torture from their unseen jailor. Somewhere beyond the bridge, beyond the boundaries of vision, a nomadic drumming emerges, it's barbaric beat in sequence with each dreary step taken by those frightened children.

From the burning waters, fireballs shoot out to scorch these little ones, who are forced to walk across this hellish passage; the bridge begins, and ends inside those waters. Other crosses began to rise from those fiery depths, each with a screaming human nailed to it; their sorrowful cries are the stuff of madness. Identifying their mommies and daddies among the crucified, the children weep harder. All the while, the young man yells at them to run away, but no sound will escape his lips.

Another explosion thunders inside the blackness, and once more, it is followed by that crimson light. Afterward, the men and women scream even louder as their sizzling flesh drops away from their mortal bodies. With trembling lips, the young man is forced to watch the gruesome affair of skin peeling from charred carcasses, and turning to ash.

Skeletons remain impaled to the crosses, their bones quickly crumbling to dust. With his eyes returning to that bridge, the young man bears witness to a little girl who now stands all alone there, cuddling her dolly in her fragile arms. No older than five, the horrified child cries for her mommy as tears soak her freckled cheeks; she squeezes her dolly against her body even tighter. In a state of utter terror, the young man looks on as a fireball obliterates her young life, setting her body ablaze, and hurling it over the stony flanks of this unholy edifice. As the flames continue to eat away at his body, he screams out into the blackness, **"Dear God, why am I here? What did I do to deserve this?"** His words are without sound.

3

A face materializes over the bridge!

Screaming internally, the terrified young man recognizes the face; it belongs to a demon, one that has persecuted him his entire life, especially these last few days. As the flames continue slithering up his body, feasting as if they had never tasted the delicacy of human flesh before, and with his life drawing to its end—still hanging on the cross, the young man remembers, it was...

A little more than a week earlier...

"Scott, it's already a quarter past seven!" she shouts from the foot of the stairs.

Sleepily, the young man slowly lifts his head off his soft pillows, squinting at his clock radio that is cruelly, validating his mother's acute attunement for time. Hearing his name a second time, he sits up, surrendering to the warmth and the lovely spring light streaming through his bedroom window. Rubbing the crusted flakes from his sleepy eyelids, he looks over at the framed picture on his nightstand; it displays the enchanting young lady who has recently stolen his heart. He gazes at the photograph until his exasperated mother bellows his name once more:

"SSSScoottt!"

Half-asleep, the young man scuttles into his bathroom to begin enacting his daily ritual, which consists of a shower and brushing his teeth in under five minutes, a feat mastered over the years. On most mornings, this unwearied woman can be heard pleading to her son to wake up and get ready for school——most mornings, multiple summons are needed to get the lad out of bed, and to the breakfast table.

She learned a long time ago her son prefers his pillows to eggs, and today is no exception!

Having completed his drudgery in the bathroom, Scott is ready to don his favorite wrinkly jeans, football jersey and letter jacket. Upon hearing another musical plea from his mother's highly tuned vocal cords, he races out of his room, and down the staircase to the front door.

Due to time shortage, and a serious lack of enthusiasm, morning breakfast is out of the question. Nevertheless, this charming mother always ensures that an alternative meal is readily available. Today it's a glass of milk, and a blueberry muffin that awaits him at the front door. With sneakers in hand, Scott drains the glass of milk, but what he does to the muffin is something else to have seen. Despite his mother's leniency, he will need a miracle to make it to class before the final bell; he has only twenty minutes remaining before the school doors are scheduled to close.

Darla Miller: an attractive lady in her early forties. Alluring figure, sparkling blue eyes, and blondish-brown hair, which touches her shoulders is what this adoring mom whom Scott loves very much is all about. Mrs. Miller has just started her new job; a human resource manager for a local supermarket chain. She and Scott's father met during their college years, became engaged, and married two years later; however, they have recently separated.

The current year is 1984.

Scott and his parents reside in a major city in upstate New York, where a heavy snowfall blanketed the area only weeks earlier. Blizzards pummel this city within the winter seasons, cocooning folks inside their homes like caterpillars waiting for the spring to reemerge as beautiful butterflies.

Prior to winter, the city was ablaze with vibrant colors as leaves dropped from the towering oak trees that dominated the landscape. Blessed it be the autumn holidays, as those majestic skies and beautiful scenery seem like masterpieces crafted by the gods themselves. With the arrival of spring, most high school seniors have already begun putting their future plans into action. A handful of these young folks will be attending college, some will enter the military, while most will join the work force. There will be those who will venture out into the world for other opportunities, bidding farewell to friends, and their cherished hometown of --

"Buffalo"

Lounging on the border between the United States and Canada---to the west of New York City is Buffalo. Its waters spill into one of the seven natural wonders of the world: Niagara Falls. Buffalo, situated in the Rust Belt region, is recognized as the location of Bethlehem Steel, which ranked among America's largest steel mills in the early twentieth century.

Stepping out onto his front porch, Scott breathes in the cleansed air, compliments of the laborious thunderstorm the night before. Damp wooden steps leave watery telltale signs on the back of his jeans, after he sits down on them to tie his sneakers. Glancing the length of the street, a surge of blissfulness sweeps over him. After whispering her name, a smile shapes his lips,

"Lisa..."

An angry car's engine fills the morning air, stirring those who are still beneath the covers on their beds. Not the least bit concerned, Scott is well-acquainted with the owner of the overly clean, mint-green, '79 Mustang' that is speeding down the street toward his house.

Scott Miller: a good-looking eighteen-year-old with blue eyes, and shoulder length blond hair. Standing at six feet with an athletic build, he's a natural to play quarterback on his school's football team. He has a sereneness about him, making him popular with teachers and students alike, and because of his flair for the game, top colleges around the country are courting him, some going as far as to extend full scholarships. Like any other talented athlete, he dreams of playing at the professional level, which has prompted visits to several universities with his father, and a few others with his two best friends.

Mr. and Mrs. Miller have been separated a tad longer than two months, and with his father living in an apartment on the other side of the city, Scott finds himself spending less and less time with him----time that was once spent as a family. Knowing his parents still care for each other, Scott often hears his mother crying inside her bedroom at night. More than once, he has wanted to go and comfort her, but he never does and, when he is with his father, he detects the same sadness in him as well.

It isn't long until the highly buffed beauty is stopping in front of his house, the driver being one of his best friends. Without missing a beat, Scott rises and makes haste over to the mustang. Opening the passenger door, he looks over at his mother who is standing on the porch----her right index finger pointing at the diamond studded watch on her slender wrist----a worried look on her face.

Looking at the driver as he climbs into the car, **"You do realize we only have ten minutes,"** Scott says.

"Yeah, yeah," the driver nonchalantly responds.

Closing the door, Scott adds, **"Well?"**

"Well, what?"

"Do you think we'll make it this time?"

"No."

"Me neither, Davey boy," Scott laughs. **"Besides, we don't really want to spoil all the fun we have sneaking into school, now do we?"**

The Mustang's tires begin to smoke as they dig into the pavement, beginning their melodramatic launch to the end of the street. Moreover, the noise stirs several household curtains----angry eyeballs cursing the two brats who have interrupted their sleep, yet again. All the while, Mrs. Miller shakes her pretty head, knowing her son is more than likely going to be late for school, again.

◦────────◦

David Knoll: Shorter and slimmer than Scott, he has short, wavy-brown hair, and hazel eyes. Dave inherited a rather large nose from his father, a genetic trait that has tormented him. Over time, he used this noticeable imperfection as a way to interact with others, by cracking jokes, and taking on the role as class clown. Unfortunately, his brand of humor inside the classrooms has led to disciplinary actions from some of his teachers, resulting in multiple referrals to the vice principal, and two suspensions this year.

Born with health anomalies, Dave has undergone five major open-heart surgeries, making him a bona fide medical wonder. With the passing of years, he accepted the reality that his life will be shorter than most, making it his priority to live like a normal kid, refusing to be pitied. Scott and Dave have been friends since their memorable encounter in the third grade at school, #28. Scott saved the poor boy from a lynching and to this day, he teases his friend about the comical event, which went along the line of ---

Ten years ago.
One dark, stormy day!
{Actually, it was sunny and bright}

It was Friday, and the end of a school day had arrived. A horde of children from the third grade were chasing little Davey home like an angry mob after a criminal. It was said that he had done something so awful that they were going to beat him up. Running for dear life, Dave screamed as if the Devil himself was nipping at his heels. To avoid being cut off from other boys who had joined in on the pursuit, Dave accidentally bumped into Scott, who so happened to be walking on the same dirt path to his house.

Though their eyes connected for only a second, it was long enough for Scott to feel sympathy. Dave continued running down the path trying to get home to safety, but the mob was hot on his heels. They pursued Dave into a yard enclosed by a high-chained-link fence, preventing means of escape. Scott watched as the infuriated girls call him bad names, while the little boys threw small rocks and sticks at him. Dave was crying.

Scott intervened by bribing Dave's judge and jurors with homemade chocolate chip cookies if they would pardon Dave...so to speak. To his surprise, it worked, and after that day the two became inseparable...like brothers. It was later revealed that Dave had looked up one of the little girls' dresses.

"So, how did it go last night with...Lissaaa?"

"Okay, I guess," Scott answers coolly, looking out the passenger side window, his elbow resting on the ledge.

"WHAT?"

"It was alright," Scott snickers, knowing full well that the absence of details is going to drive Dave utterly insane.

"What do you mean, it was alright?" Dave barks, staring at Scott with those, 'you better start talking' eyes.

Purposely continuing to be mum on the vital particulars, its only after an extended moment when Scott finally offers the stingiest answer he could think of. **"We hung out for a while. It went okay."**

"WHAT HAPPENED?" Dave roars, hinting the perils his friend faces if he doesn't supply details. Receiving no answer, Dave turns onto the street that leads to school. Moments later, Scott takes delivery of a punch on his left arm for deliberately prolonging crucial information. **"Tell me what happened!"**

"Damn, do you need to know everything?"

"YES!" Dave howls. **"I need to know, everything!"**

Following several seconds of tormenting the hell out of his friend, Scott finally speaks, **"we had a wonderful time."**

Displaying a most ill-behaved smirk, **"did you get any nookie?"** Dave snickers. Scott shakes his head in disbelief, never imagining his friend was this bad. **"You went to that holy garden of — Oh my God, you lucky bastard!"**

"Are you done?" Scott scoffs, staring at Dave who still bears that ill-behaved smirk.

"Played a little hide the salami, didn't you?" Dave jeers rowdily, making obscene gestures with his right hand, while his left hand grips the steering wheel.

"Did you get any last night?" Scott sasses.

"No, I didn't as a matter of fact." Dave smiles. "But, I do masturbate quite well." As the Mustang pulls into the parking lot directly across from their school, the two know they are in trouble, because the parking lot is not only full, but also void of any students. And, with the tolling of the morning bell, signifying the start of the first class for the day, the two are quick in exiting the mustang.

"Do you see him?" Scott asks.

"No!" Dave replies, his eyes roaming the exterior of the school, spotting several students sneaking into one of the secondary entrances located on the righthand side of the building; the door leads to the basement floor.

"Well, we have no choice," Scott mutters.

Unfortunately, with everyone already inside, these two delinquents find themselves in the same state of affairs they have been in so many times before. They must undertake the perilous task of sneaking past the school's security team without being caught, but that is not all, as they would also still need to avoid...

'Curly.'

South Park High: a four-story building, built in the latter part of "1 9 1 5" —— known as the first school in buffalo that had successfully segregated in the sixties. There are two interlinking gymnasiums, with one being slightly smaller than the other. The school has a large, Olympic-size swimming pool on the basement level; however, the grand prize is the auditorium with its high, theatrical ceiling. In addition to the main entrance: four large wooden doors with oversize glass windowpanes, there is a single door on each side, and two more on the back side.

Curly: is the head of the school's security team, a mammoth black man with a shiny bald head, and arms the size of tree trunks. One could easily argue that Curly takes his job a tad too serious...for he is relentless on his watch, especially toward those who fail——or won't, follow the policies of this esteemed institution. Displaying a lone wolf personality, Curly can easily be mistaken as someone who doesn't like people, explicitly those foolish mortals who try to sneak in late for class. Curly was not only a former drill instructor for the Marines, but he also received a purple heart during his tour in Vietnam—carrying a wounded soldier for two miles through hostile territory. Today's conundrum is what door will Curly be hiding behind? And...if it is not him, then which of the other three security guards will it be?

Presently, the hulking behemoth is lingering just outside the front entrance doors, standing atop the concrete steps. Because of their chronic tardiness, Scott and Dave have become priority targets. The giant of a man in his washed out uniform hungers to start the week off with his two crafty and elusive adversaries spending quality time with the vice principal. He yearns for them to receive their much overdue chastising on tardiness.

It is Monday, and they are late again!

Curly has been monitoring the pair since they drove into the parking lot, located on the other side of the street that has the same name: South Park Avenue. Perched on the giant steps, he bears resemblance to a stone gargoyle, ready to hammer the malicious spirits that dare to invade his domain. This unrelenting supervisor can already taste the fruits of victory that will be his once he apprehends these perpetrators—these two who have eluded him on way too many occasions.

He waits for the two mice to enter his inescapable trap, waiting to strike down with his mighty gauntlet of justice!

After crossing the street, Scott and Dave stop dead in their tracks...for they spot the massive security sentinel atop the steps. Realizing he has already spotted them, they stare at each other, anticipating what move their opponent is going to make. The dramatic scene unfolds like a classical Western showdown, drawn straight from history books, the one where the town sheriff — in this case being Curly — is determined to not only catch these two villains — Scott and Dave — but lock them away in some flee infested jailhouse, or detention hall in this case.

As cheers of encouragement descend from above, all three tilt their heads and eyeballs up toward the students, and the handful of teachers poking their heads out of the first, second, third and fourth floor windows. Dreading this unwanted attention, the two mice return their attention to the snarling mouse trapper who is less than twenty to thirty yards away. Convinced there is a betting pool of some type for this recurring event, Scott realizes the pressure is now on Curly to catch them, because if he fails, he will look bad, whereas if he doesn't, well...it will be worse for the two mice. Having to act fast as their opponent is more determined to catch them, Scott and Dave bolt like an arrow toward the rear of the school, hoping to find an unguarded door and gain safe passage inside.

Regrettably for these two infamous outlaws, Curly has prophesied which door they are heading for, and scurrying back inside he runs like a madman down the empty hallway toward the rear of the building.

"Run faster, Dave!" Scott roars.
"I'm running as fast as I can!" Dave roars back.

Making track toward the backside, the two are pleased to discover the water puddles generated by the heavy rains that came in the night have evaporated; the soil provides a favorable degree of traction. Rapidly closing the distance to that staircase at the end the hallway, which leads down to the basement level, the snarling supervisor nearly topples a middle-aged teacher from the ninth grade home economics class. The woman gawks in utter terror at the two hundred and sixty pounds of man-train barreling down the hallway, with a force that will indubitably pulverize her if she remains within his destructive path.

"MY LORD!" the woman screams.

With mere seconds to dodge the human locomotive, the teacher pitches the papers she is holding into the air and scampers into the room directly in front of her. Grunting, Curly continues down the empty hallway, passing the room that holds the teacher. From past experience, Scott knows the beefy supervisor is fully cognizant of what door they are heading for. Stopping on a dime, he immediately shouts out to his partner in crime -- **"Stop!"**

"What?!" Dave barks, just as he is about to open that first door on the backside; the same door they used only last week to sneak inside. Without responding, Scott runs for the other door, fully aware he is taking a chance in doing so; there's an important game on Saturday, and he can't afford to be caught because pressure may be brought to bear that could keep him on the sidelines.

Of the few times Curly netted him, one being before an important game, Scott was not allowed to play...well, not until they were down by a pair of touchdowns heading into the fourth quarter. The principal allowed the coach to bend the rules to bring in their stellar performer, especially since they were playing a rival school. It's common knowledge that the school's headcheeses ran private bets on these games. Upon reaching the second door, Scott opens it, trusting his hypothesis is correct. Rushing inside, they encounter zilch on the basement floor and, to their salvation, a nearby staircase is also unoccupied. Waiting to make sure nobody is descending the stairs, they make their move, disappearing like phantoms up them.

"That was close," Scott says.

"It didn't help with those fools yelling!" Dave scoffs.

"No, it didn't."

"I wanted to throw my shoe at them!" Dave sneers.

"Thank God you didn't," Scott chuckles.

"You're hilarious."

"Let's keep moving."

Pausing momentarily at the first floor landing, **"why is Curly so mean?"** Dave asks, struggling to catch his breath.

"Have you looked into his eyes?" Scott responds.

"Yeah."

"Then you know why, the man hates everyone. I'll see you later." Without pause, Scott makes like a thief down the first floor hallway, whereas Dave continues up the stairs, having two more floors to go before his epic journey is over. Upon hearing the closing of a hallway locker, Scott pokes his head around the corner, discovering the corridor to be deserted. Quickstepping over to his locker, which is across from the room he seeks, he unravels the combination to his lock and pulls open the metal cubbyhole. Reaching inside he snatches a notebook, pen, and a small backpack, along with a cumbersome, hardcover book that reads, 'American English.' Following a quick scan of the hallway, he promptly advances to the closed-door of—

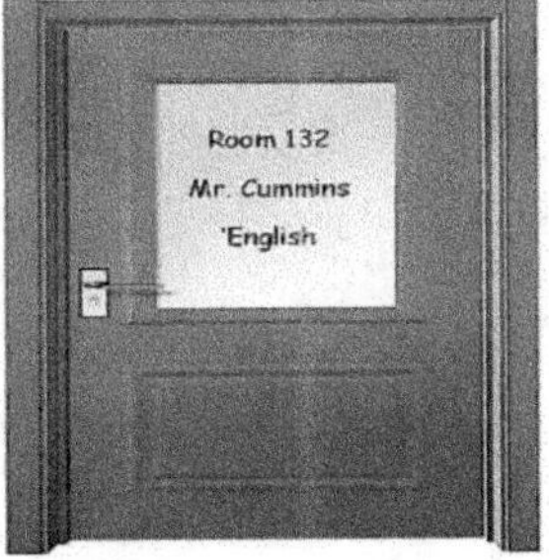

18

Like a seasoned burglar breaking into a jewelry store, Scott opens the door with a polished grace and spots the teacher at the blackboard, writing words upon it. With his backside facing him, Scott employs stealth, attempting to slip into his assigned desk by the back window. And, with his objective mere feet away ---

"**I see we are late again, Mr. Miller.**" Cursing internally, Scott stops dead in his tracks, and slowly turns toward the teacher who continues scribbling words on the blackboard, his back side facing him. "**Don't stand there like a statue, take your seat and write these words down.**" Obeying the teacher's directive, Scott hastens to his desk and opens his notebook. As he begins writing down the words, the boy seated on his right---wearing his favorite, Barney and Fred baseball cap, sneaks him a small bag of BBQ chips, which he graciously accepts.

"**Thanks, Keith.**"

"**You get away with too much,**" the boy scoffs.

"**I do?**"

"**Yeah, you do, and it sickens me.**"

"**It's called, public relations skills.**"

"**You mean, ass-kissing skills,**" Keith jeers; Scott winks and smiles. Shaking his head, the boy resumes writing down the words, whereas Scott slips a few of those tasty BBQ chips into his mouth. Given Mr. Cummins's placid demeanor, Scott knows he isn't going to catch hell from his teacher.

Furthermore, Scott isn't the least bit concerned of Curly showing up, and hauling him off to the vice principal's office; this wasn't his style. No, the security supervisor wants to catch him in the act, making the chastising all the sweeter.

"There's going to be a test on these words next week," Mr. Cummins says, slowly turning from the blackboard to face his class. **"You will be required to spell each word, then, you will be asked to use it in a sentence that contains both an adverb and pronoun."** *The class moans in displeasure.*

Before the minute hand on the clock moves its seventh time, a boy with short black hair walks into the classroom, holding a piece of paper inside his left hand. Upon seeing the lad, Mr. Cummins walks over and says hello, taking the paper and reading it. In the interim, Scott takes advantage of the distraction by depositing a couple of the tasty chips into his mouth, all the while, continuing to record the words into his blue, composition notebook.

Mr. Cummins: five feet, eight inches. He has long, thinning brown hair, which he mostly keeps in a ponytail; this man of fifty was a true rebel in the sixties, wearing much of the same jewelry to this day. He is a tolerant teacher, always on the side of clemency; at all times will you see a smile on his face. Regrettably, tragedy struck last year, victim of a negligent driver, which is reason for his walking stick; the motorcycle accident also made him a widower.

"My beloved, students," Mr. Cummins says, **"I need to leave for a while. I expect you all to behave like adults."**

Seconds after the teacher leaves with the boy, a petite, very pretty girl sitting in the desk directly in front of Scott turns around and shyly whispers hello. She receives a smile and salutations of her own, but that is as far as it goes as Scott's attention drifts away, leaving the brokenhearted girl to turn around and resume her studies.

One thing occupies his mind — Lisa.

Contrary to what Dave thinks, nothing remotely sexual happened with the blonde beauty. They patronized several stores at the downtown mall, finishing off the day with a late lunch at one of the finer eateries there. Before dating, they always said hello when they passed each other in the halls, but it never went further than that. With Scott being the football hero, and Lisa being every teenage boys fantasy, it was destined to happen. This delectable young lady has tormented the hell out of countless young men throughout her years, unintentionally and intentionally.

Twisting his body around, and resting his elbows upon the ledge of the windowsill, Scott gazes at the small park behind the school. Inserting chips into his mouth, his nostrils take joy with the flowery fragrance that comes with spring, delivered by a friendly gust of warm air that nuzzles his face. Continuing to satisfy his belly, his mind transports him back in time to when he was a small boy playing in this same park with his parents, remembering the happiness they shared with him, and each other. Elevating his chin, he stares into the cloudless sky. It's a handsome day.

Something is wrong!

An internal warning grips his being, a familiar tingling in his stomach, which from past experiences had proven to be accurate---something is amiss! Scanning the area behind the school, starting with the neighboring houses, then the corner store, he sees nothing unusual. Choosing to ignore the oddness, he resumes writing down the remaining words from the chalkboard into his notebook, but before his pen touches the paper it dawns on him: *the silence!*

Normally at this time of the day, a car would be driving down the street that borders the other side of the park.

He doesn't see any joggers, nor any bicyclists shaking off the cobwebs from the long frosty winter.

What is more, he does not observe:

Birds flying in the sky.

Children on the swing sets.

Someone walking their dog.

Not a single couple admiring the beautiful gardens the city planted inside the park just last spring, nor does he hear a sound coming from the residential homes no further than a hundred or so yards away. He hears nothing, absolutely nothing; furthermore, he believes he is being...*watched!*

It's been this type of abnormality, this unnerving brand of bizarreness that he has been forced to endure his whole life. Even when he was just a babe being pushed down the street inside his stroller, he felt the presence of Evil, even though he knew not what Evil was. This strange awareness only intensified the older he got—often lasting no longer than a beat or two of his trembling heart. Staring into those heavenly blue skies, he is quick in noticing a weirdly shaped cloud moving steadily in his direction.

Strange, that cloud wasn't there a second ago!

It's not the sudden emergence of the cloud that concerns him, but the disturbing green tint in it. Seconds later, the cloud begins turning brown. Inching his head closer to the window, he notices how the cloud is changing to blood-red, swearing on his soul something is taking shape inside it.

Grinning face—fanged teeth—demonic eyes!

The school bell rings, signifying the end of first class.

A bit startled, Scott removes his eyes from the waning vision and directs them to the front of the room—to the door to which Mr. Cummins now stands at—saying goodbye to his students as they walk by him.

He pokes his head back out the window. **"Nothing."**

"Did you say something?" Keith bids, positioning his notebook inside his backpack.

"Where did the face go?" Scott whispers to himself.

"Where did what go?"

"What?" Scott turns to face Keith.

"You just said, where did the face go?"

"I did?"

"Duh, yeah."

"I was just looking out the..."

"Are you okay?"

"Yeah." Scott's attention shifts back to the classroom door, where students are inquiring about the forthcoming test as they exit, engaging Mr. Cummins with questions.

"See you later," Keith says as he is about to walk away.

"Hey, did you see a strange looking cloud in the sky?"

"Scott, I think you're strange."

"What do you mean?"

"I mean, you've lost your mind," Keith says, walking over to the window, and looking out. "There aren't any clouds in the sky." Shaking his head, Keith heads for the door.

Returning to the window, Scott sticks his head out into the warm, breezy winds. "He's right," he concedes, his gaze descending to the cars driving on the street——on both sides of the park. "I must be imagining things again." Grabbing his backpack, Scott places his books inside, along with the half-eaten bag of chips, and heads for the door. As he is about to leave, a small tin wastebasket becomes visible by an outstretched hand. When the initial bafflement vanishes from his face, Scott reaches into his backpack and extracts the munchies, dropping them into the litter bin.

"Thank you kindly, Mr. Miller," Mr. Cummins says with a smile. "Have yourself a wonderful day."

"You too, Mr. Cummins." Scott rolls his eyes as his feet steer him through the door. He has long held that teachers were born with eyes in the back of their heads, and the main reason for this is that they know too damn much!

Once inside the hallway, Scott becomes conscious of a cool draft blowing freely inside the hallway, brushing his face like a spider's web. Reaching his locker, he scans the lively corridor for the source of the breeze after another one is felt, confirming the first was not imaginary. Shrugging off the queerness, he opens his locker. But, before his book titled, 'American English' slides off his palms to rest upon the metal shelf, that image from the cloud appears inside his head—soon replaced by a carousal of emotions that begin choking his senses. Against his will, his mind conjures a most unwanted memory.

When he was eight years old, Scott liked to stargaze from his bedroom window using an apprentice telescope his father had gotten him. It was during one nocturnal occasion that he first laid eyes upon...*Him!*

GARBED IN DARK CLOTHING.
STANDING NEXT TO THE OAK TREE.
STARING AT HIM FROM INSIDE THE SHADOWS.
ACROSS THE STREET, BY THE NEIGHBOR'S HOUSE.

25

Scott routinely summoned his father to his room, and together they searched for the mysterious man. But, they never found him; Mr. Miller simply tucked his son into bed.

'Helios'

By invoking the story of this legendary sun god, Mr. Miller found a way to comfort his son, making him believe the mighty guardian would safeguard him while he lay asleep in his bed. Nevertheless, after his father left, Scott would return to the window, and there the man would be, staring up at his bedroom window. Shooting back into bed, he would haul his sacred blankets, to which is what his father called them over his head, daring not to remove them until morning.

As the years aged Scott, sightings of the secretive man became scarcer. Strangely, one such sighting, when he was thirteen years of age enters his mind:

The lad played on the city's junior football league for a team called...the South Buffalo stingrays. It was a Friday, and practice had run late. Because he was in a hurry to get home -- his mother having told him earlier she was making his favorite for dinner -- and because it was beginning to rain, he had cut through a park called, Potter's Field. Moving at a steady pace, Scott was halfway across the spacious field when the clouds opened, and the sky darkened. He firmly believed he saw a pair of demonic eyes inside those dreary clouds; the rain really came down hard that day.

Turning his face from that watery cascade, he spotted the man he would later dub, "the Stranger." Shrouded in shadow, standing next to a tree some thirty yards away was the silhouette of a tall, lanky male. The cryptic man wore an oversized, black spooky hat, and a long, black trench coat. Though Scott couldn't see his eyes, he felt them upon him. As the rain intensified, he heard sinister laughter from the man's cruel lips, as well as from those murky skies above him. Reaching down into the mud, the lad picked up a rock, but when his eyes returned to the tree, the man and the laughter had vanished, as if they were never there. Scared out of his wits, Scott ran all the way home, stopping once to retrieve his football helmet that had slipped out of his wet hand.

Life became troublesome for the lad, as omens of the Stranger began appearing regularly:

A swift moving shadow.

Hair-raising laughter in the winds.

Silhouette of a man inside an alleyway.

Sounds of footsteps, with no one in sight.

Chilling nightmares, often ending with screams.

And of course, the constant sighting of the Stranger, standing across the street next to the tree, partially hidden inside the night.

One of the worst days for him was the day the black hat appeared on his front lawn; Scott acted sick so he wouldn't have to leave the house and go to school. He was tormented by the strange man, continuously reminded of his presence. Many times he felt the fiend was close—watching—waiting!

As Scott tries shaking off those memories, the worst one — an unpleasant chapter in his life — one he has labored to erase, consumes him. Staring into his locker with empty eyes, an awful event that occurred eight years ago imprisons his mind, forcing a tear to run the length of his face. In the intervening time, every student in the hallway is unmindful of the vacant gaze inside Scott's eyes, unmindful of the slight shaking of his hands.

He cannot move!

He cannot blink!

He is not in control!

Not now!!

October 31st, 1976

At the tender age of ten, Scott, Dave and Mike had exhausted an entire afternoon working on their costumes; it was Halloween, and they had decided to become pirates. The three buccaneers left early that evening in pursuit of sugary treasures, and chocolate bar riches. By nightfall, they had raided an ample number of houses, but time was growing short. Nevertheless, there was simply far too much room inside their plunder sacks to return home; therefore they elected to stay out a little longer and raid a few more unwary dwellings of their tasty treasures.

Mike dressed up as...'Black Beard.'
Dave dressed up as...'Captain Hook.'
Scott dressed up as...'One-eyed Willy.'

The trio dared to venture down a particularly spooky street in their conquest to knock out a few more houses, but this street offered only a handful of residences...for arson had ravished the area. To render things more ruinous for the little pirates were all the fear-provoking stories about this street called...

Thankfully, the majority of the street's lampposts were illuminated, especially since there was marginal lighting at best coming from those houses left standing. It was known that these generous homeowners kept their porch lights on longer, in hopes the little trick–or–treaters would come to their humble abodes for sweets. All the same, their candy baskets remained untouched throughout the festive night, as most kids as well as their chaperons avoided this street like the plague, because of the...

'OLD SKINNER HOUSE'

The three-story house has been abandoned for nearly six years. Rumor has it that old man Skinner hanged himself from the tree in his backyard, after taking a splitting-axe to his adulterous wife!

The three pirates were having a bounty of fun, while collecting heaps of chocolate treats from those forgotten dwellings; these neglected proprietors always gave out the really good stuff. After plundering the last house, Mike and Dave scouted an aperture between a pair of scorched houses. Deciding to cut through to the next street, which was on route to home, and without telling their fellow pirate, the two made haste through that narrow opening, cringing as they momentarily glanced at those spooky edifices that were once occupied by loving families. Now, they can only believe they are haunted by ghosts; Mike and Dave had increased their speed.

Meanwhile, Scott's attention was focused on a choice piece of candy he had received from the last address, and as a result, he fell behind. It was only after chomping down on another one of the tasty caramel nuggets that he took notice of his missing friends. Yummy sounds swiftly faded into the night when he surveyed the vicinity, realizing he was standing all alone in front of the Skinner house.

Wooden planks were missing from the porches charred stairs, and the lower windows, as well as the front door were boarded up; most of the roof tiles were gone, leaving gaping holes. Braving a few steps closer, Scott hoped to acquire a better view of the interior —— via the only non-boarded up window. But, all he was able to see was the gloom within!

With no warning, the wind picked up suddenly, making it much harder to see inside the house and forcing Scott to take off the pirate patch from his left eye. Furthermore, all the houses on the street had turned off their porch lights, and those flickering candles inside their pumpkins were all snuffed out. Making the scene even scarier, every lamppost was dimmed. This was peculiar, even for a ten-year-old.

Littering the streets were the semi-decomposed bodies of at least a hundred dead birds; these birds were not there moments ago. Scott attempted to walk away, but stopped after hearing a rattling noise from behind. This is when he turned around, his baby blue eyes elevated...

"Ahhh!" Scott cried.

Framed by the house's second-story window stood the Stranger, his creepy, oversize, black fedora seen inside the shadows, along with the upper portion of his trench coat. However, it was the man's facial features that frightened Scott. Though the fiend was mostly concealed in shadow, his face was sufficiently lit by the brightness of the full moon, giving Scott a clear view of his spinechilling façade, which to say was alarming!

The light from the moon revealed a gruesome, pastel profile that consisted of pointy teeth and thin grinning lips; Scott cried. Hideous laughter came to life inside the winds, and from beneath his large spooky hat, the man's black eyes became red as the fires in hell. Terrified, Scott dropped his bag of candy and ran hard toward the end of the street. Yet, he did not get far as the winds worsened, inhibiting him from gaining distance from the house.

CRACKLE

A lightning bolt struck a tree! Tumbling over a severed branch that had fallen to the ground by the sudden surge of electricity, Scott suffers a nasty cut on his right leg, along with various scratches on his hands and stomach. Several painful seconds later, Scott stood up. With tears running down his cheeks, he turned toward the house, crying harder when he saw the Stranger standing outside it, staring at him with those evil, jet-black eyes, illuminated from within by that diabolical reddish glow. Scott remembers the fiend walking toward him, a devilish sneer shaping his thin lips, and a horrid grunt soon following. He also remembers looking up at the trickery induced, oversized moon that was directly above the fiend. Moreover, he remembers that within the ghostly white orb were a pair of giant, colorless eyes looking directly at him; the eyes had an unusual shape to them!

"I SEE YOU"

Riding atop those blustery winds, as if one of the four horsemen of the apocalypse charged to deliver the master's message, was the voice of a demon. Completely paralyzed by this soul-stealing entity from beyond, Scott suffered more taunting, more wickedness…

"SCOTT…MILLER"

Instinctively, Scott placed his right hand over his heart, noticing its irregular beat, his first direct encounter with his internal senses. The otherworldly phenomenon infused him with heightened courage, bestowing him the mettle to break the hold placed on him, and run as fast as he could toward the end of the street. Menacing winds hurled rubbish, as well as the carcasses of those dead birds at him, making his flight to the corner all the harder, yet he continued. Running past a house, Scott observed what appeared to be a bluish silhouette of someone standing in the driveway.

Upon reaching the corner, Scott foolishly stopped for a looksee, however the only thing he saw behind him was the night...for every house, and streetlamp had become black as death. Using the sleeve of his pirate's costume, he wiped his teary eyes, hoping the spooky man was gone. No such luck, he spotted someone in a shadow by a tree.

THE LONG TRENCH COAT.
THAT MENACING BLACK HAT.
BLACK MANE DROOPING BELOW
HIS SHOULDERS.

Not more than twenty yards away, Scott could clearly see more of the fiend's facial features, which you could say mirrored those of a ghoul:

34

RED VAMPIRIC EYES.
GHOSTLY PALE FACE.
CRACKED, WILLOWY LIPS.

Infused with additional strength and courage Scott ran to the next street, hoping to find his two friends. Arriving at the midway point on this lifeless street, he found them not to be there. Scott cried out for his father, who was at home on the couch snuggling with Mrs. Miller, watching spooky Halloween movies. The snapping of a tree branch betrayed the whereabouts of the Stranger. Spinning around, Scott spotted him once more standing next to a tree.

A true embodiment of Evil, the Stranger walked out into the middle of the street, blocking access to the corner and cutting off the sole avenue of escape. Scott yelled at the fiend to leave him alone, but his plea was answered with laughter. Out of the corner of his eye, Scott spotted an opening between two houses and as the man advanced, he bolted for that gap. Without stopping, Scott ran from one backyard to the next. It was a particular yard with a lofty, chain-link fence that presented a challenge. Knowing the fiend was not that far behind him, Scott decided to scale the fence, swinging his right leg over to the other side after reaching the top. He was halfway down, when...

"Ahhh!" Scott screamed.

No further than fifteen yards from the fence stood the cryptic brute, his Dracula-black eyes fixed intently on him. Overwhelmed by a deep fear, Scott couldn't bring himself to climb down---paralyzed by the malevolence he saw in the fiend's narrowing eyes, as well as the menacing grin curling on his cruel thin lips. Clinging to the metal links, Scott felt an unholy sensation---as if the Devil himself was standing in front of him trying to rob his soul. With a monstrous burst of speed, the fiend rammed the fence, pushing hard against it, forcing Scott to lose his balance and fall to the ground. In an act of cruelty, the fiend stepped closer and pressed his face against to the fence to show Scott...all of him!

The Stranger: his pastel profile, with his timeworn wrinkled face gives the impression he has lived an awfully long time. The other characteristics of this dweller of the shadows include his Dracula-black eyes, which contain both ancient wisdom, and a sense of ageless evil. Though he's extremely tall and lanky, with oversize hands, his movements are swift and sudden. To cast your eyes upon him, would prove to be as no less challenging than seeing a ghost!

With his face still pressed against the fence, the fiend scares Scott even further by displaying his ghastly jagged teeth through the parting of his thin lips. Just when Scott believed there would be no escape, the fiend had suddenly turned around—as if something had caught his attention. This distraction, along with more internal mettle allowed the lad to stand and run away from the fence, and into another backyard; moments later, he heard the festive sounds of Halloween music. Locating the source, he spotted Mike and Dave walking down the driveway of a decorated house swarming with smiling tots, who were all dressed up in their darling little costumes, and accompanied by their parents. The two pirates were grinning from ear to ear, a clear sign they had received favorable treats. Running over to them, Scott had made it verbally clear that he wanted to go home, immediately: the adults' eyes registered concern.

As the three made haste to the corner, Scott glanced over at a random backyard, uncovering the Stranger in a shadow, staring at him with his glowing, diabolical red eyes. Mike and Dave both noticed multiple slits in their friend's costume, as well as blood trickling out of a nasty cut on his left leg. After he returned home, Scott went straight to his bedroom window and looked out. Sure enough, the man was across the street:

Inside the shadows...
Looking up at his window...
Standing next to that tree...
Oddly, he wasn't wearing the big hat.

37

In the forthcoming years, Scott continued to hear that menacing laughter inside the winds, and he continued to see those "Evil Eyes" within the clouds. During thunderstorms, when lightning rippled across the dreary skies, a chill always ran down his spine...for those electrical bolts looked like the claws of Satan reaching down to snatch him. On nights he couldn't sleep, he would look out his bedroom window only to have the winds bring unto him that familiar voice...

"I SEE YOU"

By age sixteen, he no longer saw the Stranger, and the menacing eyes had vanished from the clouds. Scott never spoke to anyone about that awful night, except his father.

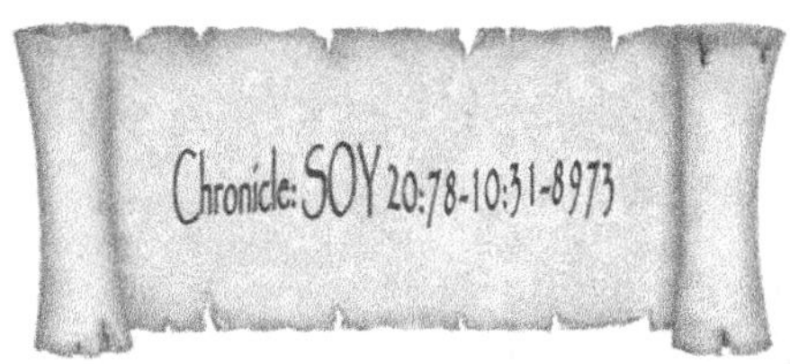

Regaining his composure, Scott reaches into his locker and grabs another book, one he will need for his next class. Before he can turn around, gentle hands wrap around him from behind; turning about he's greeted by a kiss. Gazing into the young lady's seductive cobalt eyes, his hands move to cuddle hers. **"I missed you, today,"** he confesses.

"You did?" she teases, releasing a devilish smile.

Drinking in the girl's curvaceous body, in addition to her lovely neckline, which is perfectly draped by her gorgeous, long and wavy, blonde hair, Scott declares, **"Yes, I did."**

"I am so happy you asked me to dance." — this was two weeks ago at a dance club called...the Rockit.

"I'm happy you said yes, Lisa."

Following another kiss, Lisa utters, **"I'll see you later."** After casually strolling away, she suddenly stops and tosses him a look over her right shoulder—all the while reinstating that devilish smile. Scott's eyes remain on Lisa, as do the eyes of the other young men who are lining both sides of the hallway. Some are talking to friends, their heads adjusting slightly for a peek at the beauty as she walks by, whereas a few others are acting like lost puppies, their smitten eyes glued to her every move. Turning the distant corner, Dave spots Scott in front of his locker and heads in his direction,

38

shyly saying hello to Lisa as he passes her. Ordinarily, she never acknowledges Dave's presence, but since he is best friends with her man, she says hello; Lisa begins chatting with a brunette, and another blonde near the end of the hall.

"Lisa is hot!" Dave declares, walking up to his friend.

Displaying a troubled look. "I agree," Scott says.

"What is with the look?"

"I just wonder if Mike still likes her."

"Scott, it's been three months."

"I know, but still —"

"But, nothing." Unraveling the combination to his lock, and upon opening his metal compartment, which of course is next to Scott's, he says, "It's over between them."

"I don't know if I can believe that."

After closing his locker, Dave utters, "What's so hard to believe. It just didn't work out for them."

"It's got to be hard giving up a girl like Lisa," Scott says, gazing at the beauty. "We had such a great time yesterday. Her touch is soft as rose petals, her scent is like a piece of heaven. How can Mike get over that?"

"I tell you, it's over between them!" Dave voices sternly.

Just as Dave finishes his declaration, someone throws an arm around both of their shoulders from behind. "The nose is correct, lover boy," a voice with a Spanish accent confirms. "It is over between us." Turning around, the two face the final member of their unique trinity.

Michael 'Angel' Rivera: a ladies man to the core. His girl absorbing, chestnut-brown eyes are well-complimented by his darkish brown, medium length hair with black highlights; a combination that drives the young girls crazy. Nearly as tall as Scott, this tanned youth has a slenderer physique, and is a loyal friend to both Scott and Dave. Eight years ago, he moved to Buffalo with his parents, and his pretty sister Magdalena——his junior by more than two years; they previous lived in a village in Madrid, Spain.

"I hope that's true, Mike," Scott says.

"Damn it," Dave grumbles, "I'm going to be late for Mr. Cummins's class." Quickstepping it down the hallway, he stops upon completing his seventh step, and turns around. "What mood is he in today?"

Walking up to Dave, Scott reaches into his backpack and brings out a small bag of cheese popcorn. Behind an impish grin Mike joins them, and after the bag is opened, he grabs a healthy handful with Scott following suit. With their mouths full of the tasty popcorn, they both bequeath their snarling friend the most joyous of smiles.

"You're welcome!" Dave storms away.

As the muttering teen makes haste by Lisa, who is still talking with those two girls, Scott's eyes promptly shift to her. Noticing the sparkle in his friend's baby blues, Mike concedes to himself that it is the same sparkle he once had for her. Pilfering more popcorn, Mike says, "Lisa and I are done. Just don't get too attached to that girl. Her heart is blacker than her panties."

"How do I know you're not just jealous?" Scott scoffs.

"Because, I'm not."

"That's good!" Scott scoffs again. Proceeding toward the staircase at the end of the hallway, he and Mike move in the direction opposite to where Lisa stood.

"I was done with that girl as soon as I found out she was messing around with that punk," Mike utters, his right hand placing more popcorn into his mouth.

Scott knows exactly who his friend is talking about; he heard the rumors of Lisa's involvement with this one specific boy, one he doesn't think to fondly of. "Whitey has always been trouble for us!" Scott sneers.

"I couldn't believe she was seeing him behind my back."

"Of all people. Why him?"

"I asked myself that same question."

"I don't understand what makes Whitey the way he is?!" Scott remembers how the kid harassed them when they were younger. Whitey was the neighborhood bully.

"He's strife," Mike grumbles, "that's why!"

"You can say that again."

"Listen brother, don't go overboard with her. After one good night, abandon ship."

"Thanks for the great advice!" Scott snaps.

"I'm sorry," Mike says. "I shouldn't have said that."

Reaching the staircase, Scott utters, "I have to hurry if I am going to make it to my next class on time."

Punching Scott playfully on his right arm, "I'll see you later," Mike says.

"Okay, see you later." After punching Mike on his left arm, a smidgen harder than playful, a smiling Scott ascends the staircase to the third floor.

Watching his friend vanish up the stairs, Mike quietly remarks, "Don't fall in love with her brother. Lord knows, I almost did." The Spanish youth knows Lisa is a lioness on the hunt, and though he has never been hurt by a girl, he has never come across a temptress such as Lisa. Remaining on the first floor, Mike saunters casually down the hallway, his flirtatious smile reaching every lass in sight.

'The marvelous teachings of Mr. Canton.'

Arriving on time for his next course, which is a favorite of his, Scott observes the sophisticatedly dressed teacher leaning ever so slightly over a student's shoulder, remarking on a rather tough assignment that is due at the end of the week. It wasn't that long ago when Mr. Canton was leaning over his shoulder, talking to him about a report he was doing on the French and Indian War. No one taught history as passionately as Mr. Canton: these infamous words echoed in the halls of the school.

"A time in history…is like a breath in a man's life."

Mr. Canton: a refined gentleman in his sixties. Standing tall at six feet, he possesses a fabulous collection of tailored suits and vintage ties. The rectangular, wire-frame glasses he wears compliment his slender face. His trimmed, cottony white mustache bestows upon him the appearance of a man with southern ancestry.

Standing in the front of the class with his back facing the blackboard, Mr. Canton addresses his students. **"Good morning ladies and gentlemen. Last week we started talking about the evolution of war. Today, I would like to continue that discussion."** He turns and extends his left hand toward the blackboard, pulling on a string that lowers a large map of the world. **"We covered the earlier conflicts like Korea, Vietnam, World Wars I and II. Let's discuss World War III, and how nuclear weapons will change the world."**

A boy suffering from mild acne, seated by the window next to Scott raises his hand. **"Excuse me, Mr. Canton."**

"What is it Jason?"

"Can I open the windows?" the boy asks. **"It is getting really warm in here."**

"Go ahead, it is warm in here," Mr. Canton replies; the boy proceeds to open the windows. **"As I was saying, what effects will these types of weapons have on the human race?"**

Mr. Canton picks up a piece of chalk. "If a war like this were to break out, it's likely the eastern states would get hit the hardest. Can anyone tell me why?"

A pretty girl sitting in the front row raises her hand.

"Yes, Mary."

"Is it because the main branches of government are in the eastern states?"

"That is correct." Mr. Canton writes "government" on the chalkboard. "Now, can anyone tell me what –" like an illusionist captivating his audience he pauses a moment, his eyes wielding suspense, "— these weapons will do to us?"

A skinny, freckled, auburn-hair boy sitting three desks behind Mary raises his hand. "Radiation?"

"Correct, Martin." Mr. Canton writes "radiation" on the chalkboard. "Nuclear weapons will saturate our planet with radiation, making the planet uninhabitable. However, history has shown that the human race is resilient, so much that it might acclimate to such extremities. So, we need to consider what will happen to the survivors of the War, and how radiation will change them?" Mr. Canton begins jotting down genetic alterations on the blackboard. "I believe man will convert back to the primordial days of survival, and as food stores become depleted, he will look elsewhere."

Out of nowhere, Scott finds his thoughts flooded with intense visions of this war. And, while the teacher continues to talk, he slips into a strange, dreamlike trance.

Children living like animals, hiding in the ruins!
Strong bodies perfected into killing machines!
Fierce beastly eyes, reflecting eerily inside the night!
Unspeakable acts of violence, and horror!
With his mind succumbing to these visions, that face he saw earlier in the clouds appears, only this time...

The face is laughing at him!

Like a scene straight out of a horror flick, the face talks in a voice mimicking that of Mr. Canton's, the words being those of their discussion on the war. Without any warning the face explodes, discharging a throng of colored beams that not only jolts Scott out of his trance, but out of his seat altogether.

Moving briskly toward his fallen student, Mr. Canton inquires, **"Mr. Miller, are you all right?"**

Lying flat on his backside, and staring up at the ceiling, Scott responds, **"I'm, okay."**

With laughter mounting from his students, Mr. Canton tries his best to control his own mirth by cuffing his left hand over his mouth. Climbing back into his chair, Scott signals his teacher that he is fine; his gesture received. **"Everyone back in your seats,"** Mr. Canton says.

"Too much coffee this morning, I guess." Scott snorts.

"Ladies and gentlemen, let us return to our discussion, and Mr. Miller, take it easy on the coffee, okay."

As Mr. Canton returns to the blackboard, Scott turns to face the back window, his baby blues looking beyond the little birdie that is perched on the windowsill; that face has haunted him twice in one day.

 *Time passes…*

Upon hearing the bell, the students begin heading for the door. Grabbing his books, Scott advances as well, but before stepping out into the hallway, he turns toward his teacher, wishing to apologize for disrupting the class. Sitting at his desk, Mr. Canton appears to be lost in thought, his eyes glued to the elegantly framed picture of a child who could only be his precious granddaughter.

 *Time passes…*

With the last bell of the day resounding throughout the hallways, Scott departs his final class, metal shop; the only class he and Dave share. Though they are not related by blood, the two share a special bond comparable to that of brothers——with Mike completing their most unique troupe. They have been labeled as… 'The Three Misfits.'

"Hey, what's up with you?" Dave asks.

"What you mean?" Scott retorts.

"You haven't said a word since this morning."

"Really, I'm sorry."

"Are you okay?"

"I'm having a rough day," Scott responds.

Displaying the same ill-behaved smirk from the morning, Dave snickers, **"A rough weekend too, huh?"**

Ignoring his friend's childish remark, Scott walks over to his locker and opens it. After placing his books inside, he turns toward Dave, and in a stern voice says, **"Don't you have a doctor's appointment today?"**

"Yeah, but I'm not going."

"You have to go!"

"Do we need to go over this again?!" Dave barks.

"Yeah," Scott barks back, closing his locker, **"we need to go over this again!"**

"They can't help me, so leave it alone!" Dave storms away, saying not another word, prompting Scott to lean back against his locker. His heart pains for his friend, his gut telling him something is wrong, but, Dave isn't talking. It has been at least three weeks, if not longer since Dave has gone to one of his appointments. Glancing over at the circular clock on the wall, a much needed smile surfaces on Scott's lips. Turning his head, his baby blues travel the full length of the hallway, knowing the moment is rapidly approaching and the performance, which is usually quite entertaining, is about to begin. Every day at this time, our most prestigious performer—our grand compere of the senior class makes his grand appearance;

"The Michael Rivera Show"

The program opens with Mike slowly making his way to his locker, which is next to Dave's. Needless to say, the Spanish lover finds it impossible to walk down the hallway without acquiring one or two phone numbers, and hitting on every pretty girl in sight. The young women who are in the know are conveniently by their lockers, preparing to smile at him when he walks by them. Scott finds this most amusing when their overzealous boyfriend's show up---desperate to salvage whatever relationship they had with their lovestruck ladies. Truth is, most girls are simply not able to reject the honeyed charms of this smooth-talking criminal; for instance the one he has just accidentally bumped into, halfway down the hallway.

The attractive girl just so happens to have an extremely jealous boyfriend, and their conversation is well underway by the time her young man turns yonder corner. Growling, the boyfriend hastens his pace upon seeing who his lady is talking to. He doesn't like Mike and, he is not alone in this sentiment, particularly amongst those with cute girlfriends. Whenever they caught their ladies staring at him, it made them dislike him more. The young man is swift in stepping between his girl, and the detested intruder who never saw him. Fortunately, the "Rudolph Valentino" possesses a set of skills that help him neutralize situations that could turn ugly, really fast. In other words, Mike charmed the angry young men until the danger subsided. And, to top it all off, he usually receives a handshake or even high-fives from the poor souls; nonetheless, if it came to fisticuffs, Mike would never back down, no matter how big or strong the other guy was. All the same, he prefers to utilize his persuasive talents and ease any, and all possible concerns. In the case at hand, the Spanish heartbreaker makes the set of circumstances appear totally innocent, and after receiving a halfhearted handshake from the girl's boyfriend, he strolls away, leaving the quarreling couple to themselves.

As Mike approaches Scott, a devious smirk shapes his lips. **"Man, you are just plain awful,"** Scott says, staring at him, and shaking his head.

"I was just being friendly," the Spanish lover scoffs.

"Kissing a girl is a little more than just being friendly."

Looking down the hallway, the girl can be seen yelling at her man. **"Oh boy, you may be right,"** Mike snorts. **"I'm glad she didn't stick her tongue in my mouth. That would have been pretty bad, huh?"**

Scott looks at his friend like the guy who had just stolen a baby's lollipop. **"You're horrible."**

Lowering his eyes, the Spanish lover stages a comical pose of someone seeking forgiveness for wrongdoing. **"I was bad again, wasn't I Scotty?"**

"Yes, you were bad again."

"Well, I suppose the right thing for me to do is go give back her phone number."

"You're a lost cause," Scott proclaims, as he and Mike resume their viewing of the squabbling between the young man and his angered lady. Moments later, she storms away, leaving the disheartened lad to trail close behind. **"Do you see what you did?"**

"I like women," Mike scoffs. **"Is that a crime?"**

Scott rolls his eyes, and after checking out a pretty girl who had just walked by and smiled at him, he says, **"Let's go, Dave's waiting for us."**

Opening his locker Mike places his books inside, and after grabbing his leather jacket, the two press forward to meet Dave, who is waiting for them by the glass doors at the main entrance...cooling off after his heated exchange with Scott. Rounding the corner at the end of the hall, the two nearly collide into a triad of hotties, and as expected, Mike is quick to initiate conversation, because it's imperative that he does so. Shortly thereafter, he is explaining to a pair of brunettes why he does not partake in school sports, while at the same time, a petite young Asian girl with flirty eyes is telling Scott just how much she loves watching him play.

Before long, the three are on their way, leaving Scott and Mike to debate who had the cuter girl. Their dispute concludes upon their arrival at the glass doors when they spot the brawny, security supervisor Curly talking awfully close to Dave...as if he is giving him a lecture. Scott knows full well what the scolding is all about.

"Oh shit!" Scott curses, as the two simultaneously spin around, their feet ready to flee the disaster zone.

"**Well, well...if it isn't the other two stooges!**" a fearsome voice bellows from behind. As the two slowly turn to face the approaching juggernaut, their gaze travels beyond the supervisor to focus on Dave who looks rather upset, aware they were thinking about leaving him to deal with the man eating beast alone. "**You boys are trouble for me,**" Curly snarls. "**One day I'm going to catch you guys in the act, and that will be that.**" The grumbling supervisor lays into them on how it isn't wise to piss him off. In the interim, the nearby students clear out as Curly continues to scold the trio for a minute or so, before eventually walking away.

"**That guy is so lucky he left!**" Dave scowls. "**I was just about to lean into him!**"

"**Sure, Dave,**" Mike snickers, "**he's the lucky one.**"

"**Some friends you are. Both of you were getting ready to take off!**" Dave barks, redirecting his anger.

"**You have it all wrong, buddy,**" Mike utters. "**We were trying to get Curly to follow us, so you could slip away.**"

"**Yeah, right!**" Dave snaps. "**You guys nearly vanished down that hallway!**" Unable to contain themselves, Scott and Mike burst into laughter at the sight of their friend's angry glare. But, it only lasts seconds before Dave joins in with his own laughter, as its understood by all that if Curly catches you, well...you're on your own.

As the three slowly make their way toward the entrance. "My God," Mike remarks, "did you guys smell his breath?"

"It made my nose hairs stand up," Scott snorts.

"Mine too," Dave adds in.

"How did Curly catch you?" Scott inquires; however, he refrains from further questioning upon noticing a look of embarrassment developing on Dave's face. As the three walk through the giant glass doors—and though its seventy degrees out, Mike decides to put on his jacket. Standing atop the concrete steps, they observe those students from the other side of town board the city's yellow buses parked along the street in front of the school.

After waving to an admiring young lady, Mike begins cleaning his designer sunglasses with tissue retrieved from his jacket pocket. "What time are you gents going to the Rockit on Friday?" he asks, huffing on the lenses.

Dave responds excitedly, "I'll be there about nine."

"How wonderful, Davey," Mike snickers.

"Oh, shit," Scott chuckles; looking away.

Dave scowls at both of them.

"And, who will you be bringing?" Mike asks, pausing a longwinded second before continuing. "Your hand, Davey? Are we bringing our hand again?"

With the daily ribbings officially beginning, and with the subject being girls, Dave knows he's in trouble. "I'm bringing your sister, that's who!" he growls.

"Oh, really, stud muffin. By the way, when was the last time you were actually with a girl?" Mike jests. "I'm sorry, did you just say...never?"

Scott interrupts. "Guys, I have to split."

"Don't you want a ride home?" Dave asks.

"No thanks, I feel like walking home today. I will see you guys tomorrow."

"I'll call you later," Mike utters. Scott reacts by waving his hand as he walks down the steps. "What's up with him?"

"I don't know," Dave replies. "Something is bothering him. C'mon, I'll give you a ride home."

Covering his face with his hands, Mike cries out, "OH NO! There goes my reputation, being seen with you and that big nose." Dave is about to say something unfriendly, but Mike puts his arm around his shoulders, and smooches his left cheek. "I heard you guys were late, again." Walking across the street, toward the parking lot, Mike is provided details on his friends' morning jaunt with Curly: he laughs.

Meanwhile...

Serenated by the singing robins perched on the giant oak branches, accompanied by his face being cuddled by the gentle spring winds, Scott's stroll down the Avenue is an enjoyable one. The footpath home travels through one of the city's most sought after attractions, an intersection south of downtown Buffalo.

'The Four Corners'

It's a special place where one can appraise the unique cultures this amazing city has to offer. South Park Avenue is the principal street that runs into this epic, four-cornered juncture to which Scott is presently on. It is his favored side, one that truly fancies his palate:

A zesty, Mexican-style taco shack.

Ice cream parlor, featuring fifty different flavors.

A popular comic bookstore with miniature figurines, trading cards, posters, etc...

A submarine and sandwich shop.

Huge arcade room with all the beeps and zaps.

Then, there is Scott's favorite: an Italian pizzeria that caters to the younger folks.

Stopping in front of the eatery, he tilts his head toward the blue sky, scanning the clouds for signs of that face, or anything else that shouldn't be there. After looking through the establishment's rosy windows, he enters; his nostrils are accosted by the invigorating aroma of pepperoni, sausages and cheese! An outdated jukebox from the fifties sits by the wall to his right, and to his left, are several rectangular shaped dining tables with nearly all of them being occupied. Televisions have been mounted to the walls, transmitting up-to-the-hour music videos. In the back is a pool table, and a handful of arcade games—one of them being Scott's favorite: the Phoenix.

Besides the terrific pizza, Scott comes here because the owner's twelve-year-old daughter has a crush on him, and as such, she endows him with free food and drink every time he visits. Teasingly, Scott will smile at her and make her blush, forcing the lovestruck girl to dash into the kitchen to brush her hair, and to make sure she does not have any pizza sauce on her adorable face. Already developing into an attractive young lady, Scott holds much sympathy for her father. In a few short years, this little darling is going to break a bunch of hearts, not to mention her daddy's wallet. Every now and then, when the girl plays the game with him, Scott teases her by telling her that when she gets a little older, he is going to come and sweep her off her feet, making her blush even more. Nonetheless, she insists she is already old enough.

Normally, Scott would go directly to the front counter where a slice or two of his much-loved, pepperoni and cheese would be waiting for him. But, not today. Instead, he makes his way over to his game, hopeful that the blasting of aliens on the black screen will further relieve his anxieties of the day. After greeting friends sitting at a table, and a handful of others gathered around the pool table, he heads for his beloved game, promptly inserting the required quarters upon arrival. No sooner does the game begin...

**"So, the great South Park all-time jock-rash
plays video games!"**

Identifying the speaker, Scott elects to simply ignore the childish taunting. But, no sooner after blasting the next batch of alien ships on the screen, a milder voice sounds off. **"That's one fine-looking woman you have. I do wonder what she sees in you."** Recognizing this second voice as trouble, and cannot be ignored, Scott turns to confront those who stand no further than forty feet from the entrance.

'Identical twin brothers'
Larger teens with short, curly red hair.
They are wearing, dark-green varsity football jackets
with the name "Timon" on the back.

'Crazy eyes'
A troubled juvenile, who has been thrown out of every high school in the city stands to the left of the twin's.
He is a tad shorter than the twins, and leaner.

And, then there is he, who has been Scott's childhood rival since the third grade.

Whitey McDonnell: this steely, blue-eyed senior with his ivory-white hair, tan face and tall, slender physique certainly stands out in a crowd. He attends a distinguished, all male school called...Bishop Timon. In their younger years, he and Scott had played against each other in neighborhood football games. Because Whitey was stronger at the time, he would start fights with Scott; however, as they got older the tides turned with Scott winning their last fistfight over two years ago on the basketball courts at Cazenovia Park, which is a popular playground in south buffalo.

Folding their arms across their chest, the twins take a couple of steps closer, while Crazy Eyes starts cracking his knuckles, while also taking a step or two.

"If it isn't my friend, Mr. Miller," Whitey jeers. "So, what are we going to do now, Scotty Pooh?"

Staring hard at Whitey, Scott snarls, "I always knew you needed help, you chicken-crap weasel!"

"Silly boy, I don't need help with your kind."

"All right then, why don't you and I go outside and take care of business!"

"I think not, and besides, why should I have all the fun while my comrades here miss out?" Whitey taunts.

"You call these clowns your comrades?" Scott scoffs. "They look like those dopey dwarfs who are always sniffing on Snow White's skirt." Several of the teenagers watching the spectacle laugh, while the young girl behind the counter glares at Whitey with mean eyes.

"You're a funny guy," Whitey sneers. "But you are not going to be funny for very long."

"As I said," Scott hisses, "you and I can go outside and take care of business. That is if you are not too much of a yellow-stinking coward!"

"I'd rather take care of business with that hot little lady of yours." Whitey laughs, as do the other three, and with the white-hair villain taking the lead, all four begin walking toward Scott, stopping within thirty feet of him. Rising to their feet in support of Scott are several of his classmen, who are sitting at the tables. Within seconds, the restaurant falls silent—as hushed as a whisper. **"Why are you smiling, punk?"** Whitey scowls, upon witnessing a grin taking shape on Scott's lips. **"Did you not hear what I just said about your little bitch?"**

"I heard you," Scott replies, still smiling. **"I really doubt my girl would find somebody like you any more attractive, than a pig in shit."**

"We're going to rip your face off!" Whitey growls.

"I seriously doubt it!" From the entrance comes a male's voice so daunting that it forces Whitey, as well as the other three to spin around. Occupying the space in front of the entrance door are five sizeable males—all wearing South Park football jackets. The owner of the voice is by far the biggest, and meanest looking one in the entire restaurant.

Kelly Barker: is a young man of eighteen who stands a bit over six feet, and hits the scale at two hundred, and thirty pounds of just plain nastiness. Sky-blue eyes, sandy blond hair parted down the center, and a sharp, mischievous wit is the best way to describe him. Friends for years, Kelly and

Scott played on the same teams in their community football league during their juvenile days. Small and chunky would best describe him as a boy; however, that all changed in his freshman year when he got big—really big. Kelly fostered an attitude toward those who had picked on him; Whitey was one of those kids who did just that.

Payback is a bitch!

Stepping forward, Scott goads Whitey, **"Well, weasel, what are you going to do?"**

Recognizing the circumstances are no longer favorable, Whitey observes the twins, noting both their trembling hands and the apprehension reflected in their eyes; Kelly is casting a most dreadful persona: a barbarian about to explode with rage and fury; even crazy eyes seems worried. Employing extreme caution, the twins make their way to the entrance, pointing their eyes at the floor. But, as they gingerly walk by Kelly, they instantly freeze in place—like icicles clinging to a frosty gutter, upon hearing a subtle growl.

After the two twins depart the restaurant, and rather quickly at that, Whitey and crazy eyes procure the same route, but minus the terrorization. Just as they are about to leave, the steely eye, white-haired teen turns and glowers wrathfully at his adversary, only to find him staring back at him with the same loathing glare. Upon Whitey's departure, everyone in the joint rises to their feet and applauds, with several offering Kelly and those with him free slices of pizza.

59

"Thanks," Scott says, walking up to the husky teen.

"No, problem." Kelly clasps Scott's right hand. "I have been waiting a long time to pay him back for what he did to me in the fourth grade. So, anytime you want me to snap that scrawny neck of his, let me know."

"I'll do that," Scott chuckles.

With a boisterous hoot escaping his lips—pointing in the direction of the serving counter, Kelly laughs, "I don't think you needed my help." Following his finger, Scott sees the owner's daughter standing a mere foot away from the counter with an iron skillet raised high above her head; her adorable little face turns as red as an apple.

The girl darts into the back kitchen.

Making his way to the entrance, while shaking his head in embarrassment, Scott knows Kelly intends to not only address the crush the young girl has on him, but even more, her wanting to protect him against the big bad wolf, Whitey, all inside a crowded boy's locker room.

TROWBRIDGE
"Ahhh!" Scott cried.

"ROCKIT"

Tick tock — the mending of the clock.

All those unpleasant visions Scott had suffered on Monday didn't hound him throughout the week, and for that, he was thankful. He has convinced himself that none of what he saw was real, not those eyes nor that disturbing face in the clouds. Furthermore, that irritating Halloween memory was merely a minor blip in time. With a childhood of awful tribulations, he has mastered the art of denial. On a positive note, sightings of the mysterious Stranger have long since been washed away by Father Time.

Tuesday:
Scott attends football practice after school.
Later, he hangs at Dave's house with Mike, watching
television for most of the night.

Wednesday:
Scott spends time with Lisa, then retreats back over
to Dave's house where he's provided a fabulous supper
by Mrs. Knoll.

Thursday:
Scott consorts once more with Lisa at a popular rolling
rink, spending most of the evening with her, and sneaking
into his house later that night.

Friday:

Mayhem's here, and the weekend belongs to the younger folks of the city. With many going to --

'The Rockit.'

Built in 1979, the Rockit is a huge dance club located on Buffalo's upper north side. It can accommodate several hundred people at a time, and is equipped with:

A spacious dance floor, and stage area.

Cushioned booths throughout the club.

A state-of-the-art sound and lighting system.

A café/snack shop with a half-moon countertop.

Video arcade room, featuring two air-hockey tables, several pool tables, and six electric dart boards.

The mayor and a handful of prominent businessmen are responsible for the creation of the club, built specifically for the younger folks. Tonight, they are celebrating their five-year anniversary, having signed a widely revered band to provide the evening's entertainment; the club opens at eight, an hour earlier than usual.

{Scott arrives at 8:30 pm}

Walking through the outer door, he spots two members of the security team standing in front of another door that leads directly into the club, both looking to be in their early twenties. Making his way toward them, and as if rehearsed,

Scott begins to strut down the walkway, mimicking an actor from the movies, high fiving them as he enters the club; he is wearing a burgundy silk shirt, and designer blue jeans with his black, Italian leather shoes he and Mike went shopping for a week ago. His hair is combed back, and his left wrist bears the Movado watch his father gave him last month for his birthday.

Standing just inside the threshold of the club, Scott scans the interior for Dave and Mike, whom he had called an hour earlier. This was another game the three played, the loser being the one who shows up last, which is usually Mike. As the club fills up, it's becoming increasingly more difficult to locate them, assuming they're even here. Moments later, a very pretty girl walks up to Scott and asks him to dance.

Mary Reynolds: is a striking young lady with an impressive figure, and soft brown eyes, the kind boys lose themselves in. Well-mannered, she is the type of girl your mother would instantly approve of, while your grinning father pats you jubilantly on the back. Mary enjoys a strong relationship with her parents, particularly with her mother who regularly picks her up after school. The two spend considerable time together: shopping, movies, and the routine lunch. Scott has known the cute brunette since the first grade, attending the same schools throughout the years, often with matching classes such as Mr. Canton's second period history.

Mary is dressed in a charming indigo shirt, complemented by a medium-length, midnight-black dress. Her magnificent chestnut-brown hair falls past her shoulders and is neatly tied back in a ponytail, giving her a polished, and composed look; in short, she's quite remarkable to behold. Accepting the invitation, Scott guides her to the middle of the floor, where they begin dancing to a lively, rhythmic song. Shortly thereafter, this affable couple is bumping into others, and laughing as they do.

Truth be told, Mary often occupies Scott's thoughts, especially when he catches her looking at him, which is either at school or his football games: Mary is on the cheerleading squad. When this tender eye contact occurs, she usually turns her head and looks away, whereas he doesn't.

Stopping to pose for a picture taken by a male student from the school's yearbook committee, the two are placed in a pickle that becomes even more of a pickle when a romantic song begins to play, enticing those still on the floor to hold their dancing partners closer. As his heart beats zealously, Scott is seconds away from asking her to stay and dance with him—the words crawling up his throat. At this delicate moment, a soft hand caresses his backside.

"Mary, would you mind if I cut in?"

"He's all yours, Lisa." Releasing a gentle smile, Mary leaves the dance floor, and heads toward the booth she was previously sitting at.

"You look absolutely beautiful," Scott remarks, turning his attention back to Lisa after observing Mary leave the floor. Showing her appreciation for the compliment, Lisa kisses him tenderly on his lips, then informs him that he looks quite handsome. Gazing into each other's eyes, a seductive light appears inside Lisa's captivating blues; meanwhile, a group of shy young men, or nerds as others would call them are admiring the beauty from afar.

Lisa Thomas: a shapely girl with long, beautiful blonde hair that falls nearly halfway down her back—except tonight it's styled back into a "royal bun." Hugging tight onto her firm body, and trumpeting her fabulous curves is a spectacular, cerulean-colored dress. Hung around her slender, lovely neck is an expensive gold necklace with many diamonds; she truly embodies the countenance of an empress.

{Mike enters the club}

Within moments of his arrival, two young girls approach, asking if he would care to dance with either of them. Politely declining, Mike kisses them softly on the back of their hands, and the pair swan away, giggling. Dressed in a frosty-white silk shirt, with the top three buttons undone...along with his brown tweeted trousers, and tan leather Italian shoes, the Spanish Casanova moves deeper into the club, scanning the interior to see what catch is worthy of his love.

Even after four months, Mike remains captivated by the allure Lisa once had over him; truth be told, the lovely lass still occupies his thoughts, and its far more than he would ever acknowledge. Shaking off the emotion, Mike's eyes continue roaming the club, eventually spotting Mary sitting all alone at a booth on the other side of the dance floor; he makes his way over to her.

"And, how are we doing this evening?" Mike flirtatiously asks. "By the way, you look simply...ravishing."

"Why thank you, Sir Michael," Mary replies, gracefully. "You are looking princely as well."

With a spice of chivalry, Mike gently takes Mary's right hand and kisses it. "Why, thank you, my kind lady."

"Now Michael, I know the ladies fancy your charming ways," Mary says, imparting him a look.

Still holding onto her delicate hand. "Whatever do you mean?" Mike asks, playacting a befuddled look.

"It means, I know you too well." Mary giggles.

"Um...you do, don't you?" Mike releases her hand, and before occupying the seat across from her, he politely smiles; then, they both burst into laughter.

On the other side of the dance floor near the entrance to the arcade room, a young man bearing a look of outright adoration has his eyes glued to Mary—as they have been for the better part of a minute. The black pinstripe suit he wears renders him more of a corporate officer than someone who is here to have a good time. Inhaling deeply, the timid young man proceeds toward the booth. **"Hello, Mary,"** he says, bashfully. **"How are you?"** Informing the young man she's fine, the enchanting brunette proceeds to compliment him on his suit. Sitting next to Mike, across from Mary, the young man adds, **"Did Scott show yet?"**

"Yeah, Davey, he's on the dance floor with the Queen of Sheba," Mike scoffs, motioning with his eyes toward the crowded dance floor. His scornful reporting triggers a slap on the forearm from Mary. Frankly, Dave is not the least bit interested in Scott's whereabouts for his eyes, and his thoughts are firmly on this captivating young lady sitting across from him. Luckily for Dave, Mary doesn't notice the puppy eyes he is making at her; however, Mike does.

Once the song concludes, the band announces a ten minute intermission to the audience; holding hands, the two young lovers slowly make their way over to the booth the three are sitting at.

"Hey guys," Scott hails upon arrival.

"Nice shirt, Scotty," Mike says.

"Thanks. When did you two get here?"

"A few minutes ago," Mike replies.

Reaching out and touching Dave's jacket, Scott asks, "what is up with the suit?" Receiving no response, he shifts his attention back over to Mike. "There appears to be a lot of girls here tonight."

Pointing his eyes at Lisa, Mike taunts, "Yes, there are plenty of those. But, tonight, I desire a real woman."

With irritation swelling in her eyes, Lisa excuses herself and heads to the ladies' room. "Behave, gentlemen," Mary remarks with a light chuckle, her eyes zeroing in on the nicely dressed, rather tall young man with short black hair who had just walked into the club. After climbing out of the booth, Mary walks in the direction of the male, who just so happens to be her date for the night.

"What kind of remark was that?" Scott barks.

"Sorry, I didn't mean anything by it," Mike says.

"Isn't she delightful?" Dave utters, shyly.

"Who's delightful?" Scott inquires, looking at Dave.

Smirking like a Grinch, Mike says, "It seems Davey has been shot by the arrow."

"Shot by the arrow?" Scott repeats.

"OH, YEAH!!" Mike laughs. Tracking their friend's love-stricken eyes, they see Mary heading toward another section of booths with her date walking next to her.

"I'm hungry," Dave grumbles. "I'm going to get something to eat." He stands and walks toward the café.

"What was that all about?" Scott asks, watching Dave cross over the dance floor.

"I guess, he really likes Mary."

"I never knew."

"Me neither."

"Dave is a mystery."

Stepping out of the booth, Mike removes his eyes from Dave, and places them firmly on Scott. "Indeed he is, and he likes his secrets."

"What do you mean?"

"His mother called me earlier today, wanting to know if he's been going to his appointments," Mike replies. "I know for a fact, he missed his last three."

"Yeah, I talked to her yesterday. I have a bad feeling. I'm really worried about him." Silence reigns until the blond beauty returns from the bathroom, several moments later.

With a satirical smirk forming on his lips. "So, Lisa, how have you been?" Mike asks.

"Exalting!" she responds, holding tightly onto Scott's right arm; looking away. With tension rising between Mike and Lisa, Scott is relieved to hear the band has returned, and will be opening with a slow, romantic song; this prompts Lisa to step away from Scott, and stroll out onto the dance floor, which is swiftly becoming populated with lovers.

"As you can tell, we don't like each other much," Mike says, with a dash of anarchy.

"Really?" Scott scoffs. "I couldn't tell."

"If you need me, I will be over there." Mike cuts his eyes toward a young lady who is sitting all alone at a booth on the other side of the club; she is looking in their direction.

Glancing over at the striking redheaded girl, Scott jests, "How do you know it's not me, she's looking at?"

"Well, if she is," Mike counters, "I am sure by now she knows you are taken, what with Lisa holding that dog leash around your neck. Woof, woof."

"Um...you may be right on that," Scott admits, seeing Lisa on the edge of the dance floor looking straight at him, agitation swelling in her sparkling blue eyes.

"You better go, before she tightens that lease around your neck," Mike jeers. "I'm going to go see who that girl is looking at, and by chance if it is you, I'll just convince her it's me she really wants." With a chuckle, Scott shakes his head and wanders over to the dance floor, whereas Mike heads for the redheaded girl. By the time Scott reaches Lisa, the slow song had already begun, rousing the beauty to snatch him by his shirt when he is within her reach. Kissing Scott obsessively on his lips, Lisa nearly buckles his knees. With cheeks touching, and arms wrapped around the other, they begin dancing in a circular motion. The first person falling into Scott's view is Mike, sitting at the booth talking to the girl. Next is Dave standing by the entrance, his eyes locked on Mary who is on the dance floor with her date.

A quarter rotation later is when Scott spots Kelly at the café, chatting with a pretty girl; he is joined by two of the young men who were with him at the pizza parlor. Judging by the smile on the girl's lips, Kelly appears to be doing well, that is until his two clumsy pals start acting silly——trying to promote him as a good guy: the girl walks away after a drink is accidentally spilled on her. The fury in Kelly's eyes is all that is needed to inform these misguided buffoons that it is paramount that they go somewhere else, and quickly at that! From past experience, Scott is aware that Kelly is not one to give up so easily. As the husky youth follows the girl to the back of the club, his 'Abbot and Costello' friends make haste into the arcade room.

After the song ends, the lead singer, wearing a black suit and dark sunglasses, greets the audience and proceeds to introduce his band:

Pair of female singers: bright yellow tank tops, and short black leather skirts.

Lead guitarist: red suit, red sunglasses.

Drummer: green suit, green sunglasses.

Keyboardist: orange suit, orange sunglasses.

Finally, there is the gangling bass player standing at the back of the stage; purple suit, purple sunglasses.

Following the introduction, the lead singer, who looks to be in his mid-twenties informs the crowd that they are going to play what they hope will be their breakout song.

Ten seconds into their promising smash hit is all it takes to put the club into a frenzy; rapt by the unique rhythm of the beat, the dance floor quickly becomes overcrowded.

Quick timing to the floor is Mike, and the redhead.

Kelly is also running onto the floor, holding the left hand of that girl from the café. Halfway into the dynamic tune, the husky youth and the girl initiate a popular dance involving all those on the floor: 'the electric-slide.'

Moments later, the song ends, and the band is rewarded with a thunderous tribute. Overcome by the positive review, the harmonious seven bow twice. With no end to the praise, they bow three more times. Showing their gratitude, they begin playing an old time classic, a beloved romantic melody that touched the hearts of many.

Scott and Lisa remain on the floor, as does Mike and the redhead. Meanwhile, Kelly is heading to the café with the girl who is giggling at something he is whispering in her ear. Holding Lisa close, as they repeat the circular motion, Scott's eyes fall once more on Dave standing in the same spot as before. But, just as they are about to rotate away, a sourness takes shape on his friend's face. Locating Mary, Scott bears witness to the tail end of a kiss that was placed upon her unsuspecting lips. Swiftly rotating back to Dave, he finds him missing. Normally, he would leave him to tend to his own affairs, but not this time, especially the way he has been acting of late. Excusing himself, Scott quicksteps it over to the arcade and searches the area. Without success, he decides to look outside the club, making haste through the exterior doors; he spots Dave walking toward his green Mustang, his head hanging a tad low.

"DAVE!" Scott shouts.

Without responding, the somber youth keeps walking.

"DAVE!" Scott shouts again, running toward him, and ultimately catching up. "Where are you going?"

With a numb expression, Dave answers, "Home."

"Why? You just got here."

"I want to go home."

Just as Dave reaches out to open the driver's side door, "Do you like her that much?" Scott probes.

"I like her too much," Dave concedes, closing his eyes.

"Why didn't you tell me?"

"What am I supposed to tell you?" Dave says, opening his eyes. "That I can't think straight when she is near. Am I supposed to tell you that? Or the fact that I can't breathe when I see her. Am I supposed to tell you that too? I never had these feelings. I don't know what to do. When I look at her, I want to live, even though I know I won't. Oh man, it hurts. I can't handle it, I simply can't."

"Dave, I don't —"

"There is nothing to say," Dave quickly interjects. "Life can be deceitful." He looks at Scott, a tear present in each eye. "Live my friend. It is the gift God gave to you, but not to me." All Scott can do is stand there silently, watching his friend get into the Mustang and drive off. At that moment, a laughing couple emerges from the Rockit, hand in hand, as music pours out of the club behind them.

Morning has cometh...

The crack of dawn arrives, heralded by a fist rapping on thy chamber door, hauling a sleepy young man away from tender dreams. After opening the door, Mrs. Miller walks over to the window and shifts the curtains apart, permitting a formidable beam of light to hit her son straight in the eyes: a bird perched on his windowsill flies away.

"Ah, Mom," Scott moans, "it's Saturday."

"It's also ten o'clock," Mrs. Miller declares, watching her son rouse from beneath his comfy blanket. "Do you want breakfast or lunch?" Normally, Scott wears a tee-shirt to bed: last night he didn't. "What are these bite marks?" his mother beseeches, walking toward him, pointing at his naked chest. In a state of panic, Scott frantically searches for something to put on, spotting a football shirt on his dresser.

Quickly reaching for the shirt, he replies, "I think the cat bit me last night."

"What is her name, this cat of yours?"

"Lisa." Scott puts on the shirt.

"Is Lisa the reason you've been sneaking in and out of the house?" Mrs. Miller probes with a meddling gleam.

"Breakfast sounds good," Scott says, quickly slipping into his private bathroom, and closing the door behind him. Remembering what it was like at his age, the innocence of young love, Mrs. Miller stares at the door and concedes her son had successfully evaded her probing: a smile takes shape on her motherly lips. Straightening her son's blanket, her gaze settles on the framed picture on the nightstand, displaying a picture of the young woman who is stealing her baby away from her. After tucking in the blanket under the mattress, just above the boxspring, her attention shifts to the sunlight pouring joyfully through the window, animating her lovely blue eyes.

 *Time passes...*

Sitting at the kitchen table, feasting on the scrumptious meal his mother prepared for him; made up of pancakes, eggs and sausages, Scott decreed years ago that whomever he married, would have to cook as good as dear old Mom.

While pouring her favorite, vanilla flavored creamer into her coffee cup, Mrs. Miller says, **"In case you forgot, today is your father's birthday."**

Scott, his mouth full of pancakes, mumbles, **"I'm meeting him at the bank in a few hours."**

"When you see your father, tell him to call me." Mrs. Miller gently stirs her coffee with a spoon, while her lovely eyes drift toward the kitchen window.

"You want me to tell him to talk dirty?" Scott laughs.

Sipping her dark-roasted coffee, his mother eyeballs him humorlessly; Scott finishes his breakfast in silence.

 *Time passes...*

Returning to his bedroom, Scott inspects the bite marks on his chest in the bathroom mirror. Tilting his head for a better view, he recalls his most enjoyable evening with Lisa. After the club closed around midnight, she drove him home where they exhausted thirty minutes—maybe a tad longer saying goodnight—the origin of the bite marks. The scent of her perfume still lingers in his nose, and the remnants of her lipstick are still clinging to his pearly whites. Dressing himself with a comfortable white shirt, slipping into his jeans, and lacing his sneakers, Scott makes his way to the front door, yelling goodbye to his mother as he reaches for the doorknob. Upon hearing her reply from within the kitchen, he opens the door and steps out onto the porch, lifting his face toward the bright sky.

"Hello, dear."

Scott directs his attention to the elderly woman seated comfortably in her favored rocking chair on her front porch. "Good morning, Mrs. Sinclair. How are you?"

"Oh, fine dear. Isn't today your father's birthday?"

"Yes, it is," Scott replies, walking down the porch steps. "I'm on my way to see him now."

"Please say hello to your father for me," Mrs. Sinclair says; the benevolent smile on her aging lips is one that has always softened his soul.

The Sinclair's have lived in the house next door for more than forty years.

After acknowledging her request, the lad makes haste for the bus stop at the end of the street, reaching it just as the number #6 heads his way. Knowing it travels downtown, he boards, moving all the way to the rear of the bus. Before his butt nestles into the plastic seat, the bus is pulling away from the curb; having brought his Walkman radio with him, he places the headphones over his ears. Five stops later, a striking lass boards the bus and heads in his direction.

"Hello, Scott," the girl says, taking the seat beside him.

"Hello Mary, where are you headed?" Scott asks, but before she has a chance to reply...

"BA...BOOM"

The bus's muffler suddenly backfired, startling several commuters. A lady sitting near the front of the bus places her right hand over her chest, and releases an angry sigh.

"I'm heading to the downtown library," Mary responds, then turns to Scott and asks him the same question.

"It's my father's birthday. We're having lunch."

"That's nice."

"I guess."

"You guess? Why do you say that?"

With sadness in his tone, Scott says, "My mom and dad are still not back together, and I'm not too sure if they ever will be." As Mary cuddles his right hand, he gazes into her beautiful brown eyes, appreciating why Dave adores her so much. "Did you have a good time at the Rockit?" he asks, seeking to change the mood.

"Not really."

"Why not?"

"I had an argument with my date," Mary replies. "He was trying to talk me into going home with him, and when I told him no, he stranded me there."

"What a jerk!" Scott snarls.

"He was a jerk," Mary agrees.

"What would you say, if I told you that I know someone who is absolutely crazy about you?"

"I don't know," Mary replies, looking deep into his eyes. "It would depend on who this person is."

Bewitched, Scott looks down at his right hand, which is still being held by hers. As a familiar sea of emotions bubble to the surface, his eyes slowly rise to meet hers. Struggling to express himself clearly, and honestly, Scott instead blurts out, "Um...what if I said it was, Dave?"

Leaning back in her seat, an air of sadness appears on Mary's face, disappointment in her voice. "I wouldn't have guessed it was Dave, who liked me."

At that moment, Scott realizes she had presumed it was he who liked her, and as Mary brings her eyes to the front of the bus, that sea of emotions continues to bubble internally; as of late, he has been thinking more and more about her, as if it was a prognostication of some sort.

Strange this is!

Before a confession can betray his lips, he locks it away like a jailor, and spends the time talking about his upcoming game, and about being scouted by a college he is interested in going to. As he gabbers on, Mary listens with an attentive heart, lasting until they both step off the bus.

"See you later, Mary."

"Have a nice lunch with your father."

"Have a nice time at the library," Scott chuckles.

"I know, it's a lousy way to spend a Saturday."

"Poor girl."

"Well, Mr. Miller," Mary sneers playfully, "not all of us are as smart as you in history. Some of us have to study." The pretty brunette smiles and heads for the library, leaving Scott to watch her disappear around a distant corner.

 *Time passes...*

Buffalo's downtown district is an architectural marvel, with many buildings dating back to the turn of the century found on every corner. Community gardens were planted throughout the inner city, and are enjoyed by the younger and older generations who occupied them, well before the morning sun had fully risen from the dead. Staking claim to the wooden benches scattered about the parks — enjoying their Styrofoam cups of fresh brews were the elder folks. The feisty seniors boasted entitlement, using the benches as a political platform for their friendly, and not-so-friendly debates, which usually went hand and hand with...

"Whose move is it?"

Games of checkers and chess are ritually played atop the concrete tables inside the parks, and it's these types of competitive, and not–so competitive contests that generate most of the appeal. Walking through one such park, Scott's attention—as well as a handful of others, is captured by a heated chess match.

"Come on, Teddy, you move like a snail."
{Italian accent}

"Dry your arse, Luzio. You always rushing me!"
{Irish accent}

"Well, if you didn't always take forever, I wouldn't have to rush you, would I?"
{Italian accent}

"I aren't a taken forever, I'm a strategizing here you see, strategizing."
{Irish accent}

Scott laughs right along with the other onlookers over the nonstop bantering of these two elders. The one named Luzio appears to be of Italian ancestry, whereas the one named Teddy looks to be Irish, or perhaps Scottish. Both seem to be in their early seventies.

"Noi hanno gigante pietre in Sicilia, che mossa più veloce di si," Luzio sings harmoniously, following yet another lackluster minute.

"Jaysus!" The man named Teddy grumbles. "Now, don't go a startin that savage spaghetti blather. You know how much I hate it when you dunce that."

Following another burst of laughter from all those who have gathered around the table, Scott decides it is time to get going, but just as he's about to walk away, Teddy finally moves and Luzio, without delay, captures his knight, inciting another dispute from the feisty Irishman, furthering his claim that he is being rushed.

The stroll into the heart of downtown is an enjoyable one...for the sun is shining, and the people are teeming with pleasantries and cheery faces. Small crowds of potential shoppers are patiently waiting for the department stores to open their doors for business. Many of them are observing the elegant window displays showcasing the current fashion trends. *It is a pair of designer jeans that momentarily steals Scott's time.*

Millions of dollars have been exhausted on Buffalo's new transit rail system, and to save time, Scott hops aboard the first one he sees coming down the tracks. Shelling out the one dollar passenger fee, he secures a window seat in the back. Gazing through the window, he notes the queue of individuals waiting patiently to board, fully aware that the available seats are being claimed too quickly. As the train continues accepting passengers, Scott's eyes revisit the department stores he just walked by—eventually spotting a man standing inside a shadowy alleyway—between a pair of wholesale retailers; the man seems to be looking directly at him. Experiencing that strange internal tingling, Scott leans forward in his seat, catching sight of a ghostly, white glint within the shadow that is partially concealing the man's face; the spot where the glow appeared is precisely where the man's eyes would be.

"Excuse me young man, is this seat taken?"

Nearly hopping out of his skin, Scott swiftly turns and finds an elderly lady standing by the empty seat next to him, a benevolent smile on her thin, grandmotherly lips.

"Not at all, ma'am," Scott replies.

After taking her seat and glancing out the same window, the lady utters, **"Oh my, isn't that a lovely rainbow."** Scott doesn't respond to her comment; instead, he continues to scan the alley for the individual who is no longer present.

Moments after the packed train leaves the platform, the giant golden dome; the crest of the bank his father works at slides into view. As his stop approaches, Scott scans the buildings, alleyways and anywhere else he believes the man could be; his thoughts are on the white reflection he saw, or thinks he saw. Stopping a mere block from the bank, Scott departs the train and immediately resumes his visual search for the individual. Less than a minute later, he sets aside his suspicions and proceeds to his father's workplace.

Enjoying the stroll, Scott cannot help but appreciate the kinship these buildings have with each other, many of them being built in the 1930's—his father's bank included. Entering the depository, he finds it brimming with people; mainly because it's one of a few banks that are even open on Saturdays. A woman, looking to be in her mid-fifties is seated behind a counter talking on the phone. Walking up, and not wanting to be impolite, Scott waits until she is done with her call before speaking.

"May I help you?" she politely asks.

"I'm here to see Mr. Miller."

"Do you have an appointment?"

"Yes, I'm his son." The woman picks up the phone and dials a three number extension.

"Mr. Miller, your son's here." {pause} **"Very good sir, I will send him up."** Hanging up the phone, the woman gives Scott directions to his father's office, which isn't needed since he's been there many times before. Thanking her, he proceeds toward the main staircase located several yards on his left----before the ingress that leads to the restrooms. Ascending the ivory marble stairs, he observes three armed guards: one at the entrance, another standing near the vault behind the tellers, the third walking the floor. From the top of the second floor landing, it is twenty or so steps until he is standing in front of a huge wooden door that features a beautiful, stencil glass inset in its upper panel; a tiny waiting room is on the other side, as well as another door that leads directly into his father's office. Reaching out to open that first door, Scott's mind becomes besieged with questions that have plagued him for the last couple of months or so. Questions that need answering:

Why did he leave?

Why can't they be a family again?

Why? Why? Why?

Since his parents' separation, his relationship with his father has suffered.

They postponed their hunting trip this year.

They stopped hanging out on weekends.

They didn't go on their annual fishing trip, and the last time the two ate a meal together was over a month ago.

Scott initially believed his parents just needed a little time away from each other; however, he didn't anticipate it to be this long. Upon opening the door, Scott is greeted by his father's personal secretary; a young, attractive lady looking to be in her early thirties.

"**You can go in,**" she says with a smile.

"**Thanks, Cindy.**" Scott smiles back.

Walking through the door, the lad spots his pop seated in a fancy brown leather chair, behind a fancy desk. "**Come in son.**" Scott walks over to his father, who promptly stands and gives him that lengthy, father-to-son hug, the one that seems to last forever. Feeling his father's love, the young man soaks it all in to the last drop.

86

Roy Miller: this handsome, hardworking man of forty-two has long since achieved notable undertakings in the financial arena. In his college years, Mr. Miller sported a mustache and sideburns; however, these days he keeps his thick, black hair short, and styled...with no mustache. Due to his striking features, on top of his mannish brown eyes, Mr. Miller was targeted by the ladies, especially Mrs. Miller who went out of her way to get him to notice her, which of course wasn't too difficult in the first place. He is well-liked by both family and friends. Retaining his healthy physique, he stands three inches taller than his son, whom he humorously reminds from time to time.

"Mother wants you to call her."

"Okay, I'll give her a call later," Mr. Miller says, sensing something is on his son's mind, noting the subtle uncertainty reflected in his reserved smile.

Following a brief pause, Scott spurts out, **"Dad, do you want a divorce?"** The lad's eyes reveal anguish, and his face reflects sorrow.

Sitting on the edge of his desk, Mr. Miller gazes upon his son with a prideful glee; he is becoming a respectable, strong young man. **"Son, I have loved your mother since we started dating in college, and I still love her, very much,"** Mr. Miller says, placing his hands on his son's young shoulders. **"This is something me and your mother need to work out."**

Three short knocks on the door.

Cindy walks in and reminds her boss of his meeting with the internal revenue service later in the day. Before taking her leave, she updates him on his lunch reservations, letting him know it has been confirmed. Mr. Miller thanks her.

Cindy leaves — not closing the door behind her.

"Son, it's my birthday," Mr. Miller says. **"Spending time with you is the best present I could receive. So, what do you say...let's go have some lunch?"**

"Absolutely, Dad. Happy birthday."

Scooching off the edge of his fancy desk, Mr. Miller leads his son out of the room, his right arm draped around his shoulders.

With the afternoon sun providing a gentle warmth, and given the restaurant's proximity just a few blocks away, Mr. Miller proposes they proceed there on foot. No more than three steps are taken when Scott begins telling his father about his potential acceptance to a certain university he's interested in attending. Hearing the excitement in his son's voice brings Mr. Miller back to his college days, when he was an all-state running back, and one of the fastest athletes in Buffalo. Less than a month after accepting a scholarship from an Ivy league university in Pennsylvania, he was injured in a non-essential game against a regional school.

And that as they say...was that!

A young lady in her early twenties greets them when they walk through the artistically designed glass door of the restaurant that holds their lunch reservation. With a smile, the hostess leads Scott and his father to their table, where upon seating them hands them a menu. A heartbeat later, a young male comes over with two glasses of chilled water and sets them down on the table in front of them. Before the menu even reaches their eyeballs, a veteran waiter arrives at the table to take their drink orders.

Five minutes later...

The waiter returns with a small, circular tray that holds their drinks, placing them down gently on the table in front of their recipients. **"Sir, I will be bringing your salads in two** shakes of a lamb's tail," the waiter says. "May I recommend our signature blue cheese dressing? We put a sprinkle of Cajun pepper in it."

"Absolutely," Mr. Miller says. "Son, I've had it before, it's really tasty."

"Okay," Scott responds, first looking at his father then at the waiter, who nods his head, acknowledging acceptance of his recommendation: the waiter takes their food order.

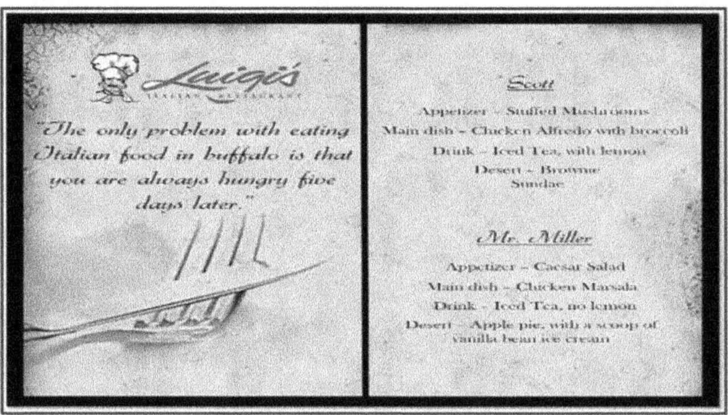

After taking a hearty swig of his iced tea, without lemon, Mr. Miller utters, "Tell me more about this university you are interested in."

"Well, dad, it's the same university you went to," Scott says; he takes a swallow of his own iced tea, with lemon.

"That is a really good school," Mr. Miller declares.

The waiter returns with their salads.

While eating his salad, Scott conveys to his father what his majors might be, as well as where this school ranks on the national collegiate football theater; Mr. Miller tells his son how he can't wait to watch him play at that level.

Listening to his son chatter away brings much joy to Mr. Miller, and after their salad plates become barren, the waiter promptly takes them away with Mr. Miller thanking him for the recommendation.

"You're welcome, Sir," the waiter says. "The chef is just finishing up with the chicken masala. It will only be another minute or so until I bring your selections."

The waiter walks away from the table.

"Dad, I'm really concerned about Dave," Scott says. "He's not going to his appointments."

"Oh, boy," Mr. Miller groans.

"We tried to get him to go," Scott adds, "but, he won't listen to me, or Mike. I'm scared for him."

"Son, I am going to have to tell his parents," Mr. Miller says in a concerned tone. "Jesus, they are going to be really upset, especially his father."

"Dad, let me talk to Dave first. I will tell him what you are going to do. I know he doesn't want his father to find out. Maybe that will force him to go."

"I'm not sure about this," Mr. Miller voices, shaking his head slightly. "Dave's parents have a right to know."

"Just a few days," Scott pleads. "When I tell him you are going to talk with his father –"

"A few days," Mr. Miller says firmly. "No more."

"Thanks, Dad. I'm going to see him later today."

"Alright son, but let me know if it doesn't work."

"I promise, Dad," Scott says.

Returning to the table with their entrées, the waiter sets one of the plates in front of Mr. Miller. **"The chicken masala for you, sir."** He sets the other in front of Scott. **"And, the chicken alfredo with broccoli for you, sir."** Upon producing a chunk of white parmesan cheese, and a grater. **"Sir, would you care for some on your alfredo?"**

"Yes, please," Scott replies.

After applying the cheese, the waiter walks away.

For the remainder of their lunch, the conversation shifts to Lisa, concluding with Mrs. Miller. Scott explains how he met her, also mentioning her attractiveness; Mr. Miller responds with a smile. After his son is done, Mr. Miller tells him that he and his mother have not reached the point of no return, putting a grin on Scott's face. After paying the bill, Mr. Miller walks his son out of the restaurant.

Strolling the bustling streets of midtown on their way back to the bank, Mr. Miller continues reassuring his son that things will work out between him and his mother. Upon arriving at the bank, Mr. Miller gives his boy another long hug. Afterwards, he heads inside, while Scott heads home.

'The Avenue'

When the Avenue first sprang into existence during the late fifties, it was a place where people came to watch illegal car races, often with the police in hot pursuit of the drivers.

'The Four Corners'

South Park Avenue, also known as the Avenue, runs from the southern town of Lackawanna, all the way into the heart of downtown Buffalo. Somewhere near the middle, there is an intersection, less than a mile from Scott's school, to which the Avenue crosses over another major street; this is the location of the four corners.

{First corner}

That corner looks like a scene straight out of a 1950s American film, featuring a classic burger joint. Tight white shorts, and red sleeveless shirts are the mandatory uniform for the roller-skating waitresses who take food orders from patrons inside their parked cars. On weekends, the parking lot is crowded with vintage beauties: Corvettes, Mustangs, Thunderbirds, not to mention the chilling, 'Plymouth Fury,' as it was portrayed in the movie. The older males proudly displayed their American-made muscle cars, bragging about them as if they were trophies of steel.

Strolling down either side of this street will place you inside a time machine, transporting you back to the yuppie days of turtleneck sweaters and thuggish leather jackets, those with fasteners that zip in the front. Young men would grease their hair back, mimicking the styles of Brando and Dean from the big screen. Sounds of the '50s wailed from the out-of-date juke boxes inside their music shops, and clothing stores. Most of the fast-food eateries feature the tabletop version of the jukebox, and for a quarter it will play your favorite oldie, but goody. Scott's pizza parlor is a block from the burger joint.

{Second corner}

Groovy tunes and a deep-rooted musical sensation are what your ears will experience here. A new genre of music embraced by rappers, and hip-hoppers. During the warmer seasons, the businesses on this corner will organize dance contests right there in the middle of the streets. And, if the younger folks aren't watching these contests, then they can be found inside their clubs, dancing away to the innovative sounds of reggae. They play this unique style of music with an uplifting energy, and to hear it would not only captivate your soul, but take you to an oasis filled with serenity and friendship. Both sides of the streets are filled with diverse ethnic restaurants, offering enough variety that you could eat something different every day for a week.

{Third corner}
This most unusual corner is commandeered by a pair of distinctive groups, each controlling an entire side:

{First Street / left side}
"New Wavers"
Teens with multicolored hair and imaginative clothing linger about their outlandish stores. Microelectronic drumbeats, synthesizers and other electric instruments reverberate from their music rooms.

{Second Street / right side}
"Gothics"
Black-clad juveniles with their mystifying piercings and eerie tattoos amass on this side. This creepy consortium of darkly dressed youths have forged their eccentric shops on every inch of real estate:
Vampirism clothing.
Wicked exotic piercing.
Cryptic jewelry and charms.
Demonic tattoos and body paints.
Nefarious and enigmatic music selections.
Dungeon-like clubs — secretive and uninviting.
A unique bookstore is located near the nucleus of this street, claiming to have the rarest assortments of books, tomes and digests on the occults and supernaturalism.

94

The mystic bookstore, and most of their other shops are painted in darker colors; however the music stores, and the spooky ass nightclubs all bear that grim shade of black. Even though these structures radiate an insane degree of creepiness, they are generally non-toxic.

In the early eighties, the youths rejoiced the nativity of the vampire movement. Long black trench coats, and jewelry looking to have been crafted by undertakers were adored as if they were mystical talismans. Their ghostly pale faces, and their black hair converted them into wannabe predators of the damned: zombies, vampires, wraiths, etc. A minority of these younger folks dress in more of a diabolical nature, applying reddish colors to their face and hair, matching that of the netherworld.

{Fourth corner}

Rowdy taverns filled with heavy drinkers line both sides of this corner. Bikers and rockers are the monarchs here, and to tell one from the other would be no easier than telling the difference between a tortoise, and a turtle. Sounds of the '60s and '70s bellow from the taverns, like gospel hymns from churches. Blue jeans, and ordinary tee-shirts are the chosen attire there.

When weather permits, bikers will line up their Harleys, Kawasaki's, Hondas and whatever else they ride in front of the taverns, creating a seemingly, never-ending succession of motorcycles. They display their club names with pride on the backs of both their denim jackets and leather vests. Anarchy—and downright meanness accurately describes these two brawling factions, which only intensify when they hold their beer drinking contests in the middle of the streets. The police routinely park less than a block away from these taverns, just in case trouble breaks out, which you can say was also routinely.

 *An extraordinary affair…*

Several of the main businesses located on the second corner, which is the musical corner, have organized a dance contest scheduled for this weekend. Receiving the proper authorization directly from the mayor's office, and with the approval from business on the other corners, a large section of the street has been closed off for the event.

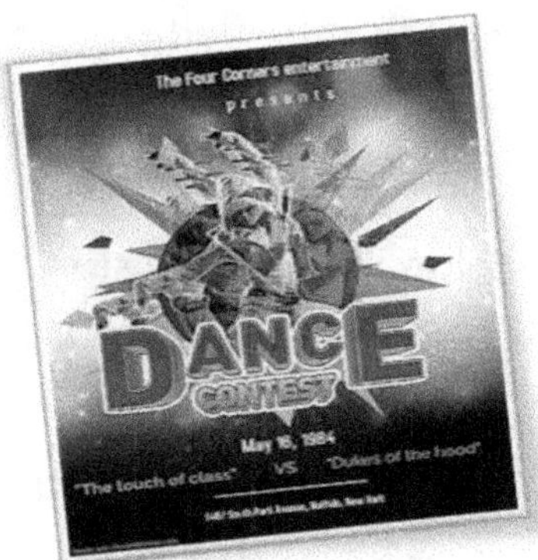

Because the young ladies attended these competitions, bachelors such as Mike flocked to the scene, contending to be the "best man of the night" — for which is what they call it; these teenage Romeos will show up in hordes.

Scott arrives on the scene with both Dave and Mike; however, the Spanish lover promptly takes his leave, intent on acquiring the most phone numbers. Fearless is a perfect way to describe Mike, which is the one thing Scott admires most about him. Though his charms are typically effective with the ladies, every so often he encounters rejection, and believe you me...it's an absolute droll experience to witness; the sour look on his face is priceless.

By climbing atop a gray, post office mailbox next to a street lamppost, and a green, metal trash container, Scott and Dave have given themselves a superb view of not only the dance contest, but of anything else that is worth looking at. Leaning against the lamppost, displaying a satirical grin, Scott utters, **"Oh Davey boy, guess who I just might have fixed you up with?"**

Dave's response is a stare that says, "I don't trust you." He has justifiable reasons for this, as Scott and Mike have pranked the poor lad throughout the years, setting him up with girls who fell below your typical standards. **"Oh really! who did you fix me up with this time?!"** Dave snarls. **"A sixty year old in a wheelchair!"**

"If you don't want to know, then I won't tell you." Scott appreciates, and often takes advantage of the fact that his friend is a most curious fellow.

Acting as if he does not give a hoot to hear the answer, though Scott knows better, Dave scoffs, **"Okay, who?"**

"Miss..." Scott pauses. **"Mary Reynolds."**

An ill-fated affair befalls poor Dave. He involuntarily steps off the mailbox and falls into the circular, green trash container. Witnessing this, the teenagers in the area laugh rowdily: Dave's butt is completely inside the container, his legs dangling helplessly over the side. Several entertaining seconds later, Dave manages to remove himself from the container and, to Scott's surprise, climbs back atop the mailbox as if nothing happened.

"Mary!" Dave gasps. **"You fixed me up with, Mary?"**

"Maybe," Scott chuckles. Dave's facial expression is that of a three-year-old who was just given his very first ice cream cone. **"I saw her on the bus today, and asked her if she would like to meet us here."**

"You're the best friend anyone could have," Dave says.

"Listen, Dave. I just got her to come here, the rest is up to you. Do you hear me? It's up to you."

"I don't know what to say."

"Don't say anything to me." Scott signals with his eyes for his friend to turn around. **"Say it to her."**

Slowly turning his head, Dave's eyes widen in genuine terror; Mary is standing next to Lisa by the curb watching the dancers warming up, less than twenty yards away.

"I don't know what to say to her."

"Dave, don't let your shyness wreck this."

"I can't!"

Scott jumps off the mailbox, and lands on the sidewalk in front of it. "I know what I want," he says, looking up at his petrified friend. "Do you?"

"Talking to girls comes natural for you and Mike, but..." Dave wheezes, "...it isn't natural for me."

"Just talk to her," Scott says. "I know you can do that."

Building up courage, Dave studders, "I can do that."

"Yeah!" Scott roars encouragingly.

"I'm going to go over, and talk to her."

"Yeah, Dave, you are the man!"

"I am the man!" Dave roars back.

"Dave—"

"I AM THE MAN!" Dave roars louder.

"Dave—"

"Yes Scott, I know...I'm the man."

"Dave—"

"What?!" Dave barks, looking down at Scott.

"Don't you think it would be a good idea if you come down off the mailbox first?" Scott snickers.

Taking in a breath, Dave jumps off the mailbox, landing to the right of Scott. With his insides twisting like a horde of worms, he follows his friend over to the pair of lovelies, and upon reaching them, he watches Scott place his right arm around Lisa's slender waist, inciting her to spin around and kiss him, several times. Both Dave and Mary are quick to look away, pretending not to have noticed.

Moments later, holding a wireless microphone, an older black man walks out into the street, welcoming the crowd to the contest. Afterwards, he introduces the first dancer of the night from the club, 'Dukes of the Hood.'

 *Time passes...*

With the competition approaching its conclusion, both clubs take pride in a job well done. Nonetheless, it is turning out to be a victory for the 'Touch of Class,' who displayed better techniques. They move to seal the win with their best dancer, 'Mr. E' walking out into the street; the young man receives a boisterous ovation; included are those from the bikers and rockers. Without delay, the dancer starts off his routine, performing flips and rolls that seem impossible for a human to achieve.

The clouds turn gloomy!
The air becomes a little cooler!
The winds become angry, when seconds ago they were passive as Christmas snow. Within seconds, this contest comes to a screeching halt, as from those dismal skies above cometh the—

Following another friendless bolt of lightning, rippling across the depressing sky, Lisa shouts, **"My car is just down**

the street!" She shepherds the others to her red Camaro; a gift on her sixteenth birthday. Lisa's parents have spoiled their precious daughter ever since she was a child, giving her everything her heart desired, and some. Upon reaching the car, all four quickly climb inside and wasting no time, with her red heart shape keychain dangling in her right hand, Lisa inserts the key and starts it up.

"VaaaRRRooooM"

The engine growls like a tigress as Lisa steps firmly on the gas pedal. As her Camaro speeds away from the curb, Dave spots his beloved Mustang, parked further down the street, crammed between a van, and a Chevy El Camino.

Heading to Lisa's suburban home in the northern part of the city, Scott unintentionally looks into the passenger side mirror and spies Dave talking to Mary. However, his attention is promptly fetched away by Lisa who has placed her right hand on the inner region of his thigh, a look of pure savagery growing inside her animalistic eyes.

 *Lisa's home...*

"Your house is beautiful," Mary remarks, as the Camero pulls into a long driveway belonging to elegant, two-story manor that features a spectacular wraparound porch; a sophisticated barn sits among a handful of tall oak trees in the back of the house.

"Thank you. It's not nearly as lovely as the one we had in San Francisco," Lisa retorts. After the Camero stops and completely shuts down, all four step out of the car; the heavy rain has stopped, and the dark clouds have lightened. While guiding her quests up the finely crafted Italian stone steps of her spacious porch, Lisa pauses and turns to face them, "Are you guys coming in?"

"I can't," Mary says, her foot resting on the first step.

"Just for a little while?" Scott beseeches.

"I promised my mother I would be home early," Mary replies. "We have relatives in for the weekend."

"How are you going to get home?"

"There's a bus stop a few blocks away."

"It's not too late?"

"No, it's still early."

"Are you sure?"

"Don't worry," Mary smiles, "I'll be fine."

"Okay," Scott says, his tone laced with worry.

After saying goodbye, Mary turns and starts walking away from the house. Thinking quickly, Scott pushes Dave, sending him tumbling down the stairs, nearly bumping into her. "I'll walk you to the bus stop?" Dave says, shyly. "I need to get my car, don't trust her alone on the streets."

Giving Scott a look, Mary replies, "I would like that."

Watching the two heading for the end of the street, Scott moves down a step, reflecting on the look Mary had just given him... with those adorable, chestnut-brown eyes of hers, as if she wanted him to know something; a pain shoots directly into his heart——into his very soul. This paroxysm of emotions corrects itself after he turns toward his woman...

"Whoa!" Scott gasps.

Leaning against the porch's support beam, Lisa stares at her man...like a panther closing in for a kill; an unrefined hunger burns in her cobalt eyes. Walking back up the stairs, Scott's eyes descend to her denim shorts, which expose her long, shapely legs——slowly traveling upward toward her delightful assets as well as her delicious neckline. And if this wasn't enough to drive the lad crazy, her slightly damp hair is hanging freely; moreover, her bangs are covering part of her face. Lisa is grinning shamefully, her non-blinking eyes sizing him up.

Nearly choking on his saliva, Scott speaks, his words slurred and raspy, **"Um...it's getting close to my beddy-bye time. Maybe I should get going as well."** Unsure of what he should do, he turns as if he is going to take his leave, but before he can plant his foot on the next downward step, the formidable female grabs him, a piping hot inferno burning inside her feral eyes.

"The only bed you are going to mister..." she hisses, **"IS MINE!"** Lisa kisses Scott with a hunger that almost buckles his already shaky legs. With eyes decreeing she is not going to accept refusal, she unlocks the front door, and grabbing onto her man's left hand, she guides him, or rather pulls him into the house, closing the door behind them.

Observing what appears to be the living room, Scott asks, **"Where are your parents?"** A captivating fireplace with an antiquated grandfather clock next to it fall into his immediate line of sight.

"Out of town." Lisa grins, impishly. **"They love to travel."**

"That's cool," Scott says, timidly.

Lisa leads her man up a swanky staircase that runs into a long hallway that curves at the end; there is a door on the right, one on the left, and two more further down. **"Baby, I have something I want to show you."** Steering Scott to the door on the right, and opening it, Lisa reveals her bedroom, a sweet fragrance satiating the air. There is a queen-size bed by the window with scores of pillows on it. Scott notes how her silky, white sheets, and her heart-pumping, pretty pink silk blanket are already drawn; a clear indication she had planned this. With her hungry, lioness eyes already feasting on her quarry, Lisa steps into her private bathroom, and closes the door.

"Oh boy...Oh boy...Oh boy," Scott mutters.

"I'm sorry baby, did you say something?" Lisa's voice is barely audible through the closed door.

"I said, this is a really nice bedroom you —" Scott is not able to finish his sentence...for the blonde beauty emerges from her bathroom wearing nothing but a see-through, white negligee; furthermore her towel-dried hair is combed back.

"Are you shy, baby?" Lisa teases.

With his jaw slightly drooped, Scott attempts to refute her questioning, valiantly, **"No, I'm not shy."** Nevertheless, his facial expressions betray him like a snitch----ratting him out that she's going to be his very first; she smiles wickedly, stripping away all his innocence.

Licking her lips naughty-like, she hisses, **"Am I going to have to rape you?"**

Scott laughs as if she is joking, however her unyielding stare tells him it's time for him to be the man. With his heart pumping feverishly, he walks toward her. When he is within reach, she grabs him, ripping off buttons and shirt. Kissing his neck and chest, Lisa works her way downward until she is on her knees----looking up into his baby blues; creatively, she removes both his pants and underwear. As his heart beats feverishly with every lustful act she executes, Scott becomes imprisoned by her sensual touching; Lisa starts to moan, becoming a slave to her own sexual ecstasy.

"I want you...NOW!" she demands.

Naked as Adam in the garden, Scott scoops Lisa up like a bride and carries her to the bed, laying her gently on it. But, before he can enjoy her, he realizes the lights are still on. Walking over to Lisa's dresser, Scott spots a candle on top of it; he kindles the candle with matches he finds next to it. After flicking off the light switch, he returns to her, only to stop cold in his tracks. Scott finds himself captivated by her curvaceous figure, entranced by the way her seductive sapphire eyes glimmer in the candlelight. Lying submissively on her bed, the blonde beauty moans oh so softly, waiting for her man to come take her; sounds of lovemaking echoes throughout the bedroom after Scott walks over to her, and begins fulfilling her desires.

106

"WATCHED"

onday kicks off with a scheduled 'Pep Rally' inside the school's auditorium: the principal is a true sports fanatic who is enjoying a remarkably good year.

Today's event is being held to celebrate the basketball and football teams, as it has been several years since both teams have achieved winning seasons concurrently, with the potential for both to advance to the finals. Awakening the spirit of the students who are still pouring in through the entrance doors, the cheerleaders begin performing on stage, executing flips and other acrobatic feats. Presently, Scott and Mike are seated in the first row, directly in front of the stage... with Dave between them, grinning from ear to ear.

"So, Mike, who was the official stud at the contest?" Scott asks; a devilish smirk satisfies his inquiry. Leaning to his left, toward Dave. **"Hey buddy, what happened with Mary Saturday night?"**

"We caught a bus to my car, and then I gave her a ride home," Dave replies. **"We talked a little bit, and I asked her if she wanted to go see a movie with me this weekend."**

"Way to go, Davey boy," Mike bellows, bestowing him a high-five. **"That's the way we do things around here."**

"It's just a movie," Dave states shyly.

"Movie or not, it's a good start," Mike adds.

Leaning in toward Dave again, Scott says, **"Just think, you may have the prettiest girl up there."** Mike pats Dave on his back, and nods in agreement. For the first time in his life, Dave feels a joy he's never known before, one that can only be inspired by a woman—and he is happy. One by one the three direct their attention to the stage—specifically to the cheerleaders who are forming a human pyramid with Mary scrambling to the top of it.

Someone begins shouting out the school's name!

From within a shadow by the stages backdoor, a husky youth comes running out toward the front of the stage, clad in full football attire: shoulder pads, leg pads, jersey; but no head gear. One side of his face is painted black, while the other is red: the school's colors. Like a man in dire need of an exorcism, he continues to scream...

Despite the distinctive facial paint, the identity of the young man remains widely recognized.

As his name echoes through the auditorium, the students and nearly all of the teachers in attendance rise to their feet and applaud. Standing by the entrance doors are the five starting members of the basketball team; upon receiving a head nod from Kelly, they start making their way toward the stage. A small staircase with only five steps is in front of the stage. After the five young men ascend to the stage using the stairs, Kelly greets each one of them with a high-five as they walk past him.

The chanting endures until Kelly steps in front of the podium, and speaks into the microphone. **"Listen up. Today our basketball team battles Kensington in our gym. I have no doubt that not only will we be victorious, but we will send them packing with their heads hanging low."**

Kelly speaks once again into the microphone. "I want to remind you people, Saturday our football team battles the city champions from last year. We are going to need you all there to cheer us on to victory. With a win, we will go to the state championship, and face our detested rivals, Bishop Timon." The school's name ignites a fierce round of boos.

Kelly waves the crowd to silence. "Now, we all know the reason we are in this game is mainly because of one person. Not only has he broken every one of our school's records, but several state records as well. With him at the helm, we are almost certain to win. So, let us put our hands together, and get our star quarterback up on stage." The students, and most of the teachers begin shouting:

Scott is fully aware that if he doesn't come up on stage, Kelly will come down with others, and carry him up. Rising from his seat, the lad waves his right hand in response to the cheers in his honor. Walking toward the staircase, he spots the husky youth out of the corner of his eye, waiting for him at the top. After planting his left foot on the very first step, he looks up at Kelly, swiftly turning rigid in fear as his black and red face has been replaced by that vision he saw in the clouds a few days ago; the grisly image stares at him.

Blood dribbles from Kelly's mouth, ghastly fangs slightly concealed behind sneering lips. But it isn't those fangs that are holding Scott in fear—nor is it the fact this vision is no further than fifteen feet away. It's something else, something far more frightening --

THE EYES...

Unaware of what Scott is experiencing, a male student slaps him kindheartedly on the back; the awful face that had taken over Kelly's vanishes. At the same time, four members of the football team hoist Scott up, and carry him onto the stage. With his name being chanted by all, he is deposited on the stage, his legs barely able to provide support.

In spite of the jubilant hubbub surrounding him, Scott remains imprisoned by fear, unable to move. His ears radio in on the crooning of the school's name, shouted from the cheerleaders who are currently amassing near the front of the stage. After releasing a fictious smile to Mary, who is looking at him with concerned eyes, he forces himself to turn his head and eyes in the direction of Kelly, whose face has already reverted back to the black and red. In the midst of the enthusiastic cheers, Scott is the only one who hears a disquieting laugh that is succeeded by an even more deeply disturbing voice...

"I SEE YOU"

The school bell rings, and the prep rally ends!

Beginning the exiting process, both the students and teachers head for the door. It isn't long until the room is as silent as a graveyard with one remaining behind...alone!

 *Time passes...*

After finishing his initial three classes, Scott proceeds to the basement cafeteria where he and Mike enjoy reserved seating within the larger of the two dining areas, at a table accompanied by several others. Spotting his dining buddy at the entrance, chatting with an extremely cute brunette, Scott approaches.

"Hey, Scott," Mike hails. "This is Susan."

"Hello, Susan."

"Hello, Scott."

"Don't we have math class together?" Scott bids.

"Yes, we do."

Gently taking hold of Susan's left hand, his tone laced with sugary goodness, Scott asks, "Why haven't we talked before?" Knowing where this is going, Mike rolls his eyes.

Revealing a truly lovely smile, Susan replies, "Because, you sit in the back, and I sit in the front."

"Perhaps I ought to sit up front," Scott teases, his tenor flirtatious; Mike shakes his head.

"I think you should."

"I'll give you a call later, Susan," Mike interrupts.

"Okay. Bye, Scott." After taking a few steps, Susan stops and glances back at Scott, releasing yet another of her adorable smiles.

"Yeah...so you get one on me once in a while," Mike scowls humorously, after Susan is out of earshot range.

"Hey there, Henry." Scott greets a fellow senior who has just walked out of the cafeteria.

"Are you okay?" Henry asks.

"Yeah, why do you ask?"

"You looked a little strange at the rally."

"I had a headache."

"Must have been some headache."

"It was."

"I'll catch you at the game." Henry saunters away, in the same direction Susan had gone seconds earlier.

"I was going to ask you about that," Mike says, as they stroll into the cafeteria. "You did look creepy. Then again, you always look creepy."

"I'm sorry, who was Susan flirting with?" Scott laughs.

Mike makes a silly face, and releases a sarcastic snicker.

Upon entering the lunch line, the two begin loading up their trays with food, especially with the flavor of the day being a favorite: Mexican. After paying the cashier, the two take their seat at their exclusive table, joining Kelly and six other players of the football team, all wearing their jerseys, all already chowing down what's in front of them.

Picking up his beef burrito from his overly stuffed plate, "Scott, what the hell was all that about today?" Kelly asks.

"I was shaking off a headache."

Before half of the burrito disappears into his widening mouth, Kelly adds, "The way you looked at me — gave me the heebie-jeebies."

Cutting into the conversation, Mike jeers, "That was a good face job, Kelly, maybe you should keep it." His jovial remark is chopped short by Kelly's unfriendly stare.

Three years back, Mike dated his sister and broke up with her after a few weeks, making her cry. Kelly never cared for Mike after that.

"Don't bring that headache with you Saturday," Kelly says, slowly taking his eyes off Mike, placing them on Scott.

Western New York experienced a major flu epidemic, creating an unprecedented postponement of all high school playoffs: football, basketball, lacrosse, and hockey. By and large, they would have been played months ago.

"Are you ready, Scott?" another teen at the table asks.

"Absolutely," Scott replies. "I'm really looking forward to beating Seneca, so we can play Timon."

"I know what you mean!" Kelly snarls. "I want a piece of Whitey myself. It sucks that he's their quarterback." The husky youths fist raps the table. "I won't get any hits on him!"

"How can you?" a third teen, sitting at the far end of the table chimes in. "You're the anchor on our offensive line."

"Well, you can believe I will get my hits on him," sneers the fourth teen at the table, "I'm defense, and I'll be looking for that horse's ass!"

"That's it!" Kelly's eyes enlarge. "I'll ask coach if I can play some defense."

"Give him an elbow for me!" Scott grumbles.

"OH YEAH!" Kelly growls.

"Fool doesn't even know what we have in store for him," the fourth teen remarks, as he reaches for his milk carton to take a drink. "Can't say he doesn't have this coming."

"For a long time at that!" the third teen snarls. "Maybe I'll ask coach to play some defense. I can't stand that guy!"

Before another threat is made against Whitey, chaos erupts when a freshman accidentally bumps into another student and spills food from his tray onto Kelly's back.

"Oh, man," the second teenager at the table chuckles. "This kid is really going to get it."

Growling like an ogre, Kelly rises from his chair and turns toward the petrified youth, who looks like he's seconds away from passing out from fright. "Get out of here, freshmen, before I kick your mangy, nerdy, butt." Truth be told, Kelly is a guy who appreciates a little fun, and besides, not much food actually fell on him. Dropping his food tray, the youth flees the cafeteria as if he were being chased by a bear.

"My, God, did you see him run?" snickers the third teen at the table. "He should be on the team."

Deciding to have a little more fun, Kelly scopes the room out like a sniper. **"Freshmen,"** he growls, **"I need freshmen to eat!"** *A frail girl sitting all alone at a nearby table is spotted.* **"You, girl, come here. I want to eat you!"** As if she was just marked as a tasty lamb by a mountain lion, the girl flees like an Olympic runner toward the exit. Afterwards, the husky youth begins harassing some of the younger teens, nearly depleting the room of them. Once he's sure his mischief has reached its peak, and with laughter rippling throughout the room, Kelly nonchalantly moseys back to his seat at the table. **"Gentlemen, let's eat."**

The bell rings...

Proceeding toward the exit, Scott and Mike are quick in spotting Dave standing just outside the cafeteria, a huge smile occupying his smugly lips, and a noticeable gleam in his brown eyes. **"I just asked Mary if she wanted to go see that movie with me after the game,"** Dave utters gleefully as the two approach.

"And..." Mike solicits.

"She said, YES!" Dave replies, enthusiastically.

"That's great," Scott adds.

Releasing a modest smile, Dave says, **"It's just a movie."**

"Oh Scotty, our baby boy is all grown up and getting laid," Mike sobs playfully, rubbing his eyes. **"Well, I guess oh, Davey won't be hanging out with us anymore, now that he has gone off and gotten himself a woman."**

"No way. You guys are my friends." Dave shoots out his right hand—the palm facing downward. **"I will never do that, till death do us part."** Slowly, Scott places his right hand on top of Dave's with Mike, even slower, following suit.

Shaking his head, Mike snickers, **"Guys, we are getting way too emotional here, starting to sound like a bunch of sissies."** All three go their separate ways, each toward their respective classes.

 *The day whizzes by…*

With less than twenty minutes before he needs to reach the gym and begin warming up for the big game, Scott is granted early leave from his teacher. In addition to football, this gifted athlete plays on the varsity basketball team, but not as one of the starters.

Coach Lewis: a tall, slim black man who walks with a limp, received during his tour in Vietnam, calls Scott over when he enters the locker room. He informs the lad that he may not see much playing time; nevertheless, he still needs to be ready if called upon. Today's contest has the fixings to be an exceptional one, as both rosters are filled with talented players; this contest is a rematch of last year's finals, which South Park won with a two pointer that scarcely beat the buzzer. Naturally, the shot was protested by the other team who claimed the buzzer had sounded off before the ball left the shooters hand.

As players from both schools walk out onto the court to practice layups, as well as their medium-and long-range shots, spectators start occupying the bleachers: the visitors' colors are green and white, the home team, black and red.

A loud buzzer comes from the scoreboard.

The head referee blows his whistle, heralding the start of the game. Heading to the sidelines, both squads receive final instructions from their coaches.

"Gentlemen, I'm proud of you," Coach Lewis declares. **"It took a lot of work to get back here. A win today, and we will return to the state championships; however, this time it's going to be different. We will bring home that trophy!"** The players place their hands on top of each other's, and in one roaring voice, they yell...

The five starters for each team walk onto the court and shake hands with the opposing players. Following another whistle, the ball is put into action, with Kensington winning the jump ball. The ball is swiftly moved down the court, where their star player performs a dazzling behind-the-back layup for two points. Behind a brilliant display of dribbling, South Park brings the ball to their opponent's basket, ending with a three–point shot by first year starter, Tim Steward.

"I SEE YOU"

In the remote corner of the gymnasium there is a black, spiral staircase that descends to an underground chamber where the school's Olympic-size pool was built. Next to the iron stairwell is a narrow, oval-shaped portico. At the very end of that shadowy passageway is a locked storage room where all the athletic equipment, as well as the school's band uniforms are kept.

The voice came from inside that portico!

Not only is he scared, but Scott's internal senses are screaming, *danger!* Staring intensely into that dark, gloomy archway, he is mindful it is normally illuminated by a ceiling light that presently isn't on. Shadows cloaking the opening is causing the archway to appear as though it's an endless wall. Complicating the situation, his mind is running amuck with images of the Stranger—perhaps he is in there!

"SCOTT…MILLER"

Even the deafening hails of the spectators fail to drown out the voice, which Scott clearly hears again; a tear runs the length of his face. Unwillingly, Scott stands and ever so slowly walks in the direction of the archway, as if *something* is pulling him there. While his traitorous feet move, his mind asks, "Why am I heading toward it, when I should be running from it?" His breathing is erratic, and his heart is struggling to maintain a normal rhythm; the screaming spectators have failed to notice him.

Still he continues, stopping when he is within feet of the stony archway---knees all but collapsing when he hears a wicked laughter from within that soul-destroying blackness. His heart all but abandons his body when a pair of shining yellow eyes, suddenly appear.

"SOON YOU WILL BE... MINE!"

Without warning, a pale muscular arm shoots out of the darkness and grabs his neck, lifting him effortlessly off his feet, until they are dangling freely in the air. Paralyzed by fear, Scott is powerless to move or scream as he is yanked violently into the blackness.

SOMEWHERE ELSE...

"Scott, are you all right?"

Upon hearing a males voice, Scott opens his eyes and discovers he is lying on the gymnasium floor just outside the archway. Caressing his aching neck, he recalls something in the dark grabbed him. Raising his head from the floor, while supporting himself on his elbows, he scans the area for the owner of the limb; the gymnasium is dark, and deserted!

Swiftly rising to his feet, **"What the hell!"** Scott cries out, his enlarged, socket-popping eyeballs locking onto the blood-red light beaming through the gymnasium windows, projecting infernal apparitions on the walls; these animated images are continuously shifting, creating a narrative as if they were summoned there to dance. That eerie light is also illuminating sections of the gymnasium floor with a diabolical sheen, creating an illusion of cracking open and swallowing the terrified lad, sending him straight to hell!

121   Adjusting his vision to the gloom, Scott notices bricks missing from the walls, which is granting him a partial view of a catastrophic scenery outside the school. He sees shadowy outlines of buildings in ruins. A hot wind blows through the gymnasium, carrying the acrid scent of rotting flesh.

In a state of absolute delirium, Scott drifts away from the archway as if he was a mindless zombie in search of fresh brains to eat. As his right foot touches the gymnasium floor for the third time, he turns to stone as he thinks he may have just heard something—or to be exact...

"GRRRR"

As if he had just stepped out of a cold shower, Scott begins to shake uncontrollably. Slowly, he turns toward the archway, his eyes unable to penetrate the unholy blackness within it; that awful growl came from an animal—possibly a dog—perhaps something worse!

"GRRRR"

Too scared to cry, Scott continues his feeble attempt to see inside the archway—to break through the dense wall of absolute gloominess. Like a repetitive hallucination, he is reacquainted with those yellow eyes!

"I SEE YOU"

If things couldn't get any scarier, eyes shining like fires from damnation materialize three feet below those yellows!

"I WANT YOU TO MEET… MY PET!"

Traumatizing laughter materializes inside the archway, and with his feet refusing to budge, Scott's only course of action is to stand there and weep. But, before that occurs, a commanding voice sounds off in his head:

"RUN!"

Breaking free of the hold, Scott scuttles through the gymnasium's metal doors, and into a hallway that runs north and south. Glancing down the gloomy passageway to his right, which is south, he elects not to take it, knowing it runs into another hallway that shoots straight into the cafeteria where he will be trapped. Not much safer is the passageway to his left, which is longer and ends at a stairwell. Staring at a large shadow on the wall directly in front of him, he spots the outline of the door to the boy's locker room. Recognizing this as his best means of escape, he runs to it and grabs the handle, twisting it open. Hearing the terrifying sound of what could only be talons scraping on the gymnasium's wooden floor, Scott freezes like ice, his trembling right hand still clasping the handle; the clawing sounds are closing in fast. Disregarding his fears for the moment, he enters the locker room with haste, frantically closing the door behind him.

123

BANG!

Something rammed into the other side of the metal door, evident by the sound he just heard. Seconds later, he hears scratching made from razor-sharp talons on the same door. With tears spilling from his eyes, Scott scans the dismal interior of the room...in the area he knows to be the location of a second door; he heads for it.

Broken light fixtures droop from the ceiling!

There are huge cracks in the concrete floor!

Most of the wooden benches in front of the lockers are missing; a number of the metal cabinets reveal telltale signs of having been introduced to a sledgehammer.

Dim lighting offers little in way of visibility, and it's the leg of a shattered bench that trips Scott up, tumbling him to the hard floor. He reached out with a hand to prevent his face from slamming into it; however, the back of his head wasn't as fortunate, whacking one of the metal lockers and drawing blood. Shaking off the wooziness, he uses his legs to push himself into a crook. Touching the back of his head, he feels wetness, and with his eyes locked on that door he had entered moments ago, he watches it slowly open with that disheartening crimson light slithering into the room!

"THERE'S NOWHERE TO RUN, BOY!"

Standing in the doorway is a fearsome figure resembling an oversized dog, its outline illuminated by that crimson light from behind, casting it as a hound from Hell!

"GRRRR"

Even though Scott is hidden in a shadow that conceals the crook, he suspects the creature will surely see him if he stays put. Finding the courage to stand, he places his back firmly against the wall, his terror-filled eyes locked onto that advancing hound, which is no further than sixty feet away.

"GRRRR"

Shuffling to his left, Scott's wandering hand locates that second door. Chancing a looksee, he removes his eyes from the doorway and spots a metallic sheen in the darkness on what is referred as a push-bar.

"GRRRR"

Another growl chills Scott's bones, prompting him to return his eyes to the hound's shadow. His gaze is met by glowing red orbs. Overcoming his fears, he exerts pressure on the push-bar and opens the metal door, rushing through it, and narrowly escaping the beast.

BANG!

While in attack mode, the beast had launched itself at Scott; the resounding bang on the other side of the door validates it had once more failed to reach its prey. A dreary stairwell with an unpleasant stench is what he experiences on the other side of the door; moreover, pitiable lighting at best comes from flickering fixtures attached to the concrete walls. Running like a madman up the stairs, and upon reaching the next landing, he immediately attempts to open the door. Whispers of torture touch his ears when his right hand fails to turn the latch. Consumed by fear, he hastens to the next landing and tries opening that door. Bless it be the lord, the latch turns. But, before opening it...

"*Jesus Christ!*" Scott screams.

That terrifying clawing he heard inside the gymnasium is alive in the blackness that rules this stairwell. Peering over the railing, he observes glowing red orbs rapidly ascending the stairs. Recognizing it to be the beast from the locker room, Scott reaches out to open the door, only to discover his legs are refusing to move—paralyzed by the scraping of razor-sharp talons on those concrete steps. Receiving yet another surge of internal mettle, Scott is able to open the door and run through it, slamming it shut afterwards!

BANG!

The forceful impact against the door startles Scott, causing him to lose his balance and stumble backwards into one of the lockers lining the hallway.

BANG!!!

Once gain there is loud bang on the door; however, this time it is significantly stronger, sounding more like a mallet, rather than an animal running into it. Scott quickly recovers his balance after realizing it was a fist that had impacted the door. Directing his gaze toward the darkness stretching in both directions, he notices the overhead ceiling lights are flickering on and off. Uncertain the door will hold, Scott steps away from the metal lockers, his left hand falling limply to the side of his leg.

"Ouch!"

A corroded screw sticking out from a severely damaged locker is certainly the source of the prick he just suffered to his left hand. While he inspects the wound, which is trivial at best, the terrifying scratching returns, heard on the other side of that door. Like a bullet shooting out of a gun, Scott sprints down the corridor for the staircase he knows to be at the end. But, before he's even halfway down the hallway, he hears a chilling sound of scraping claws on the concrete floor just behind him, which is followed by...

"GRRRR"

127 Screaming in mortal terror, Scott runs to the staircase and quickly descends it, misplacing his footing and tumbling down the last few steps. Bouncing to his feet, he sprints in the direction of the giant glass doors at the main entrance, his feet moving so fast that he finds it quite the challenge to maintain his balance. Within sight of those doors, his legs suddenly turn rigid as a corpse's.

SOMEONE IS THERE!

Shrouded in shadow, the dark outline of a hulking male is spotted standing in the middle of the hallway. Breathing heavily, Scott stares at the individual, a peculiar awareness flooding over him; from within his core, he realizes this isn't the Stranger---the tormentor who has haunted him for much of his life. His inner senses are telling him that the diabolical being before him is someone far more sinister. In the space where eyes would be, glistening yellow orbs appear, and a heartbeat later, Scott is running in the opposite direction. Before he can absorb his actions, or has the opportunity to rectify them, the creature that pursued him from the steel door---toward which he is now heading leaps on him, taking him down unmercifully hard to the floor.

A VERY DARK PLACE...

"Scott, are you all right?"

Hearing the voice a second time, Scott opens his eyes and discovers he is lying on the floor outside the portico in the same spot as before. **"What madness is this?"** he shouts, ascending to his feet: things have changed, again!

The walls no longer have missing bricks, and that crimson light is gone. Nevertheless, the gymnasium is still dark, and still very much deserted. Experiencing an agreeable warmth on his face, Scott scans the gymnasium, searching for the source of the lovely scent of blossom that has replaced the earlier foulness that had poisoned the air.

Standing just outside the portico, with his backside to it, Scott slowly turns and faces it, noting how the archway remains shrouded in gloom. Illumination emanates from the storage room located at the end of the narrow hallway; the door is ajar. With his internal senses warning him of danger, his eyes fall to his football jersey, marginally shredded by the beast's talons. Shifting his focus to the blood drippings on his sneakers, stemming from several lacerations on his chest, he gingerly touches the wounds, and experiences pain.

For reasons unknown, Scott's attention is drawn to the gymnasium's giant windows. Seconds later, he finds himself walking toward them; his internal senses is counseling him on...'what will come to past.' Reaching that middle window, he tilts his head toward the handsome blue skies, his eyes once again bulging in their sockets!

"My God, those are missiles!"

A long, sleek, cylindroid object with flames shooting out of one end soars high in that sky. Stepping closer to the window, a second...then a third is spotted penetrating the clouds; all three appear to be heading for his beloved city. As if the angel of death had paused his powerful hourglass, time decelerates! Scott witnesses the manmade instruments of destruction, trundle lethargically toward our gentle green mother. Mere seconds before the first one hits; he hears a God-like voice from beyond those midnight raptures.

The first missile snaps the spine of the city, creating a radioactive tsunami that instantly obliterates the school's exterior walls. Standing on the gymnasium's floor, enclosed by vacant space where walls once stood, Scott endures blistering winds. In the distance, screams from those caught in the deadly storm chills his blood; but he sees nothing, the concrete cloud is far too dense. Five heartbeats later that second missile also rattles downtown Buffalo, sending more waves of nuclear death rippling across the city, incinerating all those who were unfortunately still alive, silencing their cries of pain forever.

By the hand of God, Scott remains unscathed!

While his trembling legs struggle to support him on the scorched remains of the gymnasium's floor, Scott fixes his burning eyes on that third missile, which ultimately strikes the city like Lucifer's hammer!

As if they were leviathans sent by Satan, three gigantic mushroom clouds occupy the space the city once did; inside the burning winds, that otherworldly voice returns...

"THIS IS YOUR FUTURE!"

Without warning, the gymnasium's floor ignites in flames as Scott's internal senses sound off. It's only at the last second that he spots the burning car bearing down toward him at dreadful speed, pulverizing him back into blackness!

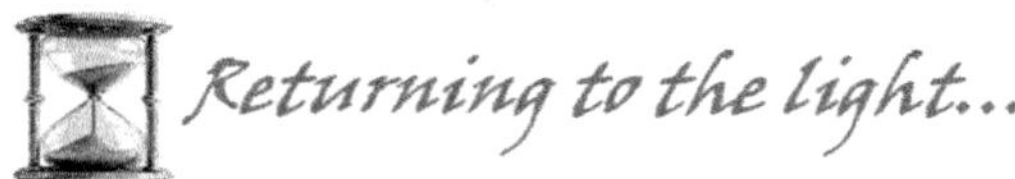 *Returning to the light...*

"Scott, are you alright?" The voice sounds staticky, as if it was being transmitted through a radio.

"Huh...what?!" Scott responds groggily, after hearing his name being repeated. Slowly opening his eyes, he finds Dave kneeling next to him on his right, with Mary on his left. Brushing away the cobwebs from his head, he spots Mike leaning over Dave's left shoulder; all three look worried and confused, especially Mary.

"What are you doing over here?" Dave asks.

"I don't know," Scott replies.

"You don't know?" Dave asks with a tone of surprise.

Realizing he is lying on the floor inside the threshold of the portico, Scott extends his hands to Dave and Mike.

"Guys, help me up." Upon standing, the first thing Scott notices is his surroundings; there are others in the area, all with their eyes on him. Hearing a faint, devilish laughter, he turns and faces the portico, noting how it is currently well lit by the overhead ceiling light, which he remembers was off. His baby blues travel the length of the passageway, all the way to the storage room at the end: the door is not only ajar, but additional light from within spills out.

"**Are you okay?**" Mary asks, her hand grasping his arm.

Behind a false smile, Scott responds, "**Yes.**" His eyes are still on that door to the storage room. "**Nothing to worry about, happens all the time.**"

"**What happens all the time?**" Dave solicits, his mouth widening—his eyebrows rising. Ignoring the remark, Scott looks over at the bleachers: there are only a small number of people, all making their way to the exit.

Curly is standing by the exit door, his eyes upon him!

Assuring everyone he is fine, Scott lies, telling them he must have succumbed to fatigue. Trusting this outlandish explanation, the congregation disperses, giving him alone time with Lisa who is standing all alone in the rear. Seeing that her man's attention is focused not on her, but on that storage room, she informs him that she will wait for him at her Camaro. Leaving the lad to his thoughts, she follows the others out of the gymnasium. Once he is completely alone, Scott drops to his knees and weeps, recalling the horrors he just experienced. That voice before the first missile hit is one he never heard before!

132

That sinister laughter retouches his ear!

Placing his right hand over his heart, Scott learns the truth about that voice, which is that it belongs to something far more powerful than a mere demon, something beyond his earthly understanding. Remembering he hit his head against those lockers, he gently touches the back of his skull, and feels wetness; there are droplets of blood on his fingertips. Inspecting his left hand, he spies a small puncture wound, compliments of the corroded screw from the locker, painful to the touch. Caressing his neck, he finds it sore.

Once more, he hears that laughter!

Returning his eyes to the storage room, Scott cringes when he notices the door is now closed! As the overhead light inside the archway dims and the sound of approaching footsteps grows, Scott hurries out of the gym and joins the crowd in the boys' locker room.

 *Time passes...*

The drive to Lisa's home is one lacking conversation, as Scott's attention is elsewhere. To address his intolerable behavior, the golden-haired beauty yanks him closer to her at the next traffic light, kissing him heatedly. Forgetting all else, Scott returns her kiss with a hunger of his own, and after pulling into her driveway, and shutting off the car, the two latch onto each other once more, eventually breaking away before it gets too far out of control.

As the young lovers stroll toward the front porch, it is Scott who is quick to notice the lights inside the house are on, as well as the ten-speed bicycle that is leaning against the back door. Staring at the bike, Scott asks, **"Lisa, are your parent's home?"**

"It looks like they are," she replies, nervously.

"Fantastic," Scott says excitedly, moving up the stairs. **"I can't wait to meet them."**

Lisa thwarts him from going further. **"Baby not tonight. It's later, and I am really tired. Besides, they are probably getting ready for bed."**

"Okay," Scott yields, his eyes returning to hers.

"Thanks. I know they would love to meet you, too."

"Maybe next time?"

"Definitely, next time."

"Well then, have a good sleep."

"Wait, I'll give you a ride home."

"That's okay," Scott retorts. **"I'll call Dave."**

"Are you sure?"

"Yeah, he isn't doing anything."

"Thanks, baby." After giving her man a tender smooch Lisa says goodnight. Once she is safely inside, Scott walks away from her house; however, he stops sharply after just a handful of steps. Intuitively, he glances up at her bedroom window, searing to the Holy Father above those curtains had just moved, a little!

Music plays to celebrate the day--

A trumpet, a trombone, a drum and a saxophone.

The cheerleader's gather on the stages floor--

For Kensington was shown the losers' door.

Last night on the ride home, Dave updated Scott that while he was having his bizarre blackout, the basketball team defeated Kensington in overtime, which is the reason for this morning's pep rally.

Scott and Mike are sitting inside the auditorium in the first row, in the same seats as they were before. "**Where is Dave?**" Scott asks, looking around for him.

Shaking his head, Mike laughs. "**Brother, you are not going to believe me when I tell you.**"

"**What's going on?**"

Mike points to the stage. "**Up there.**"

"**My sweet, Jesus!**" Scott utters in disbelief.

Dave is standing just behind the cheerleaders wearing a godawful, black and red cheerleading outfit for boys.

"**He told me ten minutes ago.**"

"**I've seen everything now.**"

"**He got upset when I started laughing,**" Mike adds.

"**Then, he would really have been upset with me,**" Scott declares. "**I wouldn't have been able to stop.**"

"**If you think about it,**" Mike says, "**how many guys would be upset picking up pretty girls?**"

"Not many."

"Not many is right."

"My God, is Dave becoming better than us at picking up chicks? Tell me it isn't so."

"All I can say is... the end of humanity as we know it, is at hand my friend." Mike laughs, as does Scott.

The band begins to play...

Underneath the cover of music, the principal, carrying a large, impressive trophy in his right hand walks out onto the stage—via the stage's back door. Walking alongside him is a heavyset, middle-aged man with thick bushy eyebrows.

"Good morning everyone," the principle says into the microphone, upon reaching the podium. **"The gentleman to my left is Mr. Clements, the superintendent of all schools in the Buffalo area."** The other man waves his left hand. **"At this time, we'd like to have coach Lewis come up on stage."**

Standing at the entrance, next to his five starters, the coach makes his way to the stage. After walking up those five steps, he heads straight for the principal and shakes his hand, likewise with the superintendent. Formerly accepting what could only be the championship trophy, coach Lewis raises it high over his head with everyone applauding. **"I am proud to accept this on behalf of our players,"** the coach says, stepping in front of the microphone. **"With that said,** we would like to thank the students and teachers who came to the games to cheer us on. Without your support, we would not be here today. On behalf of the team, we thank you." After receiving a standing ovation, the coach talks about the upcoming state championship game, scheduled to take place in Syracuse against the defending champions, who are also from that city. And, when he finishes...

As the chanting increases in volume, the cheerleaders gather at the center of the stage to erect a human pyramid, with Dave assisting them. Regrettably, the pyramid doesn't hold as one of the girls climbing to the top loses her balance and falls into the waiting arms of two of the male cheerleaders. Needing a break, Dave plops down on the floor near the back of the stage, sweating profusely. Concerned, Mary goes over and asks him if he is okay. Giving her the thumbs up, Dave gets to his feet, and rushes over to assist other cheerleaders in their efforts to build another pyramid.

"I wish to congratulate South Park on an outstanding year," the superintendent says, stepping forward and talking into the microphone. "If this school brings the championship back home to Buffalo, I will officially declare a day off the following Monday."

Erupting in blissful rejoicing, many of the students rise from their seats once more, high fiving all those around them; the band breaks out with another musical number. Many of the teachers, Mr. Canton and Mr. Cummins included are also partaking in the celebration, not bypassing Curly, who is standing by those exit doors, a prideful gleam illuminating his eyes: the massive security supervisor is even smiling.

Experiencing a rather peculiar weirdness, Scott scans the stage for Dave. Locating his friend, he observes Mary kneeling over him, as if she is kissing him. Smiling warmly, even though there's an element of jealousy on his lips, he is about to look away——that is until Mary lifts her head and reveals watery eyes; she's cradling Dave's head in her arms, his eyes closed. From somewhere inside the auditorium that devilish laughter rings out, heard only by Scott...and one other.

138

"BROTHERS DEATH"

A man in a white lab coat stands at the front entrance to one of Buffalo's oldest, and finest institutions: Mercy Hospital. The good doctor is waiting for those who have been informed of their son's situation.

A light blue corroded, Cadillac coupe Deville is driving frantically on the street in front of the hospital, turning into a parking area reserved for emergencies. After the driver's door flies open, denting the door of the minivan parked next to it, a short, potbellied man with a military "high and tight" climbs out, looking truly angry. Exiting the vehicle from the passenger side is a noticeably taller female, visibly crying; both look to be in their early fifties.

Upon reaching the doctor, the two are swiftly escorted to the elevators located in the main lobby just beyond the admissions counter, which is across from the primary waiting room. Following the closing of the elevator doors, they are given an update on their son's condition, which isn't good; the elevator stops on the floor reserved for those in need of intensive care: I.C.U. Guided to their son's room, they find him lying lifeless in a bed, an oxygen mask having been placed over his mouth, and tiny circular sensors taped to his head and chest; the sensors are connected to machines.

Doctor Fuller: is a respected surgeon in his fifties who sits on the hospital's medical review board. It was this talented doctor with his hand selected team, who had performed the complex heart surgeries on a younger Dave. He is six feet two inches tall with an average physique, short brown hair accented with gray highlights, and is clean-shaven.

Mr. Knoll: is employed as a machinist at a steel factory in Lackawanna, a town situated south of Buffalo. He has served in his current position for over twenty-five years, and intends to retire in twelve more. Standing at five feet, four inches, he owns a pudgy midsection due to his dietary habits as well as his smoking, and alcohol consumption. Mr. Knoll is the sole benefactor of his son's unwanted appendage: his large nose. He's a heated debater, especially when it comes to politics and, it doesn't matter if it is local or not, just as long as there is someone to blame.

Mrs. Knoll: is not only a compassionate woman, but a loving mother who has overly protected her son from the moment he was born. She and her husband are devoted members of their church, to which she volunteers to do their accounting. Taller than her husband, and in better shape, Mrs. Knoll is a woman who truly embraces family values. Nevertheless, she has been known to tip the whiskey bottle now and then, depending on her mood.

140

It couldn't have been no more than one or two of those unnerving clicks and tots from the medical machines when a loud buzzer suddenly erupts, and the emergency light on the wall just above Dave's bed begins flashing red. A heartbeat later, two nurses are charging into the room, one breaking away to take Mr. and Mrs. Knoll to a waiting area, a little further down the hallway. As they are being ushered out of the room, a doctor and another nurse enter. All the while, that tear-drenching buzzer continues.

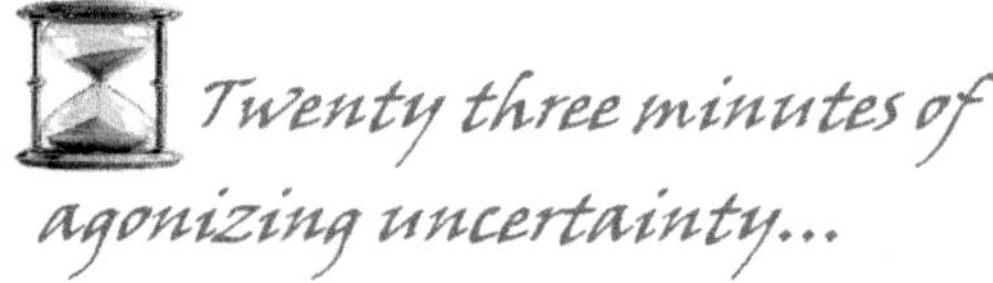 *Twenty three minutes of agonizing uncertainty...*

Bearing a sorrowful countenance, Dr. Fuller walks into the waiting room. Standing just inside the entranceway with his head hung slightly, he waits to be noticed. Dave's father is pacing back and forth, while Dave's mother sits in a chair, wiping the tears from her eyes with an already wetted tissue.

Soon enough, the good doctor is spotted.

"I'm sorry," Dr. Fuller says, mournfully. **"Dave is gone."**

Crying hysterically, Mrs. Knoll scurries into a restroom across the hall, whereas Mr. Knoll becomes enraged. **"How can this be? My son was getting his treatments!"** he yells. **"What in GOD'S name happened?!"**

Answering as delicately as he can, Dr. Fuller responds, **"I talked to Doctor Ammar before you arrived. It appears Dave hasn't been to an appointment in two months."**

"THAT'S IMPOSSIBLE!" Mr. Knoll thunders. "MY SON TOLD US HE WAS GOING!"

In a sympathetic tone, Dr. Fuller tries to explain how people, especially those young as Dave tend to avoid going to their appointments, especially if they believe nothing is going to help them.

Mr. Knoll stubbornly refutes this conception and starts blaming the school. "I'LL SUE THEM! SO HELP ME GOD, PEOPLE WILL PAY!"

{Scott enters the waiting room}

"The nurse said –"

"Why didn't David go to his appointments?" Mr. Knoll interrupts Scott, his tone less intense.

"We tried to get him to go," the emotional teen responds, "but, he wouldn't listen to us."

Grabbing Scott's arm. "LIAR!" Mr. Knoll bellows, his action prompting the doctor to step in and force release.

"It's not his fault."

"The hell it isn't!" Mr. Knoll roars. "These punks talked him into not going, and now he's gone. I want to know why my son is dead?!"

"Son, I think you should go," Dr. Fuller says gently.

The fury inside Mr. Knoll's eyes verifies the doctor's wisdom. With tears flowing down his face, Scott staggers out of the room and into the hallway.

Momentarily numb by the devasting news, Scott looks over at the entrance to the same waiting room Mr. and Mrs. Miller occupied not more than a few minutes ago, knowing the young man who waits inside will be crushed upon hearing what he hoped not to hear. Entering the small room, Scott observes Mike leaning against the wall with his eyes closed, and his head sloping downward. Opening his eyes, Mike spots Scott standing inside the entranceway, watery blues delivering the bad news. Lips quivering, and tears streaming down his face, Mike rushes out of the room, leaving his friend to sink heavily into the nearest seat.

Five ticks of the clock pass, and a woman rushes in!

Witnessing the distraught young man in the chair, Mrs. Knoll hurries over and holds him tight. **"This isn't your fault. My son loved you and Michael so much. The two of you have always been there for him, when others were not."** In a motherly manner, she places her hands on Scott's face and gives him a gentle kiss on his forehead. **"Thank you for being kind to my son."** Following another lengthy embrace, and another kiss on his forehead, Mrs. Knoll leaves to rejoin her distressed husband.

The alert buzzer inside Dave's room is silent!

It takes Scott an entire hour to assemble the necessary calmness to rise from his chair. Stepping into the hallway, he observes Dave's parents embracing each other outside their son's room, their eyes remaining wet with sadness.

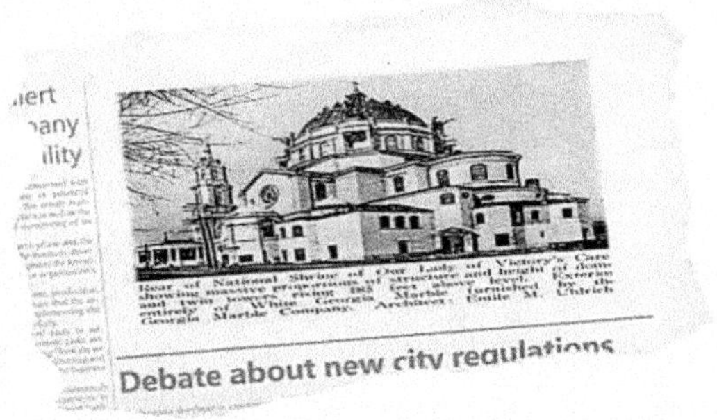

In 1926, a magnificent cathedral, 'Our lady of Victory' was built inside the main quarter of the outlying town called Lackawanna, which is south of Buffalo. Abbot Road runs directly into this town, and Scott has been traveling it for well over an hour now.

Beginning as a watery cascade, the rain has dwindled to nothing more than a drizzle, which is a good thing because Scott isn't wearing his football jacket; he left it inside his locker in his rush to get to the hospital. So, by the time he reaches this small suburban town, he is marginally soaked.

It was a beloved priest named, "Father Baker" who was responsible for both the planning, and construction of this world-renowned church. A significant amount of donated money was needed to build this once-in-a-generation jewel, with many of its furnishings imported from other countries. Walking toward the cathedral, Scott observes its massive green copper dome, as well as the life-size statues located on its embankments. Several angelic figurines were used to harvest its sacred conviction, making it a place evil wouldn't dare enter: the prize statue is the one of "Michael" wearing his golden armor and wielding his "Sword of Power," as he stands triumphantly over a dragon.

144

Though the dreary skies are beginning to clear, Scott refrains from looking up, afraid of what he might find hiding inside them. Still, he believes if there is a haven from those menacing eyes, he will find it here inside this holiest of holies. As Scott extends his right hand toward the iron handle on the cathedral's imposing medieval doors, he glances upwards at the statue of Michael, noting how the angel appears to be gazing directly at him.

145

Upon passing through those doors, he marvels at the exquisite treasures within——the beautiful murals that cover nearly every inch of the vaulted ceiling——the twelve stained glass windows, each bearing one of the apostles, perfectly illumined by the rebirth of the sun.

The architects of the church imported materials from other countries. For instance, they built a unique altar using a rare, red marble specially imported from Spain. Located in the front, the altar features a full-sized, timber cross above it with a larger than life statuette of Jesus attached to it. Standing in the corner beside the altar is a sculpted statue of the blessed Mary.

Sitting in one of the pews in the front, Scott pulls down a tiny, padded prayer stool and kneels on it. Hands clasped in front of his face, he leans forward and prays for Dave's parents, hoping they will be able to find peace. Knowing how much Mike cared for their friend and brother, Scott says a prayer for him, concerned about the way he had left the hospital. Looking up at the crucifix, Scott whimpers, **"Why?"**

"Only God knows," an unfamiliar voice replies. Startled, Scott turns around to find a man dressed in black standing slightly behind him, and to his right. **"What is troubling you, Scott?"** He presents himself as Father Gimlin.

"How do you know my name, Father?"

"You were here ten years ago, for baptism."

"That's right." Scott is baffled by the priest's memory.

"What's wrong?" Father Gimlin sits next to Scott.

"My friend died today, and somehow I ended up here."

"I'm sorry to hear about your friend."

"He had a lot of medical problems. Wasn't getting the treatments he needed. It's my fault," Scott sighs.

"Why do you think is it your fault?" Father Gimlin asks.

"I didn't push him enough to go to his appointments."

"I see," Father Gimlin responds. "You think it was your fault he didn't go?"

"Isn't it!" Scott snaps. "I'm his friend, I'm supposed to be looking out for him."

"Our heavenly father gives us the power to make our own choices. To choose our paths in life, no matter what others feel," Father Gimlin says gently. "We can only do so much for those we care about. It is ultimately their choice."

"I know your right, Father," Scott concedes. "It's just, I'm going to miss him something awful."

"You are talking about David Knoll?"

"How could you possibly know that?" Scott inquires, visibly shocked.

"David came here often. He did the talking, and I did the listening," Father Gimlin says, with a smile. "He told me a lot about you. I did not know he had passed on. But, you are wrong if you think it was your fault. David knew his time was short. I enjoyed talking to him and, I will miss him."

"Me too, Father. Me too."

"David wouldn't want you carrying this guilt," Father Gimlin says, standing. "Please, come back and talk with me again." He places his left hand on Scott's shoulder. "There is a strong life force in you, as if the angel Michael himself is here. It is a compelling strength, I sense."

After saying goodbye, Father Gimlin walks over and greets a young male dressed in priestly garbs who had just entered through a door on the western wall, which leads to the clergyman's private chambers. Deciding to leave, Scott makes his way down the center aisle, his attention drawn to a pair of confessionals by the eastern wall, several feet from another of the churches prized marvels: a hand-sculptured baptismal fountain from Italy. Although Scott feels some relief after speaking with Father Gimlin, he believes a brief confession may help him even further. However, when he approaches, he finds both occupied. Waiting for a vacancy, he strolls over to the nearest stained-glass window to read the Bible scripture engraved on its glistening brass panel, beneath the sun illuminated image of the 'Apostle Peter.'

148

Suddenly, a soft drumming sound arises!

Scanning every nook and cranny for the source of this enigmatic beat, Scott suddenly shudders with the feeling that he is being —

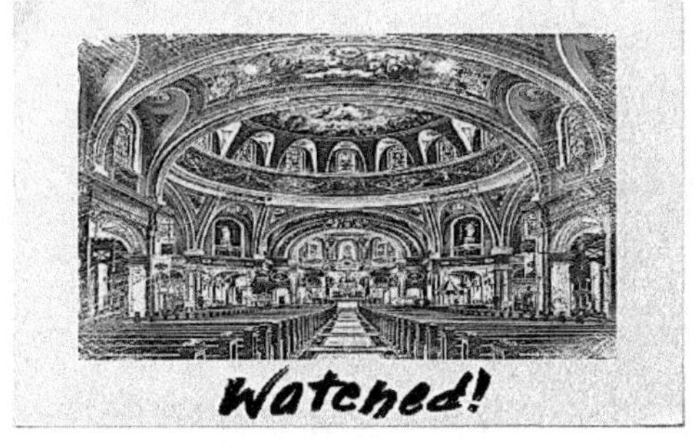

As if he was under the control of a puppet master who was pulling the strings of his prized marionette, Scott finds himself turning around and returning to the confessional. He comes to a halt as the wooden door panel unexpectedly slides open, and an elderly woman wearing a black mundane dress steps out. Peeking an eyeball, he becomes alarmed by the blackness of the interior; only a trifling amount of light is emitting through a one by one foot screen from the side where the priest sits. Believing his nerves are getting the best of him, Scott lets out a quiet laugh. **"Not a good time for me to get those heebie-jeebies, huh, Kelly."**

Upon entering the confessional, Scott pushes aside the tiny curtain on the door, exposing a small opening that permits additional light to come inside, but not very much. Before his butt touches the bench, a pastoral voice shoots out of the dark on the side where the priest sits. **"I am ready to hear thy sins. And may your God—"** a second or two of silence later **"—Bless thee."**

Scott can barely make out the silhouette of the priest through the screen, his face hidden from view. After a short moment of silence, he responds to the voice. **"Forgive me Father, for I have sinned."**

"Tell me, how you have sinned?" the voice asks.

"My friend died today. I could have done more for him," Scott answers. Receiving no reply, he presumes the priest wants him to continue, prompting him to speak for a spell.

A spidery creepiness crawls up Scott's spine after he finishes talking, and the confessional falls silent once again. This disquieting solitude compels him to look through the metal screen—with blackness the only thing staring back at him. As the silence continues, Scott assumes the priest had simply left without telling him; however, that all changes as he leans forward to rise from the wooden bench.

HA! HA! HA! HA!
HA! HA! HA!
HA! HA! HA! HA!

Not only are the whites of Scott's eyes shining eerily inside the shadows of the confessional, but fear is whacking away at his heart like a butcher's cleaver. With a trembling right hand, he reaches to slide open the exit door...

"DAVEY IS WITH US, BOY"

In the space the priest occupies, that frightening voice returns, accompanied by more of that terrorizing laughter he heard inside the auditorium. From within the darkness, a pair of red vampiric eyes glow brightly.

"Ahhh!" Scott screams, running like a madman out of the confessional. Father Gimlin, and the junior priest rush over to investigate the ruckus, as do a few parishioners.

"Scott, what's wrong?" Father Gimlin asks.

"There's something Evil in there!"

"Something Evil?"

"Yes!" Scott exclaims. "And, it spoke to me." The junior priest immediately steps forward and slides open the door, exposing an empty compartment where the priest's normally sit. Looking into the small cubicle, Scott gasps, "how can this be? Someone talked to me."

Blessed by the soothing hand of our heavenly Lord, Father Gimlin invokes holy tranquility into the heart, and soul of the troubled young man. Shortly thereafter, Scott is calm enough to leave the church and, with any luck, will be heading straight for home. Knowing of a bus stop less than a block from the church, Scott heads there. It isn't long until a bus is spotted heading his way. Having decided to allow the public transport to take him wherever it pleases, he hops aboard, taking a seat in the back.

Twenty minutes into the ride is all it takes until Scott realizes the bus is passing through the older neighborhoods of his youth; the pullcord is tugged, signaling the driver to stop. As the bus slows down, Scott gazes out the window and spots the school where he first met Dave, bringing back a rush of childhood memories.

School #28

The building looks neglected.

Windows are in need of washing.

Overgrown bushes beg for pruning.

The sun scorched brick walls are more orange than the bright red he remembers. There is a dirt trail just behind the school, and it is one Scott knows all too well: it's the path where that comical adolescent pursuit began...the one with the horde of children chasing little Davey home for peeking up the little girl's dress. As if it were just yesterday, the days that followed came to Scott, when they became friends and started hanging out after school.

Fondest memories consist of when he and Dave dreamt of being worldly explorers in search of hidden treasures and secret chambers; the real cloak-and-dagger stuff little boys fantasize about. Throughout their fairytale childhood, they explored abandoned buildings, creepy vacant houses, and other such places in their pursuit of mysteries, whodunits, or ghosts: they were fearless, and gullible.

In addition to taking him past the yard where the gang of children cornered little Davey, the path fetches him close to a single-story, gray brick building; the setting of another disquieting incident of his childhood.

Neighborhood children convinced them the building was haunted, so naturally they had to investigate. After scaling a chain-link fence, they realized that getting into the building required breaking through a door that had been boarded up. But, before the attempt could be made, an ornery old man came running, and yelling from the other side of the building, with an ugly dog growling vicious at his side. Running back to the fence, Scott took a nasty tumble and scraped his left knee bloody. Madness lived in the eyes of that lunatic!

Grabbing a chunk of a broken brick from the ground, Dave threw it at the dog just as it was about to bite Scott, hitting it in the face, and sending it whimpering in the other direction. Snarling like a beast, the old man went berserk and grabbed Scott. He attempted to stuff him inside a rusty metal barrel used for burning rubbish. Scott recalls how the man acted, as if he were possessed by demons, not to mention how strong he was, easily holding him down with one hand while igniting debris inside the barrel with the other; his grip was chilling. Coming to his rescue once more, Dave took a two-by-four that was leaning up against the building, and as the old man held Scott over his head, he snuck up and struck him in the back of his skull, sending him to the dirt.

Falling on top of the old man, Scott was able to acquire his footing first, kicking that barrel over and spilling its fiery contents onto the lunatic. Screaming in agony, as his dog barked loudly from a distance, the old man rolled around in the dirt until the flames were quenched. When he finally got to his feet, he spotted the intruders on the other side of the fence. Releasing a guttural snarl, the old man, bleeding from his head, shook that fence violently, and stomped his feet, scaring the boys into running away at top speed. An hour later, the boys returned with their parents, and the police; the old man, along with his ugly dog were gone, never to be seen again. The rubbish inside the barrel was still burning when they got there.

They met Mike the following year!

A young couple from Spain had purchased a house a few doors down from Dave. Since they had a son of similar age to Scott and Dave, it was inevitable that all three boys would start hanging out; they quickly developed a strong friendship—their special bonds being forged upon the anvil of brotherhood.

"Blizzard of 1977"

Buffalo had suffered one of the worst snowstorms in its history with temperatures dropping below the freezing mark, and snowdrifts measuring well above fifteen feet in height in the southern tiers. The folks who lived here deemed it to be the end of the world, but to Scott, Dave, and Mike, it was the greatest thing since sliced bread; the schools were closed for two weeks. During the blizzard, they shoveled snow for money, making over one hundred dollars each in three days, with many of their customers bringing them inside for some hot chocolate and cookies. Life was good.

Needless to say, the young business tycoons depleted their monies inside the video arcade rooms nearly as fast as they made it. But, they didn't care as they lived like kings those few days. After the money ran out, they went back out shoveling to earn more. They did everything together, from joining the boy scouts to playing basketball for their church on a league created by local pastors. Though Mike and Dave were not as athletic as Scott, they still played their hearts out; it was some of their most cherished times together. They were inseparable, their bond unbreakable!

A tear runs the length of Scott's face, those moments are only a memory now.

Looking at the exterior of the building, Scott notes how ruinous it has become since the five years, when he returned here with Dave and Mike. If the building could talk, it would surely beg for a demolition ball to put it out of its misery, and quickly at that. Graffiti covers nearly every inch of the brick wall, and those few spaces not defaced are severely soiled. As before, the entrance door is boarded up, plus every window is hidden behind a wooden plank. Moreover, the roof appears to be a snowstorm away from collapsing. Nomadic shrubs, and unidentifiable bushes grow freely by the sides of the building; a bizarre plant species, practically alien in nature thrives throughout this necropolis landscape. That corroded barrel is lying on its side, murky green fluid oozing through several gaping holes. The chain-link fence is missing sections, and what is left dangles feebly from its ten-foot-pole; most of these poles are either damaged, or altogether missing.

Even though Scott no longer has nightmares about the lunatic that attacked them, he has remained curious as to why the old man came after him and Dave the way he had.

What was he hiding?

When those three returned five years ago, they nearly didn't go in, as the building falsely fabricated a monster was residing within. Nevertheless they did enter, their entrance through that boarded door, made possible by the crowbar Mike had taken from his father's tool shed. Upon entering, Scott felt evil all around him; what's more, his inner senses became active. Sparse sunlight filtered through the cracks in the boarded-up windows, as well from the damaged roof above, revealing a scene so scary that it sent chills through their bones. Portions of the walls were painted with demonic symbols and cryptograms, along with words loathing with sin and wickedness!

LUCIFER

Several names were written on those filthy walls, some pronounceable, some not. In a reddish–brown substance resembling aged blood, it was a particular name that scared the bejesus out of the three of them. To this very day, that nefarious name blisters like a boil in the innermost regions of Scott's mind, seared into his memory by the devil himself, using those unholy irons you would only find inside Hell's kitchen. The name is one that fills men's heart with despair, with hopelessness...

"Antichrist," Scott mutters, uneasily.

157   Braving their fears, the three ventured deeper into this nightmarish sepulcher, keeping their scared eyes alert and their legs at the ready, just in case a hasty exit was needed. It was either the second or third room where they stumbled upon a large rat that had been gutted...near a wall that was caked in filth. It became clear its blood was used to draw the pentacle on the concrete floor.

Rather peculiar was the state of that rodent's corpse, as if it was killed recently; plus there was a godawful smell in the room, one so horrid that it junked their nostrils.

Having seen enough, Scott and Mike were preparing to make a beeline for the exit door. But, when they turned around to leave the room, they quickly discovered Dave was no longer behind them. In a heightened state of panic, their feet already three steps beyond that door, the two began searching the rooms for their misplaced friend. Ultimately, Dave was located in one of the back rooms, staring at a wall as if he were spellbound to it; his jaw hung slightly open.

Entering the room, Mike and Scott attempted to wake Dave from his stupor; however they were unsuccessful, his eyes showing minimum response. Observing words written on the shadowy wall, but unable to read them due to poor lighting, Scott hastened over to the lone window, and using the crowbar, he pried off one of the four boards nailed to it. The sunlight dribbling through the grime-caked window was enough to make out a puzzling anecdote that was written on that wall—underneath a name he had once heard in his bible studies: *Revelations*. To this day, the name still burns in his head; it seemed the name was written in rats blood.

RAPTURE

Scott remembers how the winds began pounding their blustery fists against the side of the building, the same winds that were placid and calm before they had entered. Feeling a chill running through his body, Scott stepped closer to the wall, and read...

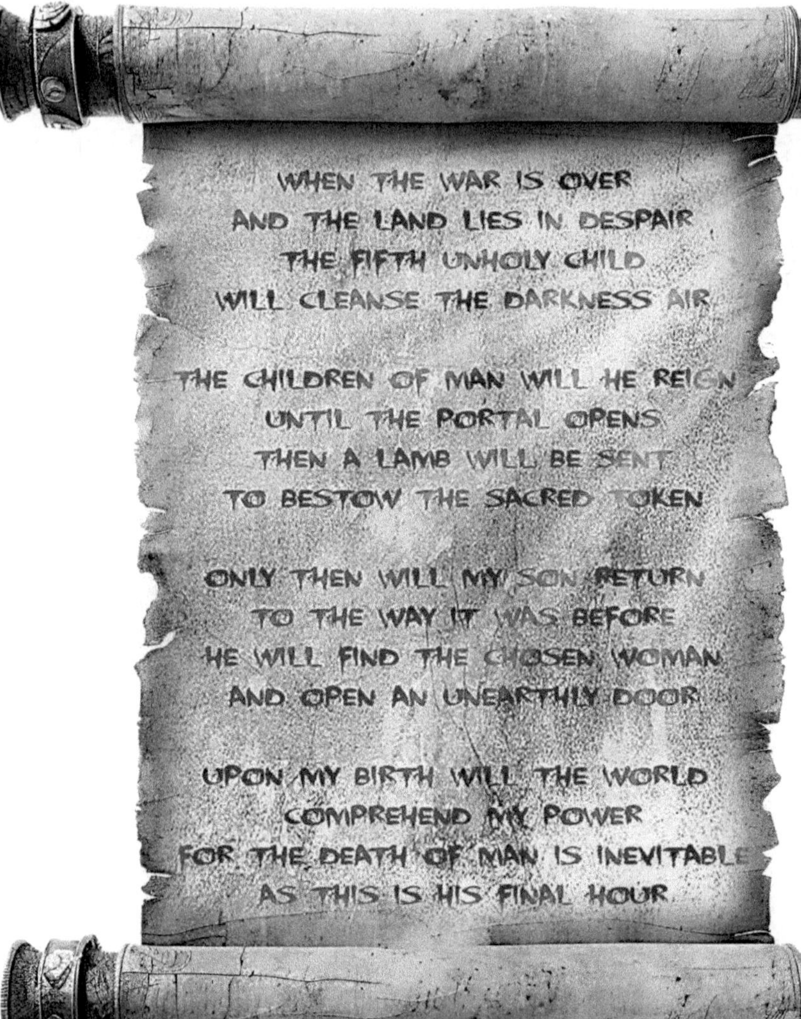

WHEN THE WAR IS OVER
AND THE LAND LIES IN DESPAIR
THE FIFTH UNHOLY CHILD
WILL CLEANSE THE DARKNESS AIR

THE CHILDREN OF MAN WILL HE REIGN
UNTIL THE PORTAL OPENS
THEN A LAMB WILL BE SENT
TO BESTOW THE SACRED TOKEN

ONLY THEN WILL MY SON RETURN
TO THE WAY IT WAS BEFORE
HE WILL FIND THE CHOSEN WOMAN
AND OPEN AN UNEARTHLY DOOR

UPON MY BIRTH WILL THE WORLD
COMPREHEND MY POWER
FOR THE DEATH OF MAN IS INEVITABLE
AS THIS IS HIS FINAL HOUR

As the three quickly moved toward the exit, it was Mike who noticed a portrait displayed on the wall across the room; however, due to limited sunlight, they were unable to discern either the portrait's details, or the name inscribed above it. After stepping over another dead rodent, Scott spotted a yellowing newspaper on the floor. Snatching it, he rolled it up tightly like a torch. Igniting it with a silver, flip top lighter acquired from Mike, he stepped a tad closer to the wall, the flickering flames revealing not only the name, but it made the portrait a little more visible.

LITTLE HORN

The name meant nothing to them, however that portrait was so fearsome to behold that all three bolted out of that room, and out of the building altogether. Standing in front of this crumbling edifice after all these years, Scott pays little attention to the weirdness of it. But, just as he begins putting distance between himself and the building, he stops sharply, and spins around...

"Son of a bitch!" he curses.

The portrait on that wall is the same face he saw in the clouds at school, the same face that occupied Kelly's in the auditorium. As he steps closer to the building, Scott begins experiencing a biblical awakening; a sinister tale of elemental evil from the unholiest dimension.

 *Time passes...*

At first, the rain was no fiercer than a kitten playing with a ball of yarn; however, it had mutated into a ferocious lion an hour or two before Scott climbed out of bed; his mother informed him thirty minutes ago that his school was closed due to anticipated flooding. Remaining in his tee-shirt and sweatpants, he heads downstairs where he's greeted by the enticing aromas of Canadian bacon and eggs. Upon seeing her son strolling lethargically into the kitchen, Mrs. Miller goes to him, and holds him tight, giving him a much needed motherly hug; she knows her son is still hurting. In her arms, he feels better.

As Scott sits down at the table, Mrs. Miller places a plate of food in front of him. Afterwards, she turns up the volume on the small television placed on the counter next to the toaster; a weatherman for a local news station is issuing a severe thunderstorm warning for the area---saying it is prudent to stay indoors, as conditions are likely to worsen throughout the day. On a brighter note, the anchorwoman, who is in her early to mid-thirties, delivers a report regarding the anniversary of Helios. She says a commemoration has been scheduled this weekend at city hall. Bemused by how the older generations still celebrate this local folklore, more than a few chuckles escape Scott's lips, accompanied by several eye rolls.

When Scott was a little boy, his father regaled him with bedtime stories about the mythical sun god, recounting how he came to Earth before the days of Christ to battle the forces of evil. According to myth, the epic battle between Helios and the devils of Hell had taken place in the lands Buffalonians call home. As Scott laid beneath his covers, he listened attentively to his father's stories that described a phenomenon occurring once every thousand years: the sun rising from the south rather than the east, accompanied by the opening of a portal, permitting Helios to enter into our world. Wearing his golden armor, and wielding his sword of power, this mighty guardian is charged with smiting evil; it was believed this mystical portal was a gateway to Heaven.

Tomorrow will mark the first day of the thousand-year cycle: the arrival of Helios!

After finishing breakfast, Scott returns to his bedroom to put on his favorite jeans. Upon slipping his head through the opening of his football jersey, he casts a glance at the photo of Lisa on his nightstand, and then heads downstairs to watch television. From his comfy spot on the living room couch, his baby blues drift toward the window; the rain is showing no signs of relenting.

 *Time passes...*

Waiting for a call from Lisa, Scott continues lounging lazily on the couch with his feet resting on the arm rest, and his eyes glued to the television, having just finished watching a thriller that starred one of his favorite actors. Switching channels to watch some music videos, he glances over at the push-dial phone lying on the end table next to him. Wanting nothing more than to spend some quality time with his lady, he finds it odd he hasn't heard from her since the day past.

"Scott, what time did your father say he was coming over tonight?" Mrs. Miller asks from inside the kitchen.

"Around five."

"Well...it's almost six," she says. "I'm going to give him a call." Scott watches his mother retrieve the cordless phone from its wall-mounted holder inside the kitchen, and dial a seven-digit telephone number.

"Roy's residence," a female answers, her tone sensual.

"I want to speak with Mr. Miller!"

"Roy, darling, there is someone on the phone wanting to speak with you," the female says, flirtatiously. Overhearing his mother speaking angrily into the phone, Scott reaches over and picks up the push-dial phone from the end table.

"Now Darla, there is no need to get upset," Mr. Miller proclaims. "She's only a friend."

"Sure she is Roy!" Mrs. Miller barks, scornfully. "Since when do friends call you, darling?"

"Darla, if you recall...it was you who wanted this silly separation," Mr. Miller snaps back, "not I."

"Now, I want a divorce!" Mrs. Miller shouts.

Gently hanging up the phone, not wanting to alert his parents to his eavesdropping, Scott stands and heads for the front door. Before turning the doorknob, he looks over at his mother who is still yelling into the receiver. Spotting his football jacket on the arm of the recliner, Scott grabs it and proceeds through the door. By the time he is halfway down his street, he is already marginally soaked.

The storm is edging toward mayhem!

Unbeknownst to Scott, there are several black crows perched on the telephone line, staring down at him with their black, beady little eyes. Reaching the corner, straining his eyes to see through the intense downpour, he catches sight of a phone booth on the other side of the intersecting road, adjacent to a neighborhood food mart. Running to it, he is swift in closing the plexiglass door once he's inside, shielding himself from the elements.

Heavy rain strikes all four sides of the booth!

After inserting a quarter into the coin slot, Scott dials his lady's home number: someone picks up on the fifth ring, pausing a moment before talking.

"Yeah, what?!" a boy rudely asks.

"Is...Lisa home?" Scott inquires, his tone confused.

"No, she isn't!" The phone goes dead.

The sound of thunder crackles in the gloomy sky!

"This shit can't be happening!" Scott snarls, slamming the receiver into its cradle.

Lisa never mentioned having a brother, and that voice sounds far too young to be her father's. Following a brief deliberation, Scott believes it was her brother, and wanting to get out of this rain, he runs farther down the street to the nearest bus stop after having spotted a bus coming his way. Good fortune shines upon him...for it's the number #4 bus, and it will drop him on the corner of Lisa's street.

 *Time passes...*

Tugging on the stop cord, Scott impatiently waits for the nearly empty bus to stop. Eager to see his woman, he hops off mere seconds after the exit door in the center of the bus opens, and runs without pause, all the way to her house. Winded on arrival, he presses the doorbell.

The house is dark — no lights from within!

Pressing the doorbell two more times, and receiving no answer, Scott walks to the side of the house and knocks on the back door; *the sound of his fist on that door echoes in the night.* Believing he may have dialed the wrong number, he snickers at his foolishness. **"I bet she isn't even home."** But, as he is about to walk away, a light appears inside the house. Upon noticing what appears to be the same bicycle he had observed several days earlier leaning against an oak tree near the barn, Scott retrieves it. He then positioned the bike against the side of the house, utilizing it as a ladder to access to the window of the room where the light went on.

The first thing Scott observes is a large, stainless steel refrigerator with double doors, and a six-burner gas stove built into a marble countertop, inside what looks to be the kitchen. As he continues his search for a body, a shameful thought enters his mind; *'What if Lisa's parents are home?'* If they are, does he want her father catching him peeking into the window like some perverted peeping Tom?

Having decided to leave and give Lisa a call from a pay phone, Scott starts to climb down off the bike. But, as he does, he spots his lady entering the room, wearing a silky white see-through shirt, red panties, and nothing more than that. Since her backside is facing him, he is unable to make eye contact; however, he is given a wonderful viewing of her shapely body as she opens the refrigerator, its interior light showcasing her wares. With zero complaints, his eyes travel downward----starting from the back of her gorgeous head to her more delightful areas. Scott convinces himself that his lady simply didn't hear the doorbell; nonetheless, all that promptly changes the moment when another person strolls causally into the kitchen...

It's Whitey, and he's completely nude!

With his face twisting in disgust, Scott watching those devious hands belonging to the ivory, white hair punk taking liberty with her body. What sickens him even more is when his woman turns around, and kisses him intensely!

"NOOOOO!" Scott silently rages.

Scott's stomach squirms as if he had just digested a can of worms, and his numbing legs are struggling to bring him off the bike; rumors about Lisa and Whitey slither into his head, the same rumors he didn't want to believe.

Well...there is no question about them now?

In an act of rage, Scott swoops up the bike and slams it violently against the door, shattering the glass in its upper pane. By the time Whitey is dressed and steps outside to investigate, he is only able to catch a fleeting glimpse of his adversary walking down the street. With a cheeky grin on his callous lips, he directs his steely blue eyes to the broken glass. **"Well, well...Mr. Miller. You are going to pay dearly for interrupting my time with your girl."** Whistling like a boy without a care in the world, Whitey casually strolls back into the house, closing the front door behind him.

DARKNESS FILLS THE SKIES...

Droplets of rainwater trickle onto his jacket by way of a leaky window his head is leaning against. Scott's thoughts are consumed by the treachery of his woman, and because his mind is on her betrayal, he is utterly unaware of the swift changing elements outside the city bus——the same bus he hopped on over thirty minutes ago. Mighty winds batter the bus unrelentingly, as heavy rain pours from the gloomy skies above. Something within the chaotic darkness outside the window snags his attention.

"Johnny's Garage," Scott mutters.

Pressing his face a little closer to the glass, a popular tavern located on the biker's side of the four corners falls into Scott's obstructed view; the rain is making it difficult to see out the window. Tugging the cord to signal a stop, the lad steps off the bus as soon as it pulls over to the curb, and the swivel door to the right of the driver opens. Heading straight for the bar, Scott hopes to catch the twenty two year old barkeep he met through Mike on duty, which so happens to be the older brother of a girl the Spanish lover once dated; they remained friends after the breakup.

Five minutes, and forty dollars later, Scott leaves that watering hole holding a brown paper bag, containing a pint of Kentucky bourbon to which he chugs half of its contents, less than ten steps from the establishment. Stumbling down South Park Avenue, while throwing punches at imaginary opponents, Scott ignores the warning of imminent danger from his internal senses. Stopping in front of his beloved pizza parlor, he downs yet another generous swig of that bourbon. Experiencing the crippling effects of the alcohol, and completely soaked from the rain, Scott extends his left hand toward the restaurants colored windows for support. Tilting his head upward, he uncovers a pair of colorless eyes watching him from within those ominous clouds.

"What do you want from me?!" Scott screams.

From out of nowhere, a vehicle the color of night turns a distant corner, speeding in his direction, its engine roaring fiercely. Blundering steps, impaired vision, and faulty motor skills are some of the things Scott suffers from as he tries shaking off the bourbon's hold on him. Moments later, he freezes stiff upon spotting a tall, lanky man standing across the street, twenty yards away...staring at him!

KNEE-HIGH, BLACK BOOTS.
LONG, DARK TRENCH COAT.
LARGE, BLACK HAT.

Identifying the man to be none other than the Stranger, Scott raises his bottle, indicating there will be no hesitation to employ it as a weapon. Lifting his head ever so slightly, the cryptic fiend reveals Dracula-black eyes from beneath the brim of his hat.

"COME ON!" Scott shouts,
"LET'S DO IT!"

As if a portal to perdition had punched a hole into our world, a blood-red burst erupts within the dark skies; what is more, that menacing laughter returns. With his attention sorely on the car speeding toward him, closing in awfully fast, Scott observes a boy hanging out of the passenger side window. **A message for Scott Miller,** the youth hollers, holding a bottle of his own, **you're wanted in Hell!**

Clumsily, Scott throws his nearly empty bottle, hitting the vehicle's bumper; whereas the boy, who had also thrown his yields far better results. The bottle breaks upon impact against Scott's forehead, causing him to tumble backwards through the window of the pizza restaurant. His momentum not only shatters the glass, but sends fragments flying into the air. Lying motionless on the glass shards in the frame of the window——with his life's blood sprayed over his entire body and face, a rather strange facial expression appears; neither the car nor the laughter stops!

170

"COME ON!" Scott shouts,
"LET'S DO IT!"

"STEEL BRIDGE"

While the siren blares loudly on the streets in front of the hospital, the man in white stands once more at the front entrance...wearing the same facial expression as when the ambulance transported in Dave. Ashes from the cigarette that is perched between the good doctor's index, and middle fingers have already fallen six times; the seventh is a puff away.

Arriving in separate vehicles, Mr. and Mrs. Miller are escorted through the lobby to the elevators. Once inside the elevator car, Doctor Fuller informs them on what the police had told him, which is Scott was involved in a fight, and the results is a head injury. He tells them their son was found unconscious, bleeding profusely as he lay dead-like inside the glass-riddled frame of the window.

"Dear God!" Mrs. Miller weeps.

After the elevator opens on the fourth floor, the three make haste to Scott's room. Stepping inside the room, a weeping mother, and a distressed father observe their son lying motionless in a bed. A therapeutic bandage has been wrapped around his head, concealing most of his forehead, as well as the left side of his face, including the entirety of his left eye. A nurse in her mid-forties is monitoring his vital signs, while a second year doctor of Asian lineage is writing on a clipboard, repeatedly glancing over at those medical machines that are next to Scott's bed, recording the digital numbers displayed on them.

**"Oh, Roy," Mrs. Miller sobs,
"that's our baby boy."**

Holding his wife tightly, Mr. Miller stares at two bags of blood hanging from a hook on a long pole, as well as the intravenous tube that is going directly into his son's left arm. An oxygen mask has been placed over his nose and mouth, which is connected to a respiratory machine.

"I'm so sorry," Mr. Miller mumbles, his heart aching with sorrow. **"I should have been there."** Mrs. Miller's tear-filled eyes rise to meet those of her husbands.

"We're giving him blood to keep him stable," Dr. Fuller says. **"The mask you see is making sure he is getting enough oxygen to his brain."**

"There was a lot of glass inside him," the Asian doctor chimes in. **"Especially in his back."**

With trembling lips, Mr. Miller pleads, **"Please, tell me my son is going to be all right."**

"It's too early to say," Dr. Fuller answers, glumly. **"Your son slipped into a coma, just before you arrived."**

"Please God...No!" Mrs. Miller weeps harder. Holding his wife even tighter, additional tears spill out of Mr. Miller's eyes; the beeps from the machine are haunting to hear!

{Mike enters the room}

Moving toward the bed, Mike looks at his brother with a face drenched in tears; his eyes have the look of a person who is lost at sea…with no hope of rescue. Released from her husband's embrace, Mrs. Miller goes to Mike and holds him tight, causing them both to cry even harder. Mr. Miller, who is visibly emotional, shields his face using both hands as tears continue to stream down his cheeks.

 *'The Ancient'*

It has been more than three hours since Scott's parents arrived at the hospital, and in that time, they have never left his bedside. With the passing of yet another hour, a senior nurse suggests they go to the cafeteria to get something to drink, while she finishes their son's hourly readings. Liking the idea, Mr. Miller rises from his chair and takes hold of his wife's right hand. Before he can successfully escort her out of the room, he releases her hand as she moves toward her son's bed. Leaning forward, Mrs. Miller tenderly kisses her baby boy's lips, telling him that she loves him. Looking over at the nurse, she asks her to notify them of any changes in their son's condition. After the elderly nurse acknowledges her request, Mrs. Miller allows her husband to retake her right hand and lead her out of the room and into the hallway. Still holding hands, they head for the elevator that will take them to the ground floor.

Less than a minute after the nurse finishes her readings and leaves the room, a man wearing a doctor's garb enters, closing the door behind him. Although he carries a medical clipboard, he has no real intention of reading it, and tosses it onto the small table next to Scott's bed. Walking toward the lone window in the room, his attention becomes absorbed by those spectral skies, where an incandescent moon hangs unnaturally. The man is wholly aware that *something* within the white orb is looking at him with detestation—looking at him from...beyond!

Torrential rain descends from those nefarious clouds, accompanied by intense thunder, as it has been these last few hours. From within the clouds, a single bolt of lightning erupts, and the ceiling lights in the room go dim, leaving the moon as the only source of light. With his ethereal, white eyes shining eerily within the darkness, the man turns toward Scott, his expression reflecting hope as well as uncertainty. Foreseeing this young man's fate, whose body not only lies in front of him, but also exists somewhere between Heaven and Hell, somewhere inside the cold, blackness of the void, he approaches the bed, speaking with a voice imbued with the wisdom of antiquity...

"Soon your journey will begin.
Soon you will see the horrors of Evil.
The Fate of this world lies in your hands.
Seek out the Christian in the land of the white tiger."

IT BEGINS!

8:02 am.

Finding Mr. and Mrs. Miller sitting in the chairs next to Scott's bed, Doctor Fuller is about to update them on their son's condition. But, as his left foot touches the floor a fourth time, a brilliant light flashes outside the hospital. Moving swiftly to the window, all three bear witness to a scene that instantly horrifies them. Rising from the south, instead of the east, the fiery, crimson sun is casting a chilling mystique over the entire city.

"**What's happening?**" Mrs. Miller wheezes.

"**That sun, it doesn't look right!**" Mr. Miller shrieks.

"**My God, look at the clouds!**" Dr. Fuller's exclaims, as his mouth sags; his eyes look as if they're going to pop out of their sockets at any moment. "**They're changing colors!**"

BROWN

ORANGE

BLOOD-RED

"**That poor woman!**" Mrs. Miller cries out.

On the sidewalk in front of the hospital, an elderly lady clings to a signpost for dear life, the winds so destructive that her legs are airborne—her shoes blowing right off her feet. The three watch in horror as the woman's grip falters, and she crashes to the ground a distance away.

176

A terrifying laughter is heard inside the winds!

Mrs. Miller takes hold of her husband's left arm as they, accompanied by Doctor Fuller, step away from the window after witnessing a vision within the clouds. The apparition resembles the face of a demon, characterized by menacing eyes seemingly directed toward them. **"Roy!"** Mrs. Miller shrieks, **"do you see that?"**

"I'm not sure what I'm seeing!" Mr. Miller gasps.

"I see...eyes!" Dr. Fuller screeches.

177

FROM THE DARKEST REACHES OF SPACE, A PORTAL OPENS!

Unbeknownst to the others in the room, Scott had sat upright in his bed, his unbandage eye opening to reveal a striking transformation—his usual blue iris's now replaced by a horrifying vampiric red. As his mouth sags, an unholy droning crawls out of his throat, sounding strangely similar to that of a helicopter's propeller; the others don't hear this sinister humming. Ever so slowly, Scott rotates his head in the direction of the three at the window whose attention remains focused on the face in the clouds. Without warning, a surge of electricity shoots through the lad's body, causing the hairs on his head to rise; his body shudders violently, and his arms fall limp to his sides. Outside the hospital, the ruthless winds continue raking the lands in their search for additional victims. And, as fast as it all began, it ends!

The homicidal winds return to normalcy.

The face and eyes inside the clouds vanish.

The sinister laughter fades.

The sun returns to its customary color.

Those clouds return to their normal state, moving freely within the heavenly skies. Catching their breaths, the three step closer to the window, their eyes locking onto the crowd of people who are rushing over to help that elderly lady who went airborne; she looks to be quite dead!

At length, the harsh vibratory sound of the respiratory machine captures the attention of Mr. and Mrs. Miller, and, with the good Doctor, all three turn toward Scott who lies asleep in his bed, his unbandage eye closed.

WITHIN THE ABYSS...

After what feels like an endless descent through a vast ocean of emptiness, Scott suddenly comes to a halt!

Blackness encloses him, wrapping him like a blanket on a bitter winter's night. And though his eyes are open, there is only the cold cruel darkness, such darkness that it makes him believe he is slipping into madness. Inching his way to the threshold of insanity, the frightened young man touches his body and feels the firmness of it—believing he is en route to that heavenly place souls travel to after death. But, as he ponders this notion, while dangling like a puppet inside the abyss, an unimaginable horror plays out before him, one that instantly terrifies his soul:

IMAGES OF BUTCHERY AND SLAUGHTER!

An unseen explosion rumbles within this cosmic vacuum, followed by a penetrating crimson light that momentarily devours the darkness. Overcome by this mysteriousness, Scott closes his eyes. But, he swiftly reopens them upon suffering an intense burning sensation on his legs; he finds himself nailed to a wooden cross, dull copper spikes impaling his hands and feet. Looking down toward the base of the cross, tears slip from his eyes, for it's completely submerged in an infinite lake of pure...

LIQUID FIRE!

Scorching flames gnaw his unshod feet, and upon lifting his miserable gaze, Scott observes a structure, archaic in nature, where none stood before. An ancient bridge made from primitive stone has appeared, with scores of children staggering across it, amidst threats of pain and torture from their unseen jailor. Somewhere beyond the bridge, beyond the boundaries of vision, a nomadic drumming emerges, it's barbaric beat seemingly in sequence with each dreary step taken by those children.

From the burning waters, fireballs shoot out to scorch these little ones, who are forced to walk across this hellish passage; the bridge begins and ends in the waters. Other crosses begin to rise from those fiery depths, each with a screaming human nailed to it; their sorrowful cries are the stuff of madness. Recognizing their mommies and daddies among the crucified, the children weep harder. All the while, Scott yells at them to run away; no sound escape his lips.

Another explosion thunders inside the blackness, and once more, it is followed by that crimson light. Afterward, the men and women scream even louder as their sizzling flesh drops away from their mortal bodies. With trembling lips, the young man is forced to watch the gruesome affair of skin peeling from charred carcasses, and turning to ash.

Skeletons remain impaled to the crosses, their bones quickly crumbling to dust. With his eyes returning to that bridge, Scott bears witness to a little girl who now stands all alone there, cuddling her doll in her tiny arms. No older than five, the child cries out for her mommy as tears soak her freckled cheeks; she squeezes her dolly against her body even tighter. In a state of utter terror, the young man looks on as a fireball obliterates her young life, setting her body ablaze and hurling it over the stony flanks of this immoral edifice. As the flames eat away at his body, Scott screams out into the blackness, **"Dear God, why am I here? What did I do to deserve this?"** His words are without sound.

A face materializes over the bridge!

Unable to break free from the cross, Scott whimpers as he instantly recognizes the face to be the same one that was painted on the wall inside that condemned building, the same face that had taken over Kelly's inside the auditorium; the face is laughing at him!

Eyes
Size: larger than normal.
Iris: identical to a snake.
Sclera: an eerie, luminous yellow.
Shape: Reptilian.

Face
Hair: blood-red; semi-spiked.
Mouth: smirking; large vampiric fangs.
A powerful sculptured jawline.
High cheekbones.

The image is discharging so much evil, so much hate that it burns like acid. Without warning, the face explodes, and a new face emerges in its place: the crazy old man from that forsaken building——his cracked-jagged, sickly yellow teeth showing between his thin sneering lips. The lunatic stares at Scott, his unnatural, jet-black eyes frightening to behold. Slowly, the old man's face begins to fade away, returning to whatever unholy dimension it had come from.

181

As his nostrils detect a sulfuric odor, Scott observes a long, sleek, cylindroid object emerging from the fiery waters.

A Nuclear Missile!

Arabic inscriptions in bold lettering adorn both sides of the missile; adding to Scott's horror, the projectile turns in his direction. No longer nailed to the cross, Scott silently screams as he begins freefalling once more.

That nomadic drumming resumes!

Speeding toward him with unholy haste, the projectile detonates——making not a sound. It does, however, create a blinding spectacle of colored beams. Covering his face with his hands, Scott pleads, **"God, make it stop!"** Following his words, flickering light becomes visible between the gaps of his fingers, and heat strokes the back of his hands. Slowly, he lowers his hands, the whites of his eyes shining like pearls in the night. Unbelievably, the source of this warmth is from a fire, but not by way of that infernal lake.

182

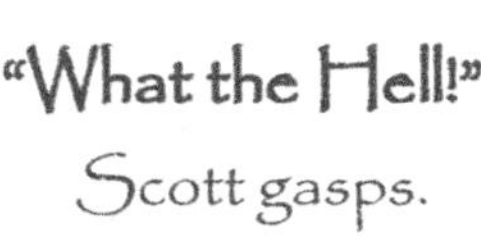

"What the Hell!"
Scott gasps.

No further than fifty yards away stands a big oak tree, entirely consumed by flames. Not sure if what he is seeing is real, or just another falsehood, Scott allows his hands to drop to his sides, falling upon something bearing the texture and roughness of wood. Removing his gaze from the burning tree, he lowers them toward the broken tree stump, which he is now seated on, located at the bottom of a two-foot-deep crater. **"Christ, where am I?!"** Scott cries, rising to his feet swifter than a jack rabbit spotting a fox.

Hearing his words for a third time, Scott places his left hand over his mouth, and touches his lips. Rotating his head and eyes toward the tree, confusion changes to horror as he beholds his surroundings. As far as his eyes can see, the landscape is one of nightmare; the terrain bears the scars of total destruction. Tilting his head skyward, his socket popping eyeballs lock onto a vision that commands his full attention; an oversized, blood-red moon hangs unnaturally in the spectral sky, its crimson light casting everything in an apocalyptic gloom. Moreover, the stench of burning wood rides the coattails of the winds, and the warm air is becoming increasingly hard to breathe. In the not-too-far-off distance are the black, skeletal remains of carbonized trees. Beyond the trees, red-colored lights flicker eerily in the night.

Squinting into the darkness, Scott observes several buildings, and a handful of houses smoldering----some like that oak tree before him consumed by flames. Returning his eyes to the crimson sky, he spots a cluster of large, black birds, silhouetted against the blood moon; they look as if they are circling his vicinity.

Climbing out of the crater, Scott continues to observe those birds in the spooky skies. At least a dozen of them, he counts in his head. After moving away from the hole, he directs his attention to his sneakers, noticing several glass shards embedded in the sides of his shoe. Struggling to find reason to all this madness, Scott's memory travels back to the incident outside the pizza parlor, just before the bottle shattered against his forehead. He recalls taking a swig of that bourbon he got from Mike's friend who works at that tavern. He remembers the car speeding toward him, as well as the kid hanging out of the passenger side window, and yelling... "Scott Miller, you're wanted in hell!"

"Am I in hell?" Scott whimpers. Remembering he got hit with the bottle, he removes his football jacket, seeing multiple cuts on the back of it. The wrinkly jeans he is wearing, now has a hole below the right knee, which wasn't there before. He remembers how bad the winds got, prowling the streets like a pack of wolves on the hunt, killing everything in sight. Finally, there is the memory of the stranger standing on the corner underneath the light. Before losing consciousness, Scott swears the fiend said...

"I will see you on the inside!"

The mysterious drumming heard moments ago returns, gently stroking the fragileness of his sanity. Feeling numb and confused, Scott's gaze wanders across the landscape until it settles on something strangely familiar. Observing a damaged road less than twenty yards away, he gains a clear understanding of his current location.

"This is Cazenovia Park."
Scott rode his bike through this park no longer than a month ago!

Limited light from the burning tree affords Scott just enough visibility to spot a basketball court with a baseball diamond next to it, both within close proximity; they appear severely wrecked. Returning his eyes to the crater he had just climbed out of a grim reflection enters his mind, causing his eyes to water and his lips to tremble. Nothing could have created such terrifying scenery, except...

"MY GOD!
IT HAPPENED!
WE DESTROYED OURSELVES!"

The words from Mr. Canton's history class sound off in his mind—spoken in the teacher's voice: "I believe humans will revert back to the primordial days of survival. They will become a bestial, savage species where the strong rule, and the weak die."

Tilting his head toward the crimson moon, Scott cries out, again, **"Why did you use those weapons? You idiots! You stupid... stupid fools!"** A profound sorrow blisters the core of his humanity; everyone he has ever loved or known is dead. Mercifully, his grief is soon followed by a renewed sense of inner strength, allowing him to rise from his knees. Once more, his eyes roam the shadowy terrain, snagging yet another familiarity, one he identifies as --

'The Steel Bridge'

The landmark structure is roughly seventy yards away and, based on his limited vision it appears to be functional. Using the sleeve of his jacket, Scott wipes away some of the tears from his eyes.

A shadow moves parallel to him!

Scott didn't see the shadow; however, he does spot a park bench that has seen better days on his left, less than thirty feet away. Walking over to it, Scott reaching down with his right hand to touch it's scorched surface.

The shadow moves again!!

As if he was a battle-hardened soldier, Scott drops to the ground behind the bench upon spotting the shadow out of the corner of his eye; he's stunned by how fast his primal instincts kicked in. Due to limited visibility, Scott cannot see the shadow with clarity, as it moves from tree to tree. At that moment, his focus shifts to the far side of the park, where he hears unusual sounds emanating from beyond the tree engulfed in flames. Unable to locate the source of the noise visually, he relies on his hearing to determine its location.

Adjusting his position behind the bench, Scott's line of sight is now directly on the burning tree. Moments later, the source of the noise presents itself; a large moving shadow is heading his way. With his backside now facing the smaller shadow, Scott drops himself closer to the dirt, his face mere inches from it. Due to the twisted wreckage of the wooden bench, its spine broken, and one end touching the ground, he is given an opportunity to peek around its drooped end without exposing himself.

Cognizant that someone, or something is still somewhere behind him, Scott remains silent, his movements mimicking that of a corpse. Several nail-biting seconds later, as well as a minor body adjustment, he becomes mindful that the large shadow is actually a cluster of individuals moving in a slow, methodical manner. Scott cannot see their faces, only their dark profiles against the foreboding backdrop. A leaning lamppost is located within ten yards from that burning tree; however, due to its damaged lamp, it offers marginal lighting at best. The lamp's soft, fuzzy glow—together with the fire from the tree reveals a throng of youths dressed in ragged clothing; the young males appear to be of a similar age to Scott. Additionally, many of their young, expressionless faces bear battle scars.

187

Scott's survival instincts flare up again as he frantically looks for a weapon, something he can use to defend himself. Apart from a seared tree branch within arm's reach, nothing else is available; he takes the branch. Gripping the wooden limb tightly in his right hand, he watches the youths as they approach the lamppost; within the gazes of the young males is a bestial reflection, an unmistakable resemblance to that of an animal: a wolf.

The similarity is troubling to say the least!

Forty-two of them Scott counts, led by a hulking youth who stands out as the largest among them. Upon reaching the lamppost they change course, turning in the direction of the bridge, and disappearing into the blackness beyond it. A grateful prayer later, Scott stands up. But, he quickly drops to the ground upon remembering there is a second shadow somewhere behind him. Assessing the unlikelihood of locating who or what it is—his eyes unable to penetrate the gloom, he slowly rises to his feet—staring hard at the area he believes the shadow may be in.

Nothing moves! Nothing can be seen!

Scott gambles a single hope, which is the gang scared off whomever or whatever was pursuing him, and with this hope, he places his attention on that bridge. For better or worse, he'll follow the fractured road before him that leads to the steel structure, and into the obscurity that lies beyond it. With as much courage as he can muster, he walks a dirt path parallel to the main road; moreover, his internal senses are telling him that a great evil is responsible for him being here, and even worse...he needs to find out why?

Heading for the bridge, a unique irregularity comes into sight. The nuclear storm had ripped a home completely off its foundation, depositing the entire upper portion inside the park's massive outdoor swimming pool, which was a popular attraction at one time for the little ones during the summer. From a distance of ten yards, Scott observes two windows on the second story of the house, along with a much smaller window that appears to be the attic. Moving a little closer, staring at one of the larger windows, he believes he sees a family picture hanging on the interior wall.

189

Before Scott is able to turn away from the house and continue toward the bridge, a shadowy individual forcefully breaks through the attic window and lands feet-first on the porch roof below. Gripping the branch tighter in his shaky right hand, Scott takes a few steps closer. Initially, he spots the shadowy outline of a young male, but as the figure slowly approaches the roof's edge, a thirteen-year-old boy, both fierce, yet vulnerable locks eyes with him. The contact lasts no longer than a second, as the night echoes once more with the shattering of glass. Scott and the young man, perfectly in sync, turn their heads and eyes toward the same window the boy had leapt from just moments before. Climbing out of that same window are two larger youths, both carrying wooden baseball bats soiled with what looks to be blood. After climbing out a different windows, a third youth hangs from his hands and drops himself to the roof. Paralyzed by fear, Scott can do nothing more than watch the three chase the smaller boy around the roof, swinging violently at him with their bats; it's clear they mean this boy harm. Each time the boy attempts to approach the edge of the roof to jump, his assailants manage to steer him away. Scott cringes when one of the males wielding a baseball bat attempts to hit the boy in the head; relying on his impressive acrobatic agility, the boy manage to dodge the blow at the last moment.

190

"Christ!" Scott gasps.

As the smaller boy makes another attempt to jump off the edge of the roof, his luck runs dry; the youth who swung at his head and missed, throws his bat at him and hits his leg, sending him tumbling. Without a shred of mercy, the three murderous youths converge on the smaller boy, kicking and punching him so sadistically hard, that Scott can hear the impact of their blows from where he stands. Horrorstricken, Scott watches the youth who didn't have a bat, pull out a curved dagger from a sheath attached to his upper right leg, and plunge it deep into his victim's abdomen; he proceeds to rip the boy apart with his blade, while the other two beat him even bloodier with their bats. Scott nearly vomits at the sight of blood pouring out from their victims wounds, not to mention the nauseating sound of bones being splintered. Struggling to maintain sanity, Scott watches those three murderous youths cease their ruthless rampage, and after howling like wolves celebrating a kill, they rotate their eyes toward their new prey. Scott notices the same animalistic reflection in their eyes, as it was in the gang of youths who had disappeared beyond the bridge seconds ago.

"The human race will turn savage."
The words from Mr. Canton echo in Scott's mind.

Dragging the deceased body to the edge of the roof, one of the killers lifts the lifeless corpse high above his head and tosses it over the side; the sickening, cracking sound of the boys head smacking the pool's waterless bottom is heard. With blood dripping off their weapons, each killer performs an Olympian's leap off of the roof, landing within yards of their next victim.

Their reflective eyes hunger for another kill!

Before Scott's mind can react to the situation, his legs are already on the move. Deemed one of the fastest athletes in all of Buffalo, he runs toward the bridge. However, hope abandons him, as he finds himself losing this race; the three are closing in on him. Making things worse, his left foot hits a piece of bomb shrapnel sticking out of the ground, and a tumbling he goes. The fall yields a nasty cut on his left leg, blood trickling from the wound. Aware the three killers will be on him as ruthlessly as their last quarry, Scott promptly regains his footing. Realizing running is no longer an option, because of the injury, Scott scans the ground for the tree branch he had dropped in the tumble. Spotting another, he grabs it and faces his assailants. Howling like starved wolves about to gorge, the three are merely walking toward him; it's obvious from the gash on their prey's leg that there's no way he is going to be able to outrun them.

There's something odd about the eyes of these killers, besides that unnerving reflection!

After hobbling to the bridge, Scott immediately places his back against its steel rail—raising the tree branch to an attacking position; the constant stinging in his leg makes it clear he has no choice but to stand and fight. Closing in on the bridge, and their victim, the murderous trio come to an abrupt halt—tilting their heads from side to side, staring at Scott as if he were part of a freak show in a traveling circus. Underneath the bridge's poorly lit lamppost, Scott is given a better view of his attackers. He observes several notable differences between himself and the others, particularly in their eyes; the color patterns are highly unconventional: their irises display uncommon hues, and their sclerae possess atypical shades of white, grey, and other colors. Each kid appears to be between fifteen and twenty years old.

The quality of muscle on their well-developed torsos, arms, and legs are also quite noticeable, and the way they hold their weapons sends a clear signal they are specialists in death-dealing; all three have visible scars, one has several, with one slicing through his lower lip.

First killer:
Knife with curved blade.
Forrest green irises, and light brown sclerae.
Short, untidy black hair with bangs hanging in his face.
Horrible scar on his left cheek.

Second killer:
Aluminum baseball bat.
Scary jet-black irises, and light blue sclerae.
Long, dark-brown hair tied into a ponytail.
Scar above his right eye.

Third killer:
Wooden baseball bat.
Creepy orange irises, and pale white sclerae.
Long, grimy, reddish-brown hair.
Two fingers are missing on his left hand.
Awful scar running the length of his neck.

Each of them is dressed in raggedy jeans, and wearing battered sneakers; the youth holding the curved blade has on a faded green army jacket, with one sleeve missing from the elbow down to the cuff. Realizing he has only moments before the homicidal maniacs attack, Scott readies himself for the predictable outcome he faces, especially having a flimsy tree branch as his only weapon of defense. But, as quick as the three step forward, they step back even quicker, their eerie eyes staring into the blackness just beyond the bridge. With the short hairs on the back of his neck rising, Scott turns his head toward the glinting eyeballs piercing that same gloom. His heart nearly skips an entire beat after the gang of barbaric teens he saw moments ago walk out of that shadowy shroud. Armed with weapons such as steel pipes, and bats embedded with large nails, they halt within fifteen yards of all four of them.

As his mind rattles, Scott shoots a look over the side of the bridge, observing a narrow creek below; he refrains from jumping upon noticing jagged rocks scattered across its dry bed—eager to take his life if he is foolish enough to leap down to them. Likewise, any attempt of fleeing into the shadows beyond this bridge is unlikely. With his attention on the horde, Scott notices that an opening in their ranks is occurring. Before he has a chance to reconsider jumping, two young males step forward, carrying the mutilated body of the boy the three had just slaughtered; his horrid wounds are visible for all to see. Staring at the dead kid, Scott can only wonder how they were able to retrieve his body from the pool so quickly.

Returning his focus back to those around him, Scott notes the similarities in clothing and physical build between the three killers and those in the gang. Allowing the branch to drop harmlessly from his hand, Scott shoots yet another look over the side of the bridge, confirming all hope is lost. At that moment, a set of different males emerge from the group and approached the three killers.

Mêlée...

Without warning, a commanding 'Battle-cry' rings out from within the horde, prompting those two young males to attack the three killers. Slack jaw, eyes wide, Scott presses his back against the rail even harder, a reluctant spectator to the brutal skirmish playing out before him. Standing their ground, the three killers fight back, led by the youth with the curved blade. Shooting forward, he slashes violently at the male attacking him. Trapping the blade between the palms of his hands, the slightly bigger male kicks the killer youth in the left side of his head with his right leg, sending him to the ground bleeding, and disoriented.

One of the youths wielding a baseball bat swings at the other male, but misses. He receives a punishing punch to his face for his failed attempt; blood oozes from his broken nose. Using stealth, the other youth with the bat sneaks up behind the male who had trapped the blade in his palms, and attempts to strike him in his head. Since the male had seen him sneaking up on him, he ducked and executed a tuck and roll, positioning himself behind the bat wielding youth; using a sweeping technique with his right leg, he takes out the legs from beneath him. Quick to rise, the unarmed killer youth throws a series of ineffective punches and kicks, all of which are blocked and efficiently countered; he receives a brutal uppercut to the mouth, resulting in a fractured jaw.

The other male connects with a crushing right hook to the body of the killer youth who was wielding the knife, after he stood up from the kick he received to the side of his head. *Scott heard the ribs break.* Snarling defiantly, and without his curved blade, the first killer youth regains his footing and attacks, receiving yet another vicious blow—this one to his face; blood trickles from between his lips.

In the interim, the killer youth who had his legs taken out from under him—and had his jaw shattered has retained his bat and is swinging at the male who just punched his partner in the face. Failing to hit his target, he is struck repeatedly by punches and kicks that drop him to the ground, never to get back up again. It's becoming clearer by the second that the three killers are no match against the two elite fighters. Executing a flying head kick to the first killer youth who had his nose broken, the second male delivers a fatal strike that drives the ridged bone of his nose into his brain, jolting the neck backwards, and leaving the kid to drop to the ground like so much deadweight.

Weaponless, and palming his broken ribs with his right hand, the remaining killer youth slides forward and throws an ill-advised, over-the-shoulder, righthanded hook at the head of the male who had just delivered the death kick to his fellow murderer. With the speed of a cobra, the elite fighter swiftly steps to the side and delivers a precise strike to his opponent's throat, instantly dropping him face first to the ground, so that he may join his murdering brothers in their much deserved deaths.

As the lifeless bodies of those three killers are tossed over the side on the bridge, the sound of their heads hitting the boulders on the bed of the creek is heard!

Mouth drooped and eyes wide with mixed awe and fear, Scott watches the two fighters rejoin their group after they had disposed of the corpses. Casting a third look over the railing, Scott reconsiders if he should jump, his eyes spotting the unmoving outlines of the three youths. Experiencing numbness, Scott shifts his focus back to the horde, noting that nearly all of them are observing him; their expressions reflect curiosity rather than hostility. From within the ranks, the biggest, scariest and most intimidating male Scott has ever laid eyes upon walks out; it's the hulking youth who led the gang into that shroud of blackness that lays beyond the bridge—the same one they just walked out of. Noticeably taller, and more broad in the shoulder than the others, the male looks to be close to Scott's age.

197

Approaching Scott, the burly youth begins tilting his head from one side to the other, fixing his gaze on him with irregular chestnut-brown irises, and eyes marked by paler brown sclera's. As the male moves his head, Scott notices a string of dull, red beads imbedded in his long, black hair. The youth has a noticeably tanned complexion, which is in sharp contrast to the lighter skin tones of those he leads, and like the others, his clothes are raggedy and worn; he's wears a shabby gray tee-shirt that features a faded buffalo graphic on it—along with jeans ripped on both sides; he has a horrible scar on the right side of his face.

Scott remains calm as the burly youth steps closer and reaches out with his right hand to touch his football jacket; a strangely familiar tattoo, etched in what appears to be ink from an ordinary fountain pen is spotted on the left side of the youths neck. Remaining like stone, his breathing shallow, Scott believes death is a crushing blow away, and just when he believes the moment has arrived, the youth simply turns away and returns to his group, vanishing with them into the darkness beyond the bridge, taking the mutilated body of the murdered boy with them. Overwhelmed by everything that just transpired, Scott collapses to the road.

 *Beyond the bridge...*

By the time Scott regained his strength and composure, an hour had passed. Rising to his feet, the throbbing pain in his leg reminds him it needs attention. Squinting into the darkness beyond the bridge, he starts to believe this is all a nightmare, but his internal senses force him to accept the horrifying reality that this is the real! Knowing of a hospital at the end of this road, he presses forward, his frightened eyes locked onto the black mantle that is slowly swallowing him whole. Only after breaking through the black shroud that he learns the truth, which is the darkness is an illusion. The haunting foliage limits the light from the crimson moon, its thick charred limbs stretching high overhead on both side of the road, creating an atmosphere that is distinctly eerie and surreal. In certain areas, beams of deep blood-red hue filter through the branches, coloring the earth below with a reddish glow----alarming to say the least!

The setting evokes the atmosphere of the tale of the 'Headless Horseman', with the only elements absent being the infamous carved pumpkin by the roadside, and an audible cry from the damned! Having decided to take advantage of the shadows, Scott heads for the nearest one, only to stop dead in his tracks before reaching it. Within a shadow on the other side of the road hides a most disquieting image:

The fur coat, and the diamond ring.
The faded blue dress, and the elegant sun-hat.
The fancy shoes with their broken heels.
The ragged, gem studded purse.

199

Scott observes the skeletal remains of what appears to be a sophisticated woman walking her dog along a different path in the park, approximately ten yards away and moving towards the bridge. Amazingly, the lady and her pooch are wholly intact, and in motion. The dog's collar is attached to a lengthy chain extending toward her outstretched, boney hand; the bone appears to be an ashen shade rather than the typical white he observed during his school visits at the Buffalo Museum of Science.

Averting his gaze from the scene, Scott continues on, trusting the shadows to provide cover. Shortly thereafter, he is eyeballing the ghostly exterior of the hospital from his position behind a car that looks to have been touched more than once by fire. *There is a skeleton inside the driver's side of the vehicle, it's boney hands still gripping the carbonized steering wheel!*

Feeling the sting on his leg, Scott turns his attention to the somber building situated approximately thirty to forty yards across a four-lane road. Before dashing across the street, he glances upward at the blood-red moon, spotting more of those strange birds he saw earlier; this sends chills running down his spine. After surveying the area on both sides, he runs across the fractured street and stops within the collapsed entrance of the hospital, standing in a shadow that could be potentially hiding a dozen or more corpses. Thankfully, it isn't!

Heart beating rapidly, and the pain in his leg throbbing, Scott prepares to enter, but not before looking up at the engravement on the concrete slab above his head; it is one he knows all too well...

'Mercy hospital'

201

"DARK WORLD"

Jagged edges, and an entrance littered in glass greets Scott as he cautiously steps through one of the glass doors that lead into the hospital's lobby: those doors are smashed to smithereens. Stepping onto the cracked marble floor, he observes bulges in the tiles, suggesting something is trying to break through from underneath. With the lobby besieged by shadows, Scott pays special attention to the darker areas, with his heart nearly stopping upon spotting several, larger-than-normal size cobwebs drooping from the ceiling; his feet immediately stop moving.

"It looks like a crypt in here!" he gasps.

After catching sight of the receptionist counter on his left, Scott stares at the gloomy corridor extending directly in front of him. Fifty feet to his right is an opening to a really large room, which he knows serves as the hospital's primary waiting area; red moonlight illuminates the space and extends into the lobby, giving the interior that quiet and grimly mood of a mausoleum. A sickly, green fungus extends across the deteriorating, paint-peeling walls; Scott deduces this may be the origin of the moisture detected in the bitter, tangy air. Also, there is a wheelchair encrusted in filth by the far wall, just beyond that counter.

Overcoming his fears, Scott moves further inside the main lobby, his limited vision prohibiting a clearer probe of the shadows, and other dark places that could be harboring trouble. He is also monitoring the cobwebs hanging above his head. Something on the receptionist's counter catches his eye, and upon a closer inspection, he discovers an old newspaper buried beneath a layer of dirt. When he tries to pick it up it begins to tear, forcing him to leave it where it is, and read it as it lies:

"So, that's how it started!" Scott snarls. "Fanatics!"

The biting pain in his leg serves as a reminder of why he is here. Walking away from the counter, he notices a rusted water fountain mounted to the wall, a handful of feet from the opening to that waiting room. A chuckle of foolishness flees his lips after he pushes the metal handle downward; the murky water not only comes out smelling of sewage, but looking of something far worse. Glancing to his left, Scott observes three elevators, along with the security personnel office; all partly hidden in shadow. After briefly surveying the entrance, he proceeds cautiously toward the archway leading to the main waiting room, compelling himself to look inside. The crimson moonlight casts an eerie glow over the space, giving it the appearance of a threshold leading into hell. Scanning the room, he notes how the chairs are caked in dirt and web. As his eyes drift —

"Murderers!" he scowls.

A massive pile of skeletons commandeers the foremost corner of the room; it is apparent they were seeking cover from the storm that unmercifully killed them. While mumbling further expletives, Scott's wandering eyes inadvertently uncover a slightly open door that shares the same wall as the skeletons. With a watchful eye, he walks over to it and inches the door open, discovering a small room lodged with dust-caked medical machines, and janitorial supplies.

Unseen is the large web occupying the ceiling!

Empty of any curative constituents for his leg, Scott leaves and closes the door, unaware of the presence above: a huge arachnid descending from the ceiling, distinguished by eight luminous red eyes, and six massive legs affixed to its furry body. Stepping away from the door, Scott's eyes lock onto five large, floor--to--ceiling windows in the room; three are cracked, the glass looking so brittle that a sneeze will do them all in. The glass in the middle window is missing, leaving behind deadly shards in its metal frame, eager to rip apart all those foolish enough to climb over them. His eyes continue to roam the room, eventually spotting a lone chair facing those windows.

Someone is sitting in that chair!

Sweating and short of breath, Scott approaches the chair quietly, each step feeling like eternity. And, to further complicate matters his mind is running wild, creating more anxiety for himself.

The skeleton sitting in the torn cushioned chair is that of a woman, holding an object wrapped in a dirty olive-green blanket, with her head slanting downward. Her bones are dressed in a faded blue dress and bonnet; the attire worn in church. Sobbing like a child, Scott knows what he will find before he even unwraps the blanket, and that is the skeletal remains of a newborn with an empty bottle in its boney jaw. Overtaken by emotion, he runs over to the closest wall and punches it. *Within the walls of the hospital, a scream rings out, one sounding female in nature!*

Startled by the scream, Scott is swift in placing his back against the wall he just punched. Rotating his eyes toward the entrance, he begins inching his way there, peeking an eyeball around the edge upon arrival. He is relieved to find the lobby unoccupied; *the screams is heard again!*

Receiving courage from within, Scott steps out into the lobby, his eyes swiftly locking onto the elevators; he notices the steel doors on the middle one are bashed in, looking as if one good tug will bring them crashing to the floor. He also notices a squeezable gap between the doors. Eyeballs into the gap reveal blackness, at first. As his eyes adjust to the dark, he spots the bottom of the elevator's car between the third and fourth floor, as well as a corroded ladder attached to the concrete shaft. Grabbing a wooden chair by the wall, Scott breaks off one of its legs and proceeds through the gap, taking hold of the ladder.

Ascending to the elevator car, Scott reaches up and unlocks the hatch underneath it—pushing it open. Pulling himself in, he finds a headless skeleton on the floor by the panel box, and both doors open. Moving toward the doors, he leans upward on his toes, elevating his head just above the fourth-floor ledge. But, before he can climb out, a dark figure shoots past the ledge and down the gloomy hallway that extends directly in front of him; the shadowy individual is running away from his location.

Ducking his head just below the ledge, Scott curses in frustration; he doesn't understand why he is in the elevator in the first place. Something within his soul is urging him to keep this course. Climbing out of the elevator—the chair leg held tight in his trembling right hand—he shoots a look down the hallway on his left, which is far more murkier than the one in front of him. Deciding to pursue the same route the shadowy figure had taken seconds earlier, Scott moves down the hallway with caution, his chair leg poised to strike anything that comes at him. That blood-red light from the moon beams through the bare windows, illuminating the right side of the hallway with its infernal glow. A pair of medical gurneys are by the wall on the left hand side, but only one contains a decomposed corpse. Upon reaching the halfway point of the corridor, Scott abruptly halts as that scream echoes once again inside the darkness; this time, however, it emanates from behind him.

207

Spinning around with his weapon at the ready, Scott's eyes fail to pierce the shadows, those that are tricking him into believing they are pursuing him down this corridor; he estimates the elevator to be in the ballpark of fifty to sixty feet away. With his attention squarely on the shadows by the elevator, he observes an eerie, bestial reflection cutting the darkness. Moments later, the probable source of the screaming—a young girl—emerges from the same darkness, running in his direction. Scott's attention shifts from the girl to the three young males behind her, dressed similarly to those who murdered that boy in the park; it appears they are chasing her. Whacking her left leg against one of those gurneys, the girl tumbles to the floor after she had unwisely turned her head for a looksee. Recovering from her nasty fall with remarkable speed, she rises so quickly that one of her assailants nearly trips over the same gurney, prompting the others to momentarily reduce their pace. Blinded by lust or blood, the three fail to notice Scott standing in the middle of the corridor——as does the girl who runs by him as though he isn't even there. With his attention remaining on the three, Scott notices how their reflective homicidal eyes are now locked on him! *Savage howling is heard!*

Endowed with pure animal viciousness, Scott acts in a manner he has never done before. Remembering what had happened to that boy on the roof, he immediately attacks the first youth entering his striking range, breaking the chair leg over his head, and sending him to the floor; blood spills out of his opened skull. Quickly converging on him are the other two...with one grabbing hold of his hair and wrapping his left arm around his neck, while the other charges with a knife in his hand. Swinging wildly with the broken chair leg, Scott is able to knock the knife out of his attacker's hand; however, his head is violently yanked backward from the kid who still has his arm around his neck. Struggling to breathe, Scott drives his body in reverse and breaks the chokehold, driving the kid into the concrete wall behind them both—the back of his kid's head smashing hard against it.

With the stranglehold loosened, and as the other youth charges with his recovered knife, Scott takes a frantic swipe at his head. However, the agile youth ducks out of harm's way, and thrusting his blade outward, his grip on the knife falters and flies out of his hand, missing its intended target. After the knife penetrates the abdomen of the boy who had applied the chokehold, the young male who lost his knife is briefly stunned by his mishap. Recognizing an opportunity, Scott advances and hits the disoriented youth in the nose, breaking it, dropping him to one knee; Scott finishes him off with a kick to the head. Removing the knife from his body, the other boy charges. A swift sidestep by his opponent at the last second throws him off balance. Unable to stop his forward momentum, the youth crashes through a window; *Scott hears a scream, then he hears no more!*

"My God!" Scott gasps. **"What did I just do?"**

Upon hearing a single footstep, Scott pivots and fixes his gaze on the wall, straining to see whatever lies concealed within the shadow that coats it like a layer of paint. Scott is jolted by the sudden appearance of that bestial reflection, cutting through the gloom like a hot knife through butter. With nothing to defend himself, but that broken chair leg, his only hope is a merciful death. Nonetheless, he doesn't get it...for out of the darkness comes not death, but a vision that instantly enslaves his soul!

"Whoa!" Scott pants.

210

Emerging from the shadow is the girl who just ran past him; as Scott casts his eyes upon the most exquisite female he has ever seen, his heart begins to beat zealously.

Her face and lips are radiant, and strikingly beautiful!
Her Egyptian, honeyed-brown eyes are mystifying!

Her coffee-brown hair is tied back into a ponytail with what looks to be string or twine. Scott is literally salivating over the girl, gawking at her magnificently shaped body, and her impressively defined arms and shoulders.

Following several seconds of ogling, Scott finally takes hold of his bearings. Spotting a metal examination table inside a dimly lit windowless room on his left, he walks toward it; his leg stings something fierce. The room contains two stainless steel cabinets: one stocked with supplies, the other empty. The glass door on the full one is undamaged, while the other has glass shards in its frame. Turning the handle on the stocked one, Scott finds it locked, prompting him to break the glass with his elbow. Sticking his hand through the broken glass, he unlocks the door and grabs some of the bandages inside, as well as a bottle of peroxide, and a half used roll of pharmaceutical tape.

{The girl walks into the room}

Pausing briefly to acknowledge her arrival, Scott notes how her bewitching eyes never leave him as she walks over to the examination table and hops onto it. Though his senses tell him she isn't hostile, he glances at the door all the same, making sure no one is following her inside. Once he is certain they're alone, he returns to the task at hand. After twisting the cap off the bottle of peroxide, he pours a lavish amount onto the slightly dusty bandage. Wanting to remain tough in front of the lady, he refrains from screaming like a sissy when the soaked bandage touches his wound; he chuckles like a lunatic at this droll reflection. After thoroughly cleansing the wound, he applies a new bandage and affixes it to his leg using the medical tape. To ensure the dressing will hold, Scott puts it to a test by taking a slow lap around the room. As he passes the girl, he spots blood trickling from a cut on her leg, compliments of the gurney in the hallway. He offers her the bandages, but she doesn't take them.

"What is your name?" Scott asks; she doesn't answer, her hands gripping the smooth edge of the table. Her eyes are locked onto his. Not sure what he should do, he slowly lowers the bandages and steps back:

Tattered denim shorts.

Scruffy sneakers.

Raggedy brown tee-shirt.

A tribal necklace featuring a peculiar pendant drapes loosely around her slender neck. She bears a scar on her left cheek and another above her right calf, both seemingly caused by something sharp. He offers her the bandages again, but when she remains unresponsive, he opts to tend to the wound himself. Gently taking hold of her superbly toned leg, Scott raises it for a better view of the cut; the girl remains calm as water throughout the procedure, even when he places the damp bandage directly onto her wound. Moments later, the wound is cleaned and dressed, yet the girl remains unresponsive. Returning to the cabinet, Scott places the unused bandages as well as the other stuff back on the shelves; he stiffens after a voice reaches his ears...

"Thank you."

Spinning about, Scott gasps, **"You can talk?!"**

"Yes, I can," the girl replies, her voice entrancing.

"Well, imagine that." Scott shakes his head and laughs.

"What is funny?" the girl asks.

"What is funny, you ask?" Scott responds; pausing a second or two before he continues. **"What is funny...is that I'm not sure if this is real or just some wild ass nightmare."**

"Nightmare?" the girl repeats.

"Yes, a nightmare." Walking back to the doorway, Scott stares out into the hallway, spotting the body of the youth he hit with that chair leg; the blood puddle next to his head has doubled in size.

"I don't understand what you mean?" the girl adds.

"That makes two of us," Scott retorts.

"What is your name?"

Looking back at the girl. **"Scott."**

"My name is Savina."

"That is a really nice name."

"You're different," Savina says. **"Where are you from?"**

"Far away," Scott replies.

"Far away?" she repeats, her voice reflecting confusion.

"Yeah," Scott chuckles. **"Really, far away."**

Scooching off the table, Savina walks over to Scott and, in a gesture of acceptance, gives him an open-handed smack on his right shoulder. **"It's nice to meet you, Scott from far away."**

Finding himself charmed by her mesmerizing eyes, Scott nearly stumbles over his words. **"It's nice to meet you too, Savina."** Before he can say anything more, Savina swiftly places her left hand over his mouth and casts a quick glance into the hallway. A frantic heartbeat later, she grabs his right hand and literally yanks him out of the room. Once inside the hallway, he looks where she does——at the shadows cloaking the elevators. Upon hearing the elevator doors close, fear grips Scott like a vice, especially when he notices a faintly, glowing green arrow aiming downward within the electrical signal box positioned above that elevator.

"We must leave this place!" Savina screeches.

Like a bullet fired at the start of a horse race, Savina dashes down the dark hallway, away from the elevators, all the while keeping a firm hold on Scott's hand; she's running so fast that he nearly trips over his own feet. An exit sign, unlit and drooping from the ceiling hangs above the door they are rushing toward. After opening the door, Savina pulls Scott inside, and together they run down a nightmare making stairwell——so dark that if not for her guiding hand, the lad would undoubtedly tumble down these stairs to his death. Reaching the basement level, Savina drags Scott through another door, and into another gloomy corridor.

"Where are we going?" Scott wheezes, stopping for a breather. **"And...for Christ's sake, what is that God awful smell?"** The answer presents itself on the stained wall before him as a single word, one that nearly drives him into a state of catatonic madness. His eyes follow the spray-painted arrow that points to another wall of absolute blackness, and like the others, his eyes cannot pierce it.

"This is our only way out," Savina proclaims, pointing in the same direction as the arrow. **"There is a room at the end of this hall. In that room is a window that leads to the outside."** Gazing intently at that impenetrable, pitch-black void, Scott's anxious thoughts envision bodies associated with the undead; zombies, ghouls, and other monstrosities that might have been spawned by the radiation. He imagines these horrors concealed within those shadows, anticipating his arrival and intent on consuming his flesh. Making things worse, there's a pale scent of decay in the air!

"This is just, wonderful!" Scott scoffs.

At that moment, the faint sound of a door being opened echoes from behind—the very door they went through only seconds ago. Retaking Scott's hand, Savina drags him into the blackness, not slowing until they are standing in front of a rickety metal door with the words, "Keep out" written on it. Due of the extreme darkness, Scott is unable to discern either the door or the inscription upon it. Once they open the door, they proceed quickly into a spacious room, which is illuminated by crimson moonlight streaming through the window that Savina previously mentioned. Straight away, the two begin barricading the door with whatever they can find: a heavy steel desk is the first thing pushed in front of the door, followed by a couple of chairs and an old-fashion wooden coatrack, which is tossed on top of the desk; the window they seek is on the back wall, completely shattered.

Obsessed with securing the room, Scott continues to pile more items on top of the desk. In the meantime, Savina has made her way to the window, and is attempting to climb through the broken glass—it's flesh ripping teeth ready to bite into her on the first mistake she makes; the agile lass climbs out and vanishes into the night. Once satisfied with the barricade, Scott surveys the room, and his eyes grow wide when he notices a row of freezers lined up against the wall; those steel cabinets are where they keep the corpses! His blood freezes when he notices one of the doors is not only ajar, but is moving side to side, creating the impression *something* has just climbed out of it!

BANG!
BANG!
BANG!
BANG!

"Savina, we got to get the hell out of here!!" Scott cries out, turning to find only empty space behind him. As he frantically searches for her, he notices an odd, asymmetrical pattern on the concrete floor, created by the light from the blood-red moon reflecting off the glass shards in the pane of the window. Absorbed by those continuously changing configurations projected off the shards, Scott enters an increasingly unfocused state that steadily diminishes his sensory awareness. In other words, he feels as if his soul is being sucked from his body. An internal blast of awareness releases him from this affair. Staring at that rosy stained window, Scott concedes the girl must have already gone through it. Spotting one of those medical rib spreaders on the floor, he picks it up and proceeds to clear away most of the broken glass in the windowpane. Without hesitation, he climbs out, and feeling the earth beneath his feet, he steps into the nearest shadow. Placing his back firmly against the hospital's external wall, he surveys the surroundings, finding no sign of Savina anywhere.

BØØM!

The sound clearly signals that the barricaded door has been broken down, and with sweat burning his eyes, Scott glances at the window, catching sight of glimmering eyeballs peering up at him; there is no doubt they have spotted him hidden in the shadow. Stepping away from the wall, Scott

217

kicks the face of the young male who is attempting to climb out, pummeling him back through that shard-lined window. Understanding that remaining in place is not an option, he proceeds swiftly toward the rear of the hospital, stopping after only thirty yards upon detecting sounds arising from further along his path. Through his internal senses, Scott notices a massive shadow by the wall to his right, partially concealing an industrial trash container. Uncertain about what to do, he rushes over, gets inside, and pulls the thick rubber lid closed.

Several terrifying moments later, Scott all but dies of fright when the rubber lid is suddenly lifted, and two young males look inside. Even with sweat stinging his eyeballs, he lies still as stone at the bottom of the container, underneath piles of rags and soiled bedding.

Something sounding like a wolf-howl comes from afar!

Luckily for Scott, the two youths never get a chance to place their eyes on him after lifting the soiled bedding that hides him. Instead, they drop the bedding and make haste toward the other side of the building, the direction the howl originated from. Scott quickly exits the container and runs into the night, leaving the hospital behind. Barely six minutes later, he is gasping for breath, feeling a sharp burning in his lungs. Standing beside a charred tree, Scott gazes at a small building that is about to fall apart, soon to be nothing but a heap of dusty concrete.

Compelled by his instincts to continue forward, Scott initiates another extended run, only halting when he is once again breathless; his left leg is paining him terribly, while his lungs burn as if he was inhaling toxic amounts of ammonia. Crouching behind a battered utility vehicle, its charred, steel frame hinting at multiple fires over the years, Scott yet again finds himself surveying his surroundings, focusing more on the gloomy silhouettes of the nearby ruins. He doesn't dare imagine what kinds of foul atrocities might be lurking in them!

"Abbot Road," he murmurs, noticing the wrecked streetlamp on the other side of the street. Its battered sign dangles from a bent pole rooted firmly in the earth. Aware of a shopping mall a couple of miles up the road, Scott decides to go there in hope of finding something he can use to get around; especially since his wounded leg isn't going to allow him to outrun anything. Perhaps he'll run into Savina there. Walking out to the middle of the road and staring down its long, deserted path, a profound emotion strikes his heart. *Everyone he knew is gone!!!*

With his eyes drifting upward, Scott spots those huge birds, silhouetting inside the blood-red moon.

219

After thirty minutes of uneventful walking, Scott finds himself less than a mile or so from the megamall. However, uneventful would not adequately describe the following: as his feet eat away at the distance, he stumbles upon a scene so terrifying, so unheavenly raw that his already troubled mind nearly succumbs to psychosis. From a distance, it looks to be nothing more than another shadow stretching across the sidewalk on the other side of the street. But as he draws level with it, everything shifts—spotting twelve massive rats feasting on something that was once —

HUMAN!

These monster rodents look to be in excess of two feet in length, weighing somewhere in the neighborhood of thirty to forty pounds: *they are ripping the corpse to pieces!*

Absorbed by the scene before him, Scott inadvertently leaves the cover of darkness and steps into the illumination of a partially functioning streetlight, thereby revealing his presence. Before he is able to correct his position, those mutant vermin notice him, their beady black eyes exhibiting a frightening reddish glow. With their sharp teeth clacking together, the rats scurry quickly in his direction while letting out a disturbing, high-pitched squeal.

With no weapon to defend himself, Scott desperately searches for something to use against those giant rats; the pain in his leg makes it clear he cannot run away. Spotting a three-foot lead pipe on the sidewalk outside a scorched, neighborhood grocery store, Scott quickly moves to grab it. But, before his feet can follow his brains directive --

"GRRRR"

Suddenly, a familiar threatening growl resonates from behind the rats, prompting each of those large rodents to pause and turn toward the carcass they were just feasting on. Shifting his frozen gaze to follow where those rats are staring, Scott observes the vague contours of two larger beasts near the partially devoured corpse, their blazing red eyes glowing satanically inside this chilling climacteric reality; the beasts are looking directly at him.

"GRRRR"

No longer interested in acquiring a fresher meal, the rats scurry past Scott toward a three-story building that is without its entire top floor, fifteen to twenty yards away; the mutated rodents swiftly scamper down a burrow at the base of the structure. Returning his attention to the corpse, Scott observes a third silhouette by those other two, and with three pairs of luminous eyes directed toward him, he begins moving away from the shadowy forms, which appear to resemble canines. While the hell hounds feast on those grisly remains, Scott, despite his injured leg, readies himself to escape by slipping into the nearest shadow. However, the way the beasts move their heads suggests they can still see him. With nothing to lose, but his life, he walks away at a brisk pace, but upon attaining distance, he accelerates into a full sprint, pushing his aching legs to the limit.

After running continuously for a mile, Scott pauses to catch his breath. Observing the area around him, he spots a barren hilltop with a towering oak tree at its pinnacle, and heads for it. Placing his back against the blackened bark of the tree, he slides down till his butt hits the dirt. Staring at the megamall, which is on the other side of the hill, his lifeless eyes drift to the horrifying landscape surrounding him; the incident with the giant rats, and those demonic canines has him shaking all over. Exhausted to the point of passing out, his droopy eyelids becoming heavier by the second, Scott begins his journey to la~la land. But, before this happens, he tilts his head toward that sinister crimson sky, and in a defeated tone, he asks, **"Why am I here?"**

'The Dream'

Lying lazily on the family couch in the living room, Scott raises his arms high above his head, and releases a much earned yawn from his sleepy lips. As his eyelids slowly open,

222

he catches the tail end of a popular music video playing on the television. **"That's a good one,"** he says, with a smile, his sluggish eyes roaming the interior of his home.

"**Scott!**" Mrs. Miller yells from inside the kitchen. **"What time did your father say he was coming over tonight?"**

Quick to his feet, Scott gasps, **"What the hell!"**

"What time was that?" Mrs. Miller asks again.

With a look analogous to that of a lunatic, but minus the drool, Scott stares at the kitchen archway. Although he is unable to see dearest Mom, he can still hear the oven door being shut inside the kitchen. With his eyes returning to the television, where a commercial for a local car dealership is playing, Scott exclaims, **"This can't be real!"** After noticing the closet by the staircase that leads to the second floor is partially open, he walks over to it, and takes a peek inside. Hanging on the closet pole are his football jacket, along with the autographed hockey jersey his father bought for him at a game, and a second pair of cleats hanging by their laces.

"Son, what time?" his mother shouts again.

As Scott removes the jacket from its hanger, he feels relieved—**"It was all just a terrible dream,"** he thinks, recalling that in his nightmare, he had been wearing this very jacket, which he now holds in his left hand. With a smile of salvation shaping his lips, he closes his eyes and begins thanking our Lord above for delivering him out of the depths of whatever hell he was in; a mouth-watering aroma invades his nostrils.

223

"Scott!" she yells once more.

Glancing at the kitchen archway, the lad remembers his mother is making his favorite for dinner: baked spaghetti. *"Around five, Mom,"* he answers, wiping the tears from his eyes. *"Talk about Déjà vu."* Remembering he hasn't heard from Lisa today, he decides to go up to his bedroom and put on a nicer shirt for when he sees her, which he hopes will be later in the evening. With a glee in his eye, and a pep in his step, Scott hastens up the staircase only to stop at the halfway point upon hearing...

The doorbell.

"That must be your father now," Mrs. Miller says from inside the kitchen. *"Can you let him in?"*

"Okay, Mom," Scott replies, turning around. Still a bit shaken from his traumatic nightmare, he misjudges a step and nearly tumbles down the remainder of the stairs. Walking to the front door, Scott pauses to reflect on the certainty it was a nightmare. Lowering his left arm, he touches the spot on his leg where he received the cut. That's odd, why does he feel pain if it was only a dream?

The doorbell rings again.

Clinging to his conviction it was all just a dream, Scott shrugs off the eeriness. Upon reaching the door, he opens it and steps out onto his porch, where all that greets him is the pleasant evening air. Finding no one there, he puts on his football jacket and proceeds down the porch steps, all the way to the sidewalk in front of his house. As whispers of chaos dance like puppets inside his mind, a pungent smell of sulfur touches his nose; furthermore, the clouds above are becoming increasingly ominous with each passing moment.

Glancing down the sidewalk to his left: nothing.

Glancing down the sidewalk to his right: nothing.

The street looks deserted.

So...who rang the doorbell?

Every house sits deathly silent, no light inside any of them—no life at all!

Returning to his porch, Scott notices how the windows of the Sinclair's house are blacker than death. Normally at this time, they would be sitting on their couch in the living room watching television, which was fairly routine for them. Shaking his head over this weirdness, Scott walks back up the stairs, and reenters the house.

"Was that your father?" his mother asks.

"No one was there," Scott replies, making his way back to the staircase; he doesn't get the chance to walk up them.

The doorbell rings a third time!

In a somewhat annoyed voice, Mrs. Miller says, **"Please answer it. I hope it isn't those Henderson boys with their pranks."** As Scott walks back to the door, a smile forms on his lips as he remembers his younger days, and the playful pranks he used to play on the neighbors, much like those

Henderson boys. Suddenly, a dark silhouette appears in the door's windowpane. With excitement, Scott opens the door and discovers a tall, lanky man in a long black trench coat, with a big spooky black hat standing there: lightning erupts inside the clouds!

"NOOOO!" Scott screams.

Just as Scott is about to slam the door shut, a strong pastel hand grabs his throat, lifting him effortlessly off his feet! **"Now don't be rude son,"** Mrs. Miller laughs, wickedly. **"Invite the man in. We have much to discuss."** Scared stiff, Scott looks down at the Stranger, who looks up at him with his Dracula-black eyes and uncompromising grin. As the darkness begins to overtake him, he can still hear his mother laughing in the distance.

'The Tree'

As his eyelids slowly open, the sight that greets him first are those scorching fires on the horizon. Rising to his feet, feeling numb and confused, Scott looks out in despair at the apocalyptic nightmare before him——something he had moments earlier held to be nothing more than an unpleasant ruse. Somehow, he's back! Madness tightens it's tentacles around Scott's mind, but before it can squeeze the sanity completely out of him, it is thwarted by a celestial surge of internal mettle.

Standing next to the tree, Scott stares intensively at the mall, which is over a hundred yards away. However, it's not the building that spooks him, even though it is creepy as hell, but the disturbing peculiarities associated with it:

First Abnormality

A flickering amber light can be seen inside the mall, visible through the building's giant glass windows.
Aside from the glow, the mall is black as death!

Second Abnormality

There is a derelict gas station sixty yards east of the mall, where two fuel pumps have toppled over and fire, fueled by its underground tanks is shooting into the air, looking so much like the flaming horns of the Devil!

With the flames reflecting like mirrors in his eyes, Scott feels an internal pull to head to the mall. Walking away from the tree, his wobbly legs fail him as one foot undercuts the other, and a tumbling down the hill he goes. Lying flat on his back, he scowls at the red sky above and curses, everything! Rising to his feet once more, he gingerly continues down the grassless slope, the fall having irritated the cut on his leg. Upon reaching the outer edge of the mall's massive parking lot, he runs, not stopping until his backside is touching the mall's exterior wall. Spotting a door fifty feet away, he moves cautiously toward it, discovering to his chagrin it is locked.

Noticing another door less than a football throw away, Scott promptly moves toward it. The unlocked entrance bears a sign stating, 'Employee's only.' Upon opening the steel door, he finds a narrow, unlighted passageway within. Harrowing to say the least, Scott bravely ventures into the blackness, sliding his left hand along the concrete wall as a guide. Because he cannot see anything, he ultimately runs headfirst into another door at the end of the corridor; his ingenuity of using his hand as a guide had failed miserably. With a trembling right hand, he opens the door just enough to allow him the safest glimpse of the area on the other side of it. Praying it is vacant, he slips in, and immediately moves into a shadow, allowing the door to close on its own.

Within the shadow, Scott observes two giant windows stretching from the ceiling to the floor on his right, both of which are undamaged. Capturing his attention are spooky, cartoonist apparitions drifting across the walls as well as the ceiling, brought to life by the mysterious glow that is hiding somewhere inside the mall. Moreover, the villainous crimson moonlight streams through those giant windows, casting a fiery glow that provides some visibility. At the same time, it hints at a deceptive tale of horrors attempting to escape from hell, via the wide cracks in the concrete floor. Moving as stealthily as possible in the shadows, Scott closes in on the department store he seeks, while keeping a watchful eye on those darker places that might harbor trouble.

Arriving at the store, Scott finds the entrance littered in glass; the windows having been smashed to smithereens, acting like an alarm to all those who may hear the crunching sounds. Carefully navigating around the shattered shards, Scott enters the store and immediately stoops behind the front counter; a portion of the crimson moonlight has filtered its way inside. After spotting a socket wrench lying inside a cardboard box underneath the counter, and grabbing it, Scott swiftly moves to the section of the store he knows to be the home of an extremely fast bike:

'The English Racer'

Foolish in allowing his mind to slip from the unbeknown perils he just might be walking into, Scott steps out of the shadows to touch the bikes frame. He remembers the day he came here with Dave to look at this bike, as Mrs. Knoll was planning to buy it for her son as a birthday gift when he turned sixteen; however, Mr. Knoll had already purchased the Mustang, making Davey boy an extremely happy young man. Lifting the bike off its rack, and setting it on the floor, Scott checks all four tires, as well as the durability of the frame, making sure it's road ready as he intends to ride it out of the mall. Very much anxious to leave, he hops aboard and immediately departs the store—heading back to the door that leads to the outside.

Along the way, Scott spots another store of interest, compelling him to stop. The steel roll-up door that secures the store after hours is lying on the cracked stone tile just outside the entrance. Leaving the bike outside, he enters the sporting goods outlet in the hopes of finding a weapon that will be more dependable than the previous ones he had. Knowing exactly what he wants, he hastens to the section that carries baseball bats; the weapon he is searching for is a long, thin, wooden bat used in a popular schoolyard game among Buffalo's youths. The game is called, 'Wall Ball.'

After locating this special bat that balances durability with lightness, Scott grabs it, and makes haste back to the entrance. *Faith carries a raw sense of irony!* Someone in a full baseball catcher's outfit is standing next to his bike with an aluminum baseball bat in their right hand. To make things even more unsettling, that diabolical blood-red moonlight wraps around this person like a shroud, intensifying their ominous presence; an animalistic glint briefly appears behind the catcher's mask. Scott's hesitation to take another step forward leads the individual to suspect fear, and therefore they charge. With his internal senses bidding him to fight, Scott lashes out with a clumsy swing when his unidentified pursuer comes in range, striking a rack of golf clubs instead of the intended target. The individual tries to strike Scott in the head with a swing of their own, but hits only empty space; undeterred, they take another swing, and miss yet again.

The failed attempt propels the person forward, causing a collision with Scott. As a result, Scott drops his recently obtained bat and steps back, inadvertently tumbling into a large plastic container filled with footballs. Quick to his feet, Scott grabs one of those footballs, and launches it like a missile at his attacker's facemask as they were preparing to swing again. Reeling from the blow, the individual drops their bat, and raises their arms to block further incomings. Taking advantage of the moment, Scott retrieves his bat from the floor and steps forward, delivering a solid blow to the left temple of the individual's head----causing them to stumble backwards. Spotting a bowling ball on a nearby rack, Scott picks it up and throws it at the individual's facemask, striking so hard that it sends them sprawling to the floor.

Without hesitation, Scott places the bat between the handlebars and rides out of the store like a fugitive, headed straight for that door. However, when he approaches to within twenty yards of it, he finds five young males wielding bats standing in his way—one of them missing his right arm. Suddenly, another youth leaves the shadows carrying a steel pipe, prompting all five to begin screaming savagely. With the fine hairs prickling on the back of his neck, Scott quickly spins his bike around and pedals furiously toward the center of the mall. Shooting out of the shadows on his left, three other males on bikes, head straight for him; one armed with a long chain nailed to a two by four.

Redirecting the Racer down a walkway, Scott spots another youth with a goalie's hockey stick—holding it as if he was preparing to joust like a knight. Noticing an elevator adjacent to a women's clothing store, its open door partly hidden in shadow, Scott guides the bicycle in that direction, narrowly avoiding a collision with a small kiosk formerly used for selling jewelry. Mimicking their quarry's action, the three riders proceed toward the same elevator. Once inside the car, Scott pushes the 'Up' button on the damaged control panel, but nothing happens. Realizing his predicament is worsening with each passing moment, he frantically presses every button, but the outcome remains unchanged. All the while, the three riders are closing in awful fast, and that kid with the hockey stick is howling like a wolf.

232

"DING"

Salvation: the elevator doors start to close!

At the sound of the digital signal, those three youths pedal faster, their fierce screams fading as the door slowly closes. With weapons hammering away on the other side of the steel door, Scott pushes the 'Up' button once more, and the elevator ascends. Uncertain about what awaits him when the doors open, he experiences relief when the metal panels split, and darkness is the only thing that greets him. Like a rocket, Scott blasts out of the elevator, riding hard toward the other side of the mall.

"DING"

The digital sound turns Scott to ice, his bike stopping on a dime. Whipping his head and eyes toward the elevator he had just rode out of a curse escapes his lips as he watches the panels slowly close. Casting aside his fears, he continues to ride hard toward the other side of the mall, pausing only out of necessity as he uncovers the origin of that strange flickering glow he seen from the hilltop. *A massive bonfire is blazing near the heart of the mall, right on the main floor!*

From his vantage point on the first floor, Scott looks beyond the steel railing and observes nearly two hundred youths circling the fire like wild savages before a big game hunt. Spotting the intruder, the youths begin howling and throwing their weapons at him; a claw hammer scarcely misses Scott's head. Riding through a wall of blackness are a half a dozen youths no further than thirty yards away; everyone one of them is flashing that beastly reflection in their eyes.

The youths by the fire scream, "Kill, Kill, Kill!"

On the verge of messing his pants, Scott looks over to his left and spots the entrance to yet another department store. Giving it no thought, he races toward the metal gate that safeguards the store, which happens to have a gaping hole in its center. Riding through it, he doesn't stop until he is deep inside, a whisker away from crashing into a circular rack filled with fancy dresses. Scott quickly lays his bike down on the ground, holding his bat tightly in his hands.

233

Because the fire is illuminating the entrance, it throws sinister shadows across the youths streaming into the shop; Scott observes them from his spot between a pair of dusty, well-dressed mannequins. Armed with fearsome weapons, the young males begin searching the frontal area, moving systematically inward. Within moments, the six youths riding bikes enter the store, unknowingly headed straight for the area Scott is hiding.

Believing he may have identified a potential means of escape, Scott focuses on the slightly curved object with bubble-shaped handrails that is hiding inside the gloom; the oddly shaped silhouette is less than forty yards away, and can only be the store's escalator going down to the first floor. Removing one of the mannequins shoes, and without standing, Scott throws it as far as possible away from the escalator; the sound of the shoe hitting something sparks a wild reaction from the howling youths, sending them into a frenzy. Hoping enough of them have taken the bait, Scott lifts his bike off the floor and rides toward what he hopes is an unguarded route to the lower level. Regrettably, three of the riders are not fooled, and spotting their quarry riding for the escalator, they give chase. Descending those steel steps, Scott had neglected to consider the safety aspect of this perilous endeavor, which was never meant for racing bikes; nevertheless he doesn't break his neck or damage the tires, and rides hard toward the entrance.

"*Bang*"— something sounding like a firecracker comes from the escalator, inciting Scott to stop for a looksee; it appears the three riders followed him down the escalator, with the first rider blowing out his front tire. Because of the damaged to the tire, the back tire is slanted, and acting as a ramp, it launches the rider behind him into the air, causing the screaming youth and his bike to crash unmercifully into a service counter below. Scowling wrathfully near the top of the escalator is that last rider, his bestial, reflective eyes flashing eerily inside the gloom. Looking over at the youth who had crashed into the counter, Scott knows he is dead, his body laying lifeless on the floor.

Upon receiving an internal directive, Scott gets his bike moving, but not before spotting a pair of glowing white orbs in a shadow next to the men's clothing rack. Driven by fresh determination—or perhaps fear—Scott races out of the store, quickly moving past one department outlet after the other. Just when he begins to believe he is going to make it, the frosty hands of calamity close their icy fingers. Blocking the door that leads out of the mall are a pair of youths with aluminum bats, their eyes fixed on him. Applying the brakes, Scott turns his attention to the intense howling coming from the distant shadows behind him. Slicing through the dark like a surgeon's scalpel, beastly reflections send Scott into a cataleptic numbness; his internal senses immediately start pumping courage into his soul, which allows him to act.

Recklessly, Scott rides the Racer straight at those two guarding the door, hoping they will move. No such luck; the two charge with bats elevated. Seconds before the impact, Scott lifts his front tire into a wheelie, just as the two swing their bats at him. The rubber section of the wheel deflects one of the impacts back toward its origin, resulting in the kid being struck on the right temple, dropping him to the floor to which he doesn't get up. Meanwhile, the other youth strikes the bikes metal frame and alters his course.

CLANG!

The sound of metal on metal echoes throughout the mall.

The sound of glass shattering!

Since his bike was redirected on that last strike, Scott lost control and had failed to return the wheel to the floor. As a result, he crashed through one of the giant windows, tumbling to the skin-removing gravel outside the mall.

From the shadows next to that shattered window, a pair of glistening red eyes emerge, followed by the chilling sight of large, bone-white, flesh-ripping teeth!

Shaking the cobwebs from his head, Scott slowly get to his feet, and wobbles over to retrieve the bat he had lost during the crash. Once he retrieves it, he turns to face an opponent that isn't there. Experiencing a stinging sensation on his left forearm, Scott examines the tear in the sleeve of his jacket, surmising the glass must have cut him as he went through it. Luckily, the wound is trivial, and therefore, he gives it no more attention, and with the bat gripped firmly in both hands, he approaches the window. The young male who struck the bike's frame with his bat is lying on the floor inside the mall on the other side of the window, with a glass shard the size of a machete piercing his abdomen; blood is steadily flowing out of the wound. Scott assumes the youth followed him to the window after striking the bike's frame; now, all Scott can do is watch as the youth's eyes—free of hatred—close for the last time.

Realizing the savage howling he heard moments ago has stopped, Scott remounts his Racer and rides it up the hill with the large oak tree. After reaching the tree, he pauses to catch his breath and glances back at the mall to check if any of the riders from the shadows are chasing him—just as they were before he crashed through the window. Shifting his gaze to the road that led him to the mall, he recalls there's a highway, a mile away; his instincts urge him to head for it.

"OH, F--K!" he curses, his lips quivering.

As his eyes revisit the mall, Scott spots two of those demonic canines leaping through the broken window, joined by a third that lands beside them; all three spin their sinister, glowing red eyes toward the hill—fixing their gaze on him!

Recognizing them to be the beasts that were eating the corpse he had seen earlier, Scott begins to panic as he isn't confident at all that he can outride them...for they look like runners. On the other hand, he knows exactly what they will do to him if they catch him. Without warning, those infernal spawns of Satan spring into action and run up the hill with terrorizing speed. Tapping into his internal strength, Scott speeds down the other side of the hill, peddling furiously with all his might, toward...

ROUTE US 240

Though the entrance to the highway is hidden away by darkness, Scott's certain he's heading in the right direction, and with God's help, he hopes to reach it before those hell hounds catch him. Pedaling with every ounce of strength he can muster from his fatigued legs, he spots a corroded sign marking the entrance to the highway.

"GRRRR"

One of the monstrous dogs, now less than ten feet away and moving alarmingly fast, lunges at Scott, its powerful jaws snapping shut just shy of his right leg.

"AHHH!" Scott screams.

As another leaping canine attempts to clamp its saliva spraying jaws down on Scott's left arm, he jerks away just in time, causing the beast to miss and land awkwardly on the ground. Quick to its feet, the enraged hell hound resumes its pursuit. Receiving more stamina internally, Scott begins distancing himself from the pursuing hounds. The terrifying dogs chase relentlessly, their growls fierce, as though driven by fear of punishment from their master in hell if they should fail in capturing their prey. Even after Scott arrives and speeds down the ramp towards the highway, those beasts refuse to give up the pursuit.

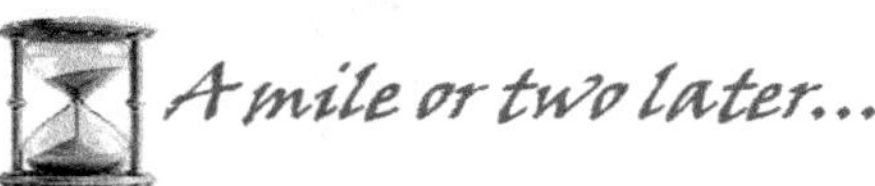 *A mile or two later...*

239

Bringing the English Racer to a complete stop, Scott twists his body around, his anxiety mounting to see if he is still being chased by the demonic hounds. Staring at the road he rode down, Scott gets his bike moving again when he observes six glowing red orbs running down it. Riding hard for another mile or two, he pauses a moment to reassess the situation. Following several terrorizing minutes, he concludes that he has indeed escaped the hounds...for now!

"It looks like a crypt in here!"
Scott gasps.
SOUTH PARK HIGH

"LIPTON"

Describing the highway Scott is riding on would be like illustrating the ideal Nomadic refuge...for there are literally miles upon miles of outright desolation. The barren forests on both sides of the expressway are daring him to enter; furthermore, he all but sheds his skin when he looks up into those crimson skies—the blood-red moon giving the illusion of being oversized, staging a falseness of touching the highway in the horizon; the giant moon continues to cast a backdrop for those mysterious black birds, their shapes outlined clearly against its fiery glow.

Engaging the Racer's kickstand, Scott climbs off the bike and walks out to the middle of the road. Blood curling, teeth grinding and lips quivering, his widening eyes zero in on the distant ruins of what can only be downtown Buffalo. What remains of his beloved city lies in despair, wrapped tightly in the Grim Reapers cloak and looking so much like a vampire's playground. Scott's internal senses are telling him that the answers he seeks are inside the ruins!

Glancing over at the spooky forestry to his left, Scott comes to believe they are home to more of those devil dogs, patiently waiting for him to foolishly venture a little closer. Making things worse are the unwelcomed thoughts of that cryptic fiend he calls the Stranger; *maybe he's in the trees with the hounds!*

Retuning his attention to the road, Scott observes the countless vehicles littering both sides of the highway, each one acting as a metal coffin for the bony occupants that still occupy them. Moments later, he notices a large, olive-green highway sign about twenty to thirty yards away, which he hadn't seen before due to his vision restrictions. Hanging askew, one end is completely detached from the overhead steel pole, while the other end dangles a foot or two above the ground. After taking in a lungful of the warm air, Scott returns to his bike and immediately rides toward the sign, his course soon revealing a section of the city he is very much acquainted with. If the sign were attached, it would point to an off-ramp swathed in gloom. Staring at the one lane road, his undisciplined mind once more produces images that do him no favors. *The disquieting silence is haunting!*

Before riding the Racer down that road where the sign once pointed, Scott scans the area for signs of those hell hounds. He also places his attention on that barren forest, and shivers—feeling as if his mind is deceiving him—making him believe those charred trees are moving around him, their creepy branches stretching out to grab him. Scott knows if not for his internal senses pumping strength and courage into his soul, he would be back inside the abyss, trapped in an eternal mind-prison. By maintaining a consistent pace, he reaches the end of the junction in under an hour, where he observes a street sign that appears almost fictional.

'South Park Avenue'

This off-ramp, which Scott has decided to travel down, runs a few miles or so, eventually leading him to the northern sector of the city where the Avenue begins. Yet, this street is unfamiliar to him now—cracks wide enough to swallow him whole run along its length, with much of the pavement having shifted out of place. Exercising extreme caution, Scott keeps an eye on the neighborhood streets after observing several homes burning. Those not engulfed in flames are blacker than a witch's heart—once homes to loving families. But, now they are nothing more than an unholy extension of this overall hellish tableau.

 *A mile or two later...*

How can he be experiencing hunger pains if this is only a nightmare? With a growling stomach, Scott searches his memory for the location of a supermarket he and his mother often patronized. Taking a detour down a familiar street on his way to the store, he suddenly slams on the brakes after passing a two-story house that had just burst into flames, which moments earlier was as peaceful as a cemetery. As he twists his body, his widening eyes mirror the intense flames that is consuming the house—a blaze raging forth without any sign of warning!

"What the hell!" Scott gasps.

Observing the fire, Scott notes its behavior is strange; instead of burning through the house as one might expect, it appears to be feeding off the building in an effort to keep itself going endlessly. Giving this weirdness no more of his time, he rides fast toward the end of the street. Arriving at the food mart a few minutes later, he enters the parking lot, stopping next to a burnt-out pickup truck. Gazing upward at the parking lots unfunctional lamps, he notices how most of them have been ripped off their posts; the absence of the outside lights hinders him from seeing inside the store. Nevertheless, his sense of smell is picking up the abated odor of rotted meat that is still lingering in the winds.

Why is he still able to smell meat?

As he rides closer, Scott notices what appears to be flickering ceiling lights inside the supermarket, barely giving off any illumination. Additionally, more than half of those storefront windows are shattered, many of them are missing altogether. In case a hasty exit is needed, Scott tactically places the bike by the entrance and enters with bat in hand, stepping over a headless skeleton on the way in. Following a quick scan of the interior, he walks over to the nearest rack of canned goods and grabs a can of sliced carrots, amazed to find so many cans still here. Reading the expiration date on the brown-yellowing label, he turns stiff upon hearing...

After returning the can to the rack, Scott readies his bat for battle; the melodious tune comes from beyond the shadows at the end of the aisle. Prepared to take a batter's swing at anything that comes out of those shadows, Scott moves at a snail's pace toward them—the singing increasing in volume with each step. Reaching the end of the aisle, he pokes his head around the bend and smacks his bat clumsily on the edge of the rack, losing his grip.

"CLANK…

"CLANK…

"CLANK…

With the sound of the bat bouncing repeatedly off of the floor, echoing hauntingly in the dark, Scott glares through the translucent gloom and spots a young male, suffering from what he can only surmise to be dwarfism, sitting on a plastic blue milk crate struggling to open a jar of salsa. Upon being alerted to the presence of an intruder, the youth takes off down the aisle into darker shadows.

"Wait!" Scott involuntarily shouts.

Utterly stunned by the speed of the male, Scott is slow in retrieving his bat from the floor. Proceeding toward the crate, he pauses briefly to make sure no one is sneaking up behind him. Seeing no one, he continues, stopping short of the shadows the kid disappeared into.

"I just, wanted to talk," Scott says, quietly.

"Why didn't you just say so," a malleable voice responds from overhead, and to his rear. Turning around, and looking up, Scott spots the youth perched on top of the food rack in the aisle he just went down—his right arm cocked back in a way that indicates he will throw the jar of salsa at the slightest hint of danger. Aside from the jar, only the eerie reflective eyes of the youth are visible, as he's nearly cloaked in shadow. Following a moment of steady eye contact, the kid climbs down. "I'm always looking for good conversation."

"Good conversation?" Scott repeats, baffled.

"Yes," the kid retorts, "good conversation."

"Okay," Scott snickers.

"They call me, Lipton."

"They call me, Scott."

"Hello, Scott," Lipton says, smacking him on his arm in the same manner Savina had at the hospital.

Looking at Lipton's eyes, which hold an unusual shade of forest green for the irises, and a mystifying, white-green for the sclera's, Scott asks, "do, you live here?"

"No, I just eat here."

"Are you alone?" Scott is finding it quite the challenge to pull his eyes away from Lipton's.

"No," Lipton grins. "You're here."

With a madman's smile taking shape on his lips, "Yes," Scott utters, "I'm here."

Lipton: Standing just under four feet tall, this youth has a strapping physique with shoulder-length, curly, strawberry blonde hair. Dressed in a white long-sleeved button-down shirt, brown corduroy trousers, and black combat boots, he resembles a dwarven warrior from a well-known role-playing game, complete with a leather sheath secured to his backside and a large blade tucked inside. Lipton appears to be close to Scott's age...maybe a year younger.

***

"Where are you from?" Lipton asks.

Eyeballing the swords hilt, which is sticking out of the sheath, Scott replies, **"ah, you wouldn't believe me."**

Returning the unopened jar of salsa to the shelf, Lipton heads toward the center of the store. Realizing he isn't being followed, he pauses and says, **"follow me."**

Bearing a degree of uncertainty about the kid, Scott complies while remaining vigilant for others. Approaching a grimy, round white plastic table surrounded by three equally dirty chairs, Lipton gestures Scott to sit as he walks behind the snack shop counter. While seated, Scott's attention remains on his host as he strategically places his bat on the floor by his right foot for easy access. A few moments later, Lipton returns from searching the shelves; he's now wearing a server's apron and holding a plastic tray. On the tray are an opened can of peaches, a can of pears, and an unopen bag of sour cream potato chips that have expired.

"Nice apron," Scott chuckles.

Lipton holds out the tray. **"Take one."**

"Thanks." Selecting the peaches, Scott also takes the white plastic spoon lying next to it. Wasting no time, he digs in. Despite being well past their prime, and extremely warm, the peaches still have taste. Consuming their humble feast, the two remain seated, and talk.

 *The ticking of the unseen clock...*

"I never imagined the world was so wonderful," Lipton says, sipping pear juice from the can.

"It was...wonderful." Scott's tone is tinged with sorrow.

"And your people destroyed it?"

"So it seems."

"Why?"

"Because we were stupid."

"What do you mean?" Lipton asks.

"The world was ruled by those with money," Scott says. **"And those who had it, cared little for the rest who didn't."**

"That's bad."

"With money came power."

"Power?" Lipton repeats.

"Power created greed," Scott says. **"And, greed made people do unthinkable things."**

"Like what?" Lipton asks.

"Wars."

248

"Did you see the War?" Lipton asks.

"No. Yet, somehow I ended up here."

"How?"

Crumbling up the empty bag of chips, and tossing it to the floor, Scott replies, "I don't know. But, it appears I am going to find out why. Lipton, did you see the war?"

"No," Lipton answers. "I was born after it ended."

The dwarfish youth recounts his time growing up in the aftermath---how he was abandoned following the death of his parents---those he never knew. He tells Scott about the woman who had found him when he was an infant. How she cared for him for eight years, or 'Black Moons' as he calls them. Scott feels Lipton's pain when he explains how the woman was slaughtered by the elder males, just before they all vanished...never to be seen again. Hiding in the ruins with other children. Feeding on whatever they could find, catch or kill. Lipton describes the horrors he had witnessed, the many deaths he has seen.

"Where did the elders go?" Scott asks.

"They just died," Lipton replies, coldly. "All of them!"

"I'm sorry to hear about the woman who took care of you," Scott utters, his hands cuddling the can of peaches.

"It's been such a long time. I still remember her."

"I'm sure you do," Scott says, picking up on the sorrow in the males tone.

"It was awful what they did to her," Lipton adds.

"What did they do?" Scott solicits, not even sure he wants to hear the answer.

"They ate her."

"WHAT!" Scott gasps.

Without responding, Lipton stands and returns to the shelves behind the counter. Following a brief absence, he returns to the table with two unopen bottles of apple juice. "I watched them eat her," the dwarfish youth says, handing one of the plastic bottles to Scott—laying eyes on the bat next to his foot.

"Why would they eat her? Scott asks. "There appears to be plenty of food left."

Seated in his chair, Lipton twists the cap off his bottle of apple juice, and consumes half of its content. Seconds later, he responds. "It seemed the elder males developed a taste for human flesh. After the women were gone, they ate each other."

"My God, he predicted this would happen!"

"Who are you talking about?"

"An extremely wise man." Scott recalls the classroom discussion. "His name is...or rather, was Mr. Canton."

"Mr. Canton?" Lipton repeats.

"My history teacher. He said, the world would become savage and hostile where only the strong will survive.

"Does he have magic?"

"Magic?" Scott implores, "why do you ask that?"

"Because, he saw the future."

"No magic. He was just a smart man who somehow knew this was going to happen," Scott retorts.

Thunder erupts outside the supermarket!

"We need to go," Lipton declares, standing up.

"Is that thunder I hear?"

"Yes," Lipton responds. "The rain will soon follow, so we should get going."

"Where?"

"Come," Lipton says, as he heads for the entrance.

 *The Rain...*

Before departing the supermarket, Scott loaded up a backpack he found lying on the floor with an assortment of can goods; the backpacks colors are a little more girly than he would have wanted. With Lipton sitting on the Racers handlebars, they traveled east.

"We need to ride faster," Lipton says, looking upward.

"Why?" Scott asks.

"We need to escape the rain."

"Why do we need to escape the rain?" Scott glances at the crimson sky, noting the darkening of the already grim clouds, while the blood-red moon glows more eerier.

"Over there!" Lipton exclaims, extending his right index finger toward a standalone structure that almost causes Scott to mess his pants.

"That's a church!" Scott gasps, as the haunting image of those blood-red, vampiric eyes he saw in the confessional at the Basilica appear in his head; moreover, that menacing laughter once again echoes in his ears. Bringing the racer to a stop by the curb in front of the spooky cathedral, Scott stares uneasily at it, noting the minimal damage it suffered. Springing off the handlebars, Lipton proceeds toward the large steps that lead directly to the church's medieval-style, wooden entrance doors. Still sitting on the Racer, Scott suddenly spins around on his bike after believing he heard a sound behind him. Yet, all he finds is the spectral winds sweeping through the handful of scorched houses that are still standing in the area, like tormented wraiths in search of fresh souls to incarcerate in some unholy penitentiary.

After he finally dismounts the Racer, Scott's troubled mind begins to betray him by conjuring terrifying scenarios that simply aren't real. Those recurring images of vampires, ghouls, and other blood-sucking creatures stream into his mind——deceiving him into believing they are waiting for him inside. Making the situation even more unsettling is the red moon bathing the entire church in an eerie, unsettling glow.

Smashed windows...
Cracked red bricks...
Scorched wooden doors...
Dark and brooding landscape...
Squawking sounds emerge from the rooftop!

Startled by that ungodly screeching, Scott pivots his head and eyes toward the roof. There, he observes over a dozen carrion birds perched next to a large, inverted iron cross near the pinnacle of the roof; those black fowls stare at him as if he is their evening meal!

"**We need to get inside!**" Lipton voices firmly.

"**Where did they come from?**" Scott gulps.

With his left hand clasping the dull brass handle on the door, Lipton reaffirms, "**We don't have much time!**"

"**Is that door even open?**"

Raising his right index finger, Lipton triggers the doors inner mechanism, causing the right half of the door to swing inwardly. "**Yes,**" he responds. Moving up those steps with a sense of urgency, Scott stops abruptly at the door upon hearing additional squawking from above; he spots several birds *hopping* down the rooftop toward him. Witnessing a faint reddish glow in their tiny black eyes, Scott promptly enters the church, shuts the door, and engages the deadbolt with a decisive, "**Click.**" Examining the anteroom, the area where the pastor typically welcomes parishioners, Scott notes the dark discoloration in both the walls and ceiling, indicating significant fire damage; furthermore, the stained glass windows of Jesus, Mary, and a Saint he has never heard of are dull and dreary; the one of the unknown Saint is cracked. It appears the scorched wooden floor has also endured the Devil's wrath.

As Lipton's feet fetch him to a pair of oversize doors that lead directly into the main assembly, Scott gambles a peek inside the compartment of the bell tower. Its burned and blackened door almost comes apart as he slowly eases it open; a piece from the upper panel snaps off, dropping to the floor and disintegrating into black dust on impact.

The sound of flapping wings echoes above!

Narrowing his eyes, Scott squints into the blackness that occupies the upper portion of the tower. In addition to the absence of the massive bronze bell, there is a sizable hole in the roof. Through this opening, one of those dark plumed birds has extended its head, and is staring at him, its glowing red eyes visible amidst the gloom. Carefully, and swiftly, Scott closes what is left of the tower door.

Avoiding a corroded nail that is sticking out of the floor, Scott moves expeditiously toward those doors Lipton had already gone through. Examining the tiny shards of glass embedded in the door's shattered windowpanes, he notes the presence of old blood. Following a swift looksee at the entrance, Scott proceeds into the assembly via the doors, where his attention is instantly drawn to the stained-glass windows along both sides of the room; several of the panes are cracked. Looking up at the vaulted ceiling that towers nearly eighty feet, Scott notices three of the ten massive support beams are splintered, while the center main beam is completely broken in half with each end hanging mere feet from the floor. Upon spotting Lipton standing by the main altar located in the front of the great hall, Scott makes his way down the center aisle, his eyes swiftly locking onto the timbered cross featuring a fully intact---full-sized ceramic statue of Jesus suspended above it. Glancing at the wall to his right, he notices bricks missing near the top, and on the wall to his left, he spots a wooden door with a distinct crack running its length. *Without warning, heavy rain begins pounding the roof of the church!*

"I sometimes sleep there," Lipton declares, pointing to the pews in the front row that are facing the altar.

"You must be kidding?" Scott gasps, eyeballing the disquieting ruby-red sheen that streaks across patches of marble floor near the pews—serving as a stark reminder that evil is ever-present; the source of the hellish glow comes from the blood-red moon, its unnerving light slithering through the gaps in the wall, as well as beaming through the stained glass windows. **"This is just great!"** he grumbles.

Since neither desires unexpected visitors during their stay here at this holiest of holies, the two begin searching the rooms---securing all access into the church.

"Let's start there," Lipton says, heading for the door with the large crack in it.

"Um, okay," Scott gulps, gripping his bat tightly in his trembling hands. **"I'm...right behind you!"** While fictitious forecasts of vampires and ghouls radio into his brain, the wide-eyed lad watches Lipton twist the knob on the door and enter the room----half expecting him to run back out, pursued by prowlers of the damned. When this doesn't happen, Scott walks into the room, where the first object visible is the priest's armoire----the cabinet for storing robes and street attire. The room also contains a vintage roll-top desk, a small bed by the wall, and two additional doors aside from the one they just entered. Taking one of the service candles from the desk, and kindling it with matches found in its drawer, Scott follows Lipton to the door bearing the image of the Nazarene on it.

The cellar: dark, moldy, and spooky would describe the crumbling basement, those decayed steps nearly collapses under their weight. The stone walls look as if they will turn to powder if touched, and the support beams look so brittle that Scott is terrified to go near them, believing the entire structure will crash down on them. Additional exploration doesn't unearth any coffins, and for this, Scott is thankful. Humoring himself, he educates Lipton on the subject of vampires who in return tells him he never seen one, making Scott feel a little better; nonetheless, he will keep a cross, and a bottle of holy water on hand when, and if, he sleeps.

The outside: the other door opens to a small foyer that leads to another door that opens to a narrow flight of stairs; four of the ten steps are fractured. The stairs fetch the two to the backside of the church. Observing no danger, they return to the foyer and engage the eroding deadbolt on the door that will hopefully secure the entry. Leaving the room, as well as the great hall altogether, they return to the front entrance door and bind the door handles with rope found inside a cardboard box in the cellar, preventing those doors from being opened from the outside.

Since the gaps in the main assembly walls are too high for anyone to reach, they pay them no mind. Revisiting the priest's chambers they look for blankets to make those hard wooden pews more comfortable. Happenstance it may be, rummaging through the armoire they stumble across a dusty, unopened bottle of sacramental wine to which both of them consume a divine religious gulp of. Okay, maybe a tad more than a gulp.

TIME PASSES...

Having settled down on their pews of choice, which are next to the others, Scott and Lipton restart their earlier conversation from the supermarket. Scott reiterates how the world once was, talking about his childhood, his school, and the ladies of his time. His words echo deep into the night until sleep overtakes them both.

As if the Devil himself had reached out from Hell to stir his body, Scott jerks violently from his dreamless slumber, and off the pew altogether. Despite his legs feeling sluggish, he manages to summon the energy to get up from the floor and stand. Retrieving his bat from the bench, he raises it to an attacking position!

But who does he swing at?
There's nobody here!!!

Following several agonizing beats of his terrified heart, Scott starts to consider that maybe...just maybe, it was the whistling winds that had awakened him, slinking through the multiple gaps in the wall. Boy, would he like to believe that falsehood, but his internal senses are sounding off, telling him he is in danger! With his heart still beating frantically, he glances over at Lipton and finds the dwarfish youth asleep on his pew, beneath his blankets with his head uncovered. As his weapon falls limp to his side, an unpromising breeze brushes his face. Shifting his gaze toward the door with the crack in it, which is now open, Scott moves slowly toward it, his feet staggering across the cracked marble flooring. Frightened, he remembers closing the door after he and Lipton left the room; moreover, that blood-red light from the outside is shining the way to the door.

"SCOTT... MILLER"

Hearing that disturbing voice again, Scott changes direction...for the voice seems to have come from the altar. With his bat poised to strike anything that moves, and his non-blinking eyes glued to the shadows veiling much of the holy platform, he inches toward it. Seven candles sit atop that gloomy altar, and all of them are ignited; strange, prior to him going to sleep, they were not!

"I SEE YOU"

This time the voice startles the bat right out of Scott's hand: the sound of the bat slapping the floor over and over again echoes throughout the church, until it ultimately fades out. Retrieving his bat, he searches for the owner of the voice, squinting hard at those darkest of places. From the corner of his eye, Scott notices that door to the priest's chambers is now closed! Absorbed in fear, he slowly walks back toward the door. Halfway to it he feels an urge...more like a compulsion to look back at the altar.

"AHHH!" Scott screams.

White ceramic eyes are replaced by illuminating yellows, and a thorny crown now rests upon the ceramic head of the statue of Jesus, whose head is now facing Scott. Adding to this nightmarish image, the statue's black lips are not only parted, but are revealing ghastly fangs dripping with human blood; the head moves as if it is—alive!

The statue speaks:

In the evilest of tenors, in a manner instilling terror into the nub of Scott's soul, the statue laughs. Several terrifying seconds later, an ungodly, yellowish beam shoots out of the figurine's eyes to strike Scott's chest, sending him to the cathedrals marble floor. Before darkness fully consumes him, he watches in a paralyzed state, the figurine of Jesus walking toward him, its ghastly white ceramic hands reaching out to take hold of his neck; an unnatural blackness begins to devour his entire being.

260

Upon a hill...

Lifting his head off the dirt, Scott spots a hill in yonder distance. Getting to his feet, his eyes lock onto the mass of individuals atop it, their backsides facing him. Just then, that enigmatic drumming he heard in the last church he was in echoes inside the blistering winds. Moving up the hill, he strains his eyes to see what they are doing. And, as his feet brings him closer to them, it becomes clear they are looking at something on the other side of that hill--something he cannot see. Charged from within to continue, Scott stops momentarily and turns around; observed so many miles away is the mammoth outline of what can only be New York City!

A monstrous roar echoes from beyond the hill, a sound Scott has never experienced before. On trembling legs, he continues up the hill—drawing nearer with each step—soon discovering the people standing there are young men armed with unsophisticated weapons of death. As if he was drawn there by some invisible force, his pale blue eyes almost lose all color once he reaches the crest---gazing out over the sweeping valley beyond the hill, where trains, railcars, and other severely corroded locomotives surround the gorge. Still, it's neither the valley, nor those trains that is making the lad's heart race, but rather the gigantic, seven-headed, red-scaled dragon at its center. Long scaly necks hold each one of the dragon's massive heads, and resting on each head is a gold crown studded with rubies the size of basketballs. Panting feverishly, Scott stares at the dragon's fourteen eyes---each one bearing the same similarity to the eyes of a demon he has often encountered throughout his life.

After the unholiest of names is whispered in the winds, Scott witnesses each one of the dragon's seven heads rise toward the crimson sky, unleashing a unified, thunderous roar that instantly turns those skies a darker red. Scott is nearly overcome with terror when he hears horrible, gurgling noises behind him; as he turns, he realizes the youths have vanished, replaced by sinister figures draped in black robes,

261

their menacing iridescent green eyes shining from beneath their hoods. Hearing another deafening roar, Scott turns to face the valley, discovering the dragon is no longer there. In its place appears what can be described as a miniaturized scaled model of the universe, with a massive black hole at its center. Unable to look away, he watches the galactic monster, this celestial terror devour entire planets and suns, ripping them apart to their core, drinking in their existence of space. Scott believes he sees the 'Eye of a God' in the center of the cosmic vacuum, an eye that is looking at him!

"The fate of this world, rests in your hands!"

The ethereal voice echoes with an uncanny familiarity, as though it belongs to the realm of dreams. Yet, rather than emerging from the black hole, it drifts in from beyond those vivid red skies. Before Scott has the chance to flee, green, slimy, scaly hands latch onto him from behind, ripping him asunder until his screams fade away inside the blackness!

"Scott...   Scott...   Scott..."

Deep within his consciousness, he hears his name called out for the third—and last time. Emerging from the dark, a white door appears, and slowly opens. Endless seconds later, a shimmering hand is leading him to, and through that door. Opening his eyelids, Scott sees the dwarfish youth kneeling beside him.

"What are you doing on the floor?" Lipton asks.

"Where is he?!" Scott shouts, terror flashing in his eyes.

"Where is who?" Lipton looks puzzled and confused.

Acting like a man who had just escaped Frankenstein's castle, Scott stands and promptly picks up his bat from the floor. Rotating his unblinking eyeballs toward the altar, he discovers those seven candles are now out, smoke wafting upward from their blackened wicks. Breathing heavily, he heads for it, slowly raising his eyes to the cross. "It's gone!" Scott cries out. "The statue is gone!"

With his own eyes locking onto the vacant timber, the dwarfish youth takes a few steps forward. "You're right."

"God, help me!" Visibly upset, Scott wanders over to his pew and sits down. Shortly thereafter, he begins telling Lipton about the terrible things that happened.

"He's looking for you!" the dwarfish youth proclaims, gazing once more at the cross.

"Who's looking for me?"

"We dare not say his name."

"Little Horn." Scott hears this name internally.

"I never heard that name," Lipton admits.

"I saw the name on a wall." Scott recounts the time when he, Dave and Mike broke into that derelict building.

"It was written on a wall?!" Lipton responds.

"Not only that, but there was a face underneath the name." Scott describes the portrait.

"I know that face!" Lipton declares. *"It's him!"*

"HIM?" Scott repeats, startled by Lipton's tone.

"We know him by another name!"

"What name?"

"To speak of it is death!"

"I need to know."

"He hears you when you say his name."

Hearing the name internally, Scott utters, **"Rapture."**

"How did you know?"

"That name was written on a different wall inside the building," Scott says. "Lipton, I don't know why I'm here, but I believe it has something to do with him."

"I will tell you one thing," Lipton says, grimly, "he is the law here, the unchallenged law, and none will defy him...not even, Alexander."

"Alexander?" Scott repeats the name.

"My chieftain."

"Your chieftain?"

"I am of the Seneca clan."

"Seneca clan?"

"Yes."

"The name of your clan is, Seneca?"

"Yes."

"Like the Seneca Indians?"

"My chieftain says it represents the inner spirit."

"Is your chieftain an Indian?"

"Keoni is the only Indian in our clan," Lipton retorts.

"Keoni?"

"A powerful warrior, born from two tribes."

"Two tribes? What do you mean?"

"He is a descendant of a great Indian war chief named, Red Jacket," Lipton proclaims. "His mother was from the Polynesian tribe of Molokai."

"Where is this Keoni and Alexander you speak of?"

"I will take you to them after the rain stops."

"Tell me more of Rapture," Scott pleads.

After walking away from the pews, Lipton comes to a complete stop a few steps later. **"The great battle, as we call it, ended twenty black moons ago,"** he says. As he turns toward Scott, the lad observes fear on his face, and terror in his eyes. **"That is when he came."**

"You're saying twenty years, right?" Scott asks.

"Yes."

"Got it."

"The battle lasted forty days," Lipton adds. "Sometime later, after the nations were gone, a plague came upon us."

"There was a plague?"

"Yes, and it killed nearly everyone who had survived the cannibalistic times that followed the battle. It came from the black waters to the east. From a city that was once called, the Jewel of the World."

"New York," Scott mutters.

"When the plague finally left us, only the children were left alive," Lipton says. "He whom you speak of walked out of those black waters."

"Antichrist!" The word escapes Scott's lips.

"I never heard that name," Lipton says.

"It refers to the Devil's son."

"Now, that's a name I have heard."

"The Devil's son?"

"No, Devil."

"Where did you hear it?" Scott asks.

After a brief pause. "Three nights ago, I had a dream," Lipton replies. "He said, the beast that rose from the black waters will soon slay us. And, that a boy with hair the color of sand will come to find an instrument for our salvation."

"What are you talking about?"

"I had a dream," Lipton says, looking at Scott.

"What's so strange about that?" Scott utters. "I dream all the time."

"We don't!" Lipton retorts, sharply. "He blocks them, and yet one came to me."

"I still don't understand what you're saying."

"My dream had something to do with you."

"Me?"

"Yes, you...Scott Miller!"

Gripping his bat tightly in his hands, Scott is quick to his feet. "How do you know my full name?!" he barks.

"He told me."

"Who told you?!" Scott barks again.

"The man with the white eyes."

"Who?"

"The man with the white eyes."

"Who is the man with the white eyes?"

"I don't know, but he was in my dream."

"And in your dream, this man told you my name."

"He told me that I need to help you."

"Help me with what, Lipton?"

"Finding what you seek."

"I don't know what you are talking about."

"In the city, there is a library," Lipton says. "I believe, I'm supposed to take you there."

"Why do you need to take me there?"

"I believe it has to do with a book I saw there."

"A book?"

"Yes."

"This is getting really weird."

"We need to find the book."

"WHAT BOOK?" Scott roars.

"The book about the Devil," Lipton says.

"You mean, about Rapture?"

"No," Lipton retorts. "About the Devil."

"The book about the Devil?"

"I don't know what a Devil is, do you?" Lipton asks.

Shaking his head over this bizarre conversation, Scott replies, **"Yes, I know what a Devil is."** At this moment, he is instructed to go to the priest's podium, which is twenty feet to the left of the altar——half hidden in shadow; his internal senses are telling him to locate something beneath the dirt. Following the internal command, Scott finds a dusty book with a golden cross engraved on its cover. Removing one of the candles from the altar, he lights it with matches lying next to it. With graceful fingers, Scott delicately flips through the fragile, yellowing pages until he reaches the latter part of the book, the section on the apocalypse: "Revelations."

{Scott reads from the Bible.}

"And I stood upon the sands of the sea, and saw a beast rise up from the dark waters, a great Dragon having seven heads and ten horns, and upon his heads were golden crowns, and upon his heads is the name of Blasphemy."

{Scott continues.}

"And the great Dragon was cast out, called the Devil, and Satan, which he deceived the whole world."

268

The moment Scott closes the holy book, heavy winds begin hammering away at the church's exterior. Touching the engraved cross on the bibles worn-out cover, he shoots another look at the naked cross, and confirms what must be done. Maddening to behold, he needs to learn more about this demon that stalks him.

 *But first, he will rest...*

After untangling those ropes on the door handles, the two open the door and proceed down the fractured steps that lead to the front of the church.

"**It's dangerous!**" Lipton declares.

"**I need to find out why I'm here,**" Scott says, glancing up at the rooftop, finding the black birds gone. "**The book you saw at the library may give me some answers.**"

"**It could be your death that you're riding too,**" Lipton says, stopping on the second to the last step. "**The inner city is controlled by a clan called, the Blackfists.**"

"**The Blackfists?!**" Scott recites the name.

"**Yes, and they kill on sight.**"

"**I'll avoid them.**"

"**You can't avoid them, they are everywhere!**"

"**Lipton, what choice do I have? You said it yourself, he is looking for me.**"

"**Yes, but —**"

"**I have to go.**"

"In this world, there is no such thing as parley!" Lipton utters, sternly. "The Blackfists will see you."

"I'll take that chance." Without hesitation, Scott climbs onto the Racer and secures his bat behind the handlebars; his backpack is fastened around his shoulders.

"Are you fast on this thing?" Lipton asks.

"I was able to outrun three hell hounds."

"I hope so." Lipton climbs up onto the handlebars.

"No!" Scott thunders. "I won't risk both our lives. I know where the library is."

"Were wasting time," Lipton refutes stubbornly.

 *Time passes...*

Less than an hour later, traveling north with Lipton on the handlebars, the ghostly contours of what remains of the downtown area creeps into view. South Park avenue loops into the very heart of the city, exposing them to open spaces where they lack shadows for concealment or refuge, robbing them of a sanctuary to pursue the "Abet of God."

Reaching the outer perimeter, Scott is again accosted by the lingering consequences of the War:

> *Streets are severely fractured!*
> *Multiple fires are burning, in and out of the city!*
> *Many structures are on the verge of collapse!*
> *Scorched vehicles clutter the streets!*
> *There are skeletons...everywhere!!!*

Mangled rebar juts the sides of the buildings, similar to swords impaling a body. Most of the structures have long since been destroyed, leaving mounds of granite as the only evidence of their existence.

"Look at that!" Scott gasps, applying the brakes.

A little more than a hundred yards away, the entire top floor of a ten-story building suddenly drops onto the one beneath it, starting a chain reaction of falling floors that doesn't stop until the entire building is gone. As the thick plume of concrete dust ascends from the ground, Lipton promptly instructs Scott to proceed without delay; it isn't long till the two are inside the business district of the city, a city truly under the control of a shadow king.

Pedaling through the inner city, Scott observes twisted tracks of iron lying waste on the streets. Community parks once filled with energy and life have vanished, their concrete tables and benches reduced to ashes. Inside a demolished police station, Scott spots a rail car on its side, it's skeletal passengers still seated in their blackened seats. Moments later, the spooky outline of the library comes into view.

"Do you see anyone?" Scott asks, bringing the Racer to a full stop in front of the structure.

Staring intensely at a building on the other side of this broad six-lane street, Lipton regrettably affirms, **"Yes."**

"Hell, I can't see anything beyond the darkness," Scott pants, staring at the same building Lipton is; the five-story structure is swathed in gloom.

"I do." Lipton touches the sheath strapped to his back.

"Shit!" Scott curses. "Can we outrun them?"

With the agility of a trained acrobatic, Lipton leaps off the bike to land firmly on his feet. "No," he firmly responds. After removing his bat from behind the handlebars, Scott disembarks the Racer——allowing it to fall to the sidewalk. Running alongside Lipton up the library's giant concrete steps, his gaze settles on a looming silhouette of what must be city hall, a massive, thirty-two story building visible three blocks ahead; a colossal chunk of its peak is missing, plus the whole edifice leans slightly to the right. Illuminating the building with a devilish red glow is the crimson moon, drawing a disturbing pictorial in Scott's mind of a burial chamber for titans, and behemoths. Without pause, the two hurry into the library through its unlocked, double steel doors.

Finding the place a little too dark for his liking, Scott unintentionally runs into a reading chair, tumbling belly first over it. Muttering under his breath, he stands up. Peering through the dim light, he notices the librarian's counter and promptly heads over to it. Rifling through the drawers, he discovers a handful of candles along with a box of matches. Kindling one of the candles, he is given a slightly better view of the sprawling interior of the library.

After setting the waxy stick into a brass candleholder, Scott ignites a second one, but rather than handing it to Lipton, who has already demonstrated his ability to see well in the dark, Scott puts it into another holder. And, with an outstretched hand holding that candleholder, he makes his way back to the doors he and Lipton went through. **"Click."** After pushing the sliding bolt that secures both doors, he turns in the direction of his traveling companion and asks, **"Lipton, where is the book?"**

"I saw it on the third floor," the dwarfish youth answers, **"lying on a small, round table."** Spotting the dark silhouette of the grand staircase to the right of the librarian's counter, Lipton moves up the stairs with speed.

In quick time, Scott makes his way to the staircase, and as his foot hits the fifth step, he stops upon hearing an odd sound coming from somewhere on the main floor. From his spot on the stairs, he scans the floor, paying close attention to the shadows encasing the bookshelves. Glancing over at the oversize windows, he is startled by the many, animal-like reflective eyeballs that are looking straight at him from the outside. **"Lipton—"** he whispers, the hairs on the back of his neck rising fast. Receiving no response, he redraws his eyes from the windows to place them on the next floor up, cursing when emptiness is the only thing looking back at him. Returning his attention to the windows, he discovers those bestial eyes have vanished.

273

Muttering further profanities under his breath, Scott hurries up the stairs, skips past the second floor, and heads straight for the third, stopping on a dime when he reaches the landing. As he leans against the dull brass railing of the staircase, his right hand trembling as it clutches his bat and his even more unsteady left hand holding the candleholder outward, its flickering light proving inadequate against the prevailing darkness, Scott again whispers Lipton's name. Noticing a shifting shadow near a window on the back wall roughly sixty feet away, Scott approaches cautiously, his eyes attentive to any movement. When he is within twenty feet of the window, he whispers, **"Lipton, is that you?"**

Following several tense moments, the dwarfish youth emerges from the darkness and immediately points to the window. **"Take a look!"**

Startled by Lipton's abrupt arrival, Scott regains his composure and approaches the window. Looking through it, **"Christ, I see them!"** he gasps. Those reflective eyes he had observed earlier in the main floor windows, now appear within the shadows consuming a building, some forty yards away; the fifteen story structure was once a landmark hotel, the large, bold letters on the side of the building affirming Scott's recognition of the site.

"I don't understand why they haven't attacked," Lipton says, anxiously. **"It's death to be here."**

"Screw the book!" Scott wheezes.

Rushing back to the staircase, they pass a small, circular reading table. Resting atop the table lies an odd looking, brown, hardcover book-box. **"Scott, that's it!"** Lipton barks, pointing to the table.

"I have seen this symbol before," Scott says, stepping closer to the table. **"It was on the wall inside that building I told you about, the place where I saw that face."**

"What does it mean?" Lipton asks, glancing from the book toward the staircase as his right hand moves to grasp the sword sheathed on his back.

"It called a pentagram, and it rarely leads to anything good," Scott replies, feeling a surge of anxiety, his internal tingling bursting from within.

"SCROLLS OF LUCIFER"

Even by merely observing the runes imbedded into the cover, Scott can sense the enigmatic importance of the book. As his fingers caress the engraved symbol, a most troubling sensation takes hold, the awareness of an unholy presence... somewhere inside the library!

Stepping away from the table, Scott stares hard at the shadows covering the walls, as well as the bookshelves.

"What is it?" Lipton asks.

Scott returns his attention to the book. **"I'm, not sure."**

"We don't have much time."

"I know Lipton, but I need to look in this book."

"Alright then, make it quick." Lipton pulls out his sword from within the leather sheath and begins shifting his eyes from the windows, over to the staircase.

Unclasping the locking mechanism on the left side of the book-box, Scott opens it and finds an aged, leatherbound journal within. Carefully retrieving the journal from the box, and setting it on the table, the wide-eyed lad turns to the first page and begins reading it. **"Lipton, this isn't a book, it's a journal,"** Scott says, flipping another page. **"It was written by a Professor Robin in 1943. He writes that it is based on what he believes to be his greatest discovery: "The Scrolls of Lucifer"**

276

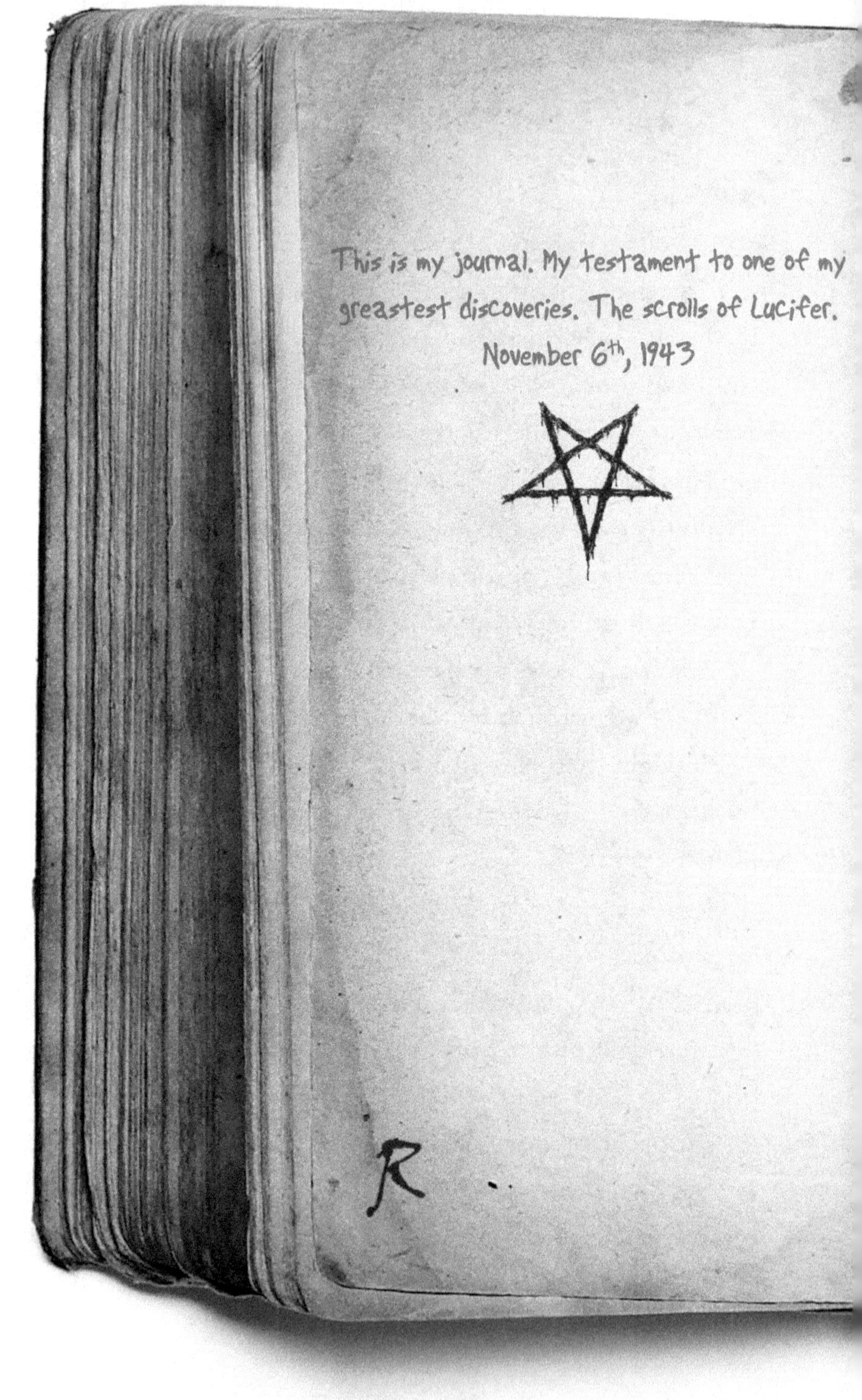
This is my journal. My testament to one of my greastest discoveries. The scrolls of Lucifer.
November 6th, 1943

Jan 2nd, 1943

I, Professor Robin, have been asked by the Vatican
to investigate the recently discovered ruins beneath
the Saint Georgeous Cathedral in Rihab. This unusual
request comes from the Pontiff of Rome himself.

Jan 8th, 1943

At midday, my team of archaeologists and I, along
with a young priest named Father McDaniel, entered
northern Jordan near the Syrian border.
We entered the city of Rihab shortly after sunset.

Jan 9th, 1943

Previous radiocarbon dating confirmed the church
was built between the years 33 and 70 AD.

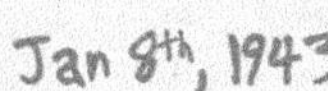

There are stone seats inside, believed
to have been for the clergy, and an
ornate circular ceiling believed to
have been the apse. On the back wall was a
collapsed tunnel, which we think was once linked
to a water source. We found pottery fragments
on the floor, and inside the walls.

It was Johnathan who discovered the hidden cache in the base of one of the seats.
The iron canister found inside contained scrolls dating back to the origin of the church.
It took a few days to decipher the scrolls, and what they revealed wasn't accepted at first by the archeologists, and certainly not by Father McDaniel.

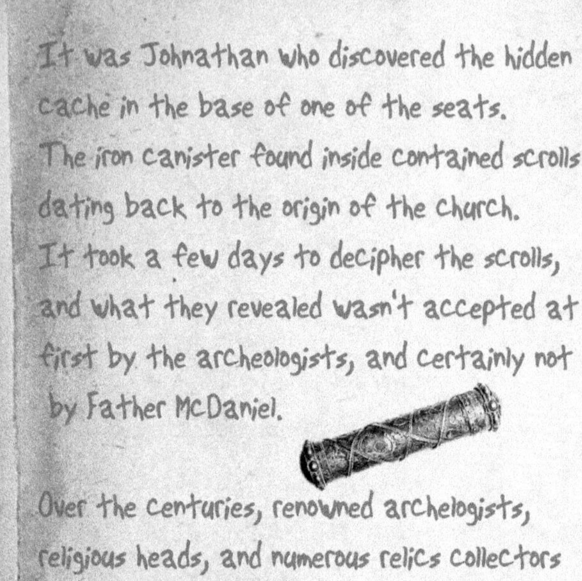

Over the centuries, renowned archelogists, religious heads, and numerous relics collectors searched the world over to find what many have called, "The tomb of Baal."
It is a place of Evil, a place mentioned only in the halls of whispers. My predecessor was among those who attempted to locate the ancient crypt, believed to be the burial site of the first Antichrist.
The scrolls gave irrefutable details about the crypt, compelling my fellow archeologist, and Father McDaniel to accept its authenticity.
According to the scrolls, the tomb is somewhere inside the territories of Ethiopia, Africa.

Two Illustrations were found on the scrolls:

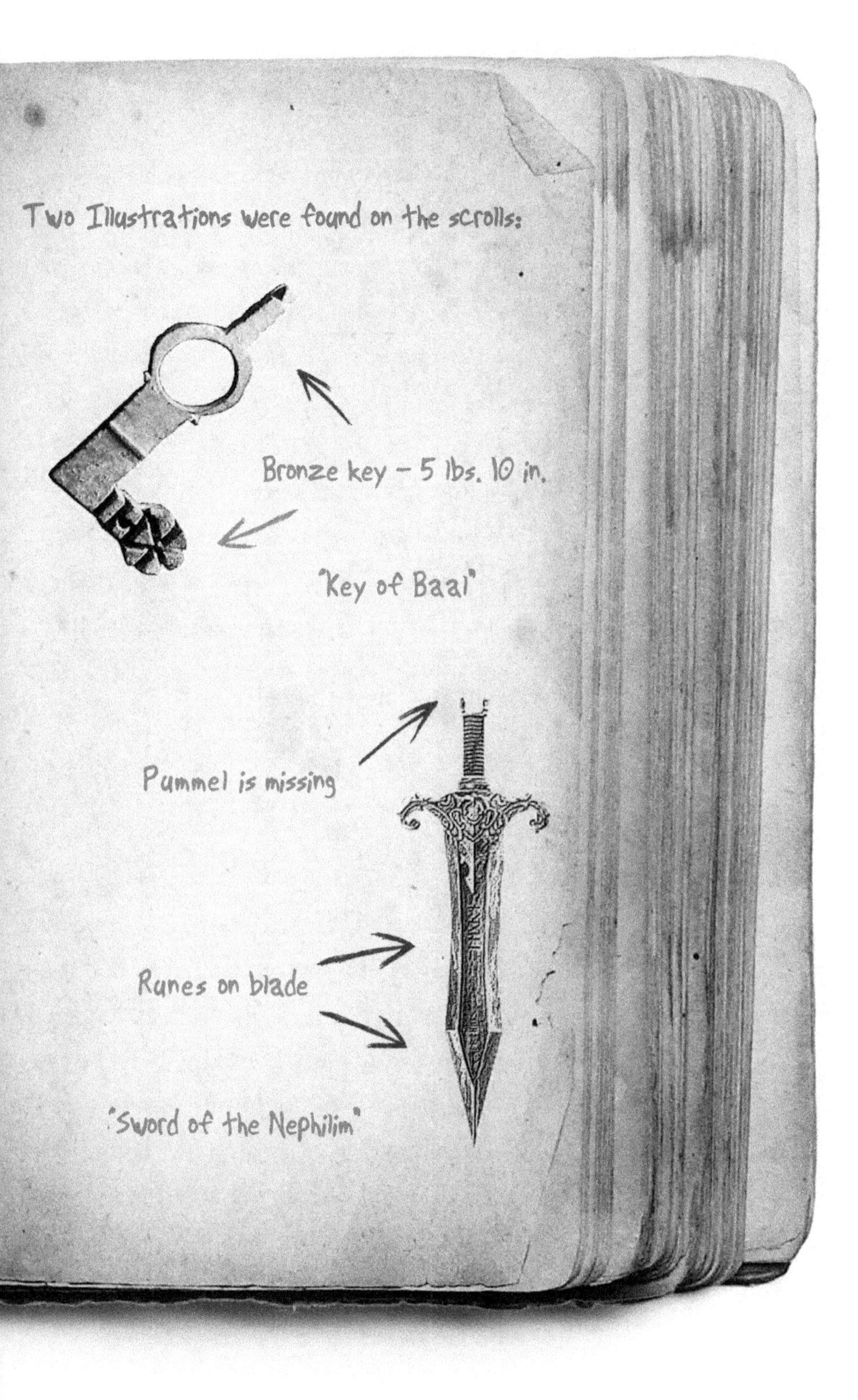

The first illustration shows a Roman key from
the first century, early in the empire.
Made of Bronze, it's said to weight nearly five
pounds, with no distinctive markings on it.
My strong suspicions to what this key unlocks
would have brought unnecessary anxiety to my
colleagues, so I didn't tell them, nor did I tell
them about a second key.
The second illustration shows the fabled sword
of the Nephilim, which is depicted without its
pommel. There were no clues explaining why the
sword was referenced in the scrolls, and there
was also no information about where the pummel
could be found. I have long since believed the
sword was inside the crypt.

Jan 10th, 1943
After much reluctance, my colleagues consented
to undertake the journey, and Father McDaniel
was instructed by the Vatican to accompany us.
Since the Germans were patrolling the skies over
Africa, we decided it would be safer to travel to
Ethiopia by land. In the morning, we headed for the
city of Jeddah on horseback across the mountains.

Jan 13th, 1943

After traveling two and a half days through some
of the roughest terrain I have ever encountered,
we arrived at the outlying town of Jeddah.
Before leaving Israel, I arranged passage aboard
a ship that would take us across the Red Sea to
the port of Sudan. The captain of the merchant
ship 'Lady Blue,' will meet us at the docks.

Jan 15th, 1943

The port was in turmoil.
News of the Germans advancing north spread fear
among the people, prompting many to flee into Egypt.
For this reason, we were unable to find any suitable
means of transportation into Ethiopia.

Jan 16th, 1943

The Germans attacked the occupied
territories of the British Empire inside
Africa. I had received word that dark agents
were inside Sudan as Hitler had learned of this
expedition. English soldiers searched the city for
the agents, but never found them. We continued
looking for safe transport to the south, again
being unsuccessful.

Jan 17th, 1943

The Germans had bombed several nearby villages,
forcing us to remain in Sudan.
We heard our first air raid alert at dinner, and
later that night, I noticed someone in the shadows
across from my hotel window.

Jan 20th, 1943

A package came from the Vatican today, hand
delivered by three royal guards. The Holy One had
provided us a major piece of the puzzle; the key.
I have known for some time the Vatican possessed
one of the two roman keys inside its scared vault.
This one was found by a Knight Templar during one
of the earlier crusades. A month later, that same
knight was found murdered.

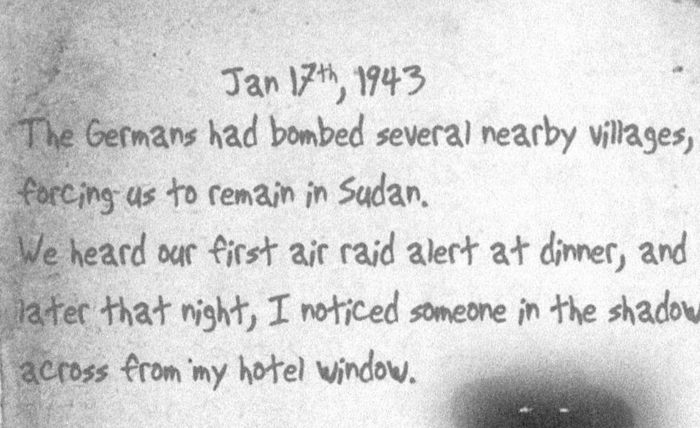

Jan 22nd, 1943

The British pushed the Germans back into Kenya,
which allowed us to continue our journey into Africa.
We boarded a passenger train headed south, and
by late evening we arrived at the ancient city of
Kassala, located in northern Ethiopia.

We were greeted at the station by the commanding
officer of the British garrison. The colonel told us a
rather strange fellow arrived a week earlier, asking
questions about us. The man has since vanished.
The garrison was assigned to Kassala ever since the
unexplained retreat of the Italian army.
Given quarter at the colonel's residence,
we were treated to a splendid dinner,
prepared by his personal chef.
Over brandy, we talked about Baal
and his legacy of terror. I could tell
by the whites of the colonel's eyes that
he was glad he wasn't being ordered to take us to
Ethiopia. We would have to get there without escort
or protection.

Jan 23rd, 1943

In the morning, we learned that an archaeologist
who recently joined us after we left Rihab had
been seen heading for the German lines during the
night. We also learned that German authorities
were inspecting all trains entering Ethiopia, and
that the directive to locate us at any cost had
been issued personally by the Führer.

Jan 24th, 1943

We were told the Germans were destroying all
tracks going into Ethiopia, ours being one of them.
Father McDaniel had sent a cable to the Vatican,
updating the pontiff on our situation.
Realizing time was against us, the colonel provided
other means of travel.

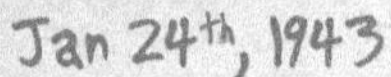

Jan 26th, 1943

On horseback, we crossed the northern border of
Ethiopia a few days later. With our water bags
nearly depleted, we stopped at the settlement of
Bahir Dar. The locals gave us quarter in a church
by Lake Tana. Weary of travel we bathed and
relished our first good night of sleep in days.

Jan 27th, 1943

Another archeologist went missing!
Assisted by the local residents, we had conducted
searches in the eastern mountain region as well as
along the southern stretch of the Blue Nile River.
His name is Edward, and he is a trusted friend.
During the night, we heard strange howling coming
from the mountains.

Jan 29th, 1943

Edward has been missing for two days.
Several of the locals had also gone missing, and blood
drippings were found in and outside the settlement.
That night, we were awakened by the disturbing
sounds of screaming and persistent howling, both
originating from the mountains to the east.

Jan 30th, 1943

That morning, we awoke to a scene of shock and
terror. Edward, and the missing locals had been
crucified, nailed to wooden crosses down by the
lake. Their bodies were ripped apart by an animal,
the claw marks monstrous in nature.
Due to the absence of Edward's head, we were
forced to identify him by his bloodied clothing.

Jan 31st, 1943

We have been ordered to leave the village.
More of the locals had disappeared with more blood
drippings found inside the settlement.
I sent word to my friend in Israel, telling him to
meet us at our destination. God speed!

Feb 1st, 1943

After departing from Bahir Dar, we proceeded southward toward the Basalt Mountains near Lalibela, which are more widely referred to as the Ethiopian Highlands. Resting on a mountaintop is a tribal village called, Mequat Mariam. The scrolls state that Baal's tomb is there.

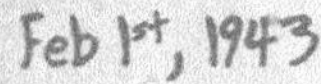

Feb 4th, 1943

Following three days of travel, we arrived at the remote village only to find it deserted. No villager or livestock, only the presence of evil inside the hot winds. My colleagues, along with Father McDaniel were ready to call it quits. We took shelter in the villagers' huts, which were built from brick, mud, and straw, hoping they would protect us from the elements. The largest hut, centrally located within the village served as our base. While we had brought enough food to last a month, it was imperative to find an adequate water source.

Feb 5th, 1943

We began our search for the tomb before the sun
had time to fully rise, especially since my colleagues
and Father McDaniel were so anxious to leave.
A mutated calf, which wasn't there the day before
was found outside the village. Later that night, we
heard howling similar to what we heard at Bahir Dar.
This place wasn't known to have wolves.

Feb 7th, 1943

We couldn't find the tomb.
The scrolls offered no clues to its exact location,
and given there are countless gorges and caverns,
locating the crypt seemed more impractical with
each passing day.

Feb 8th, 1943

Father McDaniel is missing!
Human footprints were spotted in the dirt leading
to the priest's hut. The footprints came from
outside the village. My friend is a week away.
Saying I am anxious for his arrival would be an
understatement.

Feb 9th, 1943

We still couldn't locate Father McDaniel.
A dry, merciless heat was present all day, and
those winds carried the foul stench of that
decaying calf. We had dinner inside the main hut,
while haunting gales swept over the mountaintop.

Feb 10th, 1943
WE FOUND THE TOMB!

By chance, we stumbled upon a primeval
ladder carved directly into the side of
the mountain, its tribal design keeping
it hidden for centuries. We used a rope
from the main hut to reach the ladder,
which is located twenty yards below on
the southern cliff.

The ladder drops down about fifteen to
twenty yards and ends just above an
overhanging ledge, which then leads to a
large cave. If not for the torches we
brought, we would be without light for
there was nothing but unholy blackness
inside the cave.

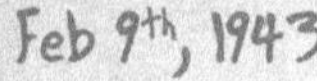

A short, downward staircase carved from the earth begins thirty feet from the cave's entrance, leading to a dark alcove. Within the alcove, an iron door has been embedded into the mountain's rock.

Looking at the keyhole, we knew what our key was for. Still, I believed the key served another purpose besides the door. Opening the door, we were greeted by a blackness no man has ever seen, and with torch in hand, we broke the threshold and kindled another torch that was attached to the wall on the other side of the door. After kindling three more, we were granted an unrestricted viewing of the mountainous tomb...the final burial place of Baal.

The ceiling is over fifty feet up, and the room is big enough to hold a few hundred people. The flooring was made from polished black marble. From within those shadows to our right came a brilliant red flash, resembling that of a beacon.

With torch in hand, I approached the shadows and found hidden within a large statue of a beastly, seven headed dragon with ruby eyes and six arms.

As I suspected, the sword was held in the third hand on the third arm of the statue, and the pommel was indeed missing as in the illustration. Most of what I know about this sword comes from stories passed down by my predecessor.

In the center of the enormous cavern rests a stone casket holding Baal's mortal remains, its imposing size is simply unsettling. Measuring more than ten feet long and six feet wide, it rests on a striking blood-red platform crafted from a rare limestone; this base is actually larger than the casket above it.

There was nothing inside the cavern besides the casket, and the dragon statue. There were no doors besides the one we entered. Runes and mystic symbols were sketched into the sides of the stone casket. Some I have seen before, some I have not. A closer examination revealed another keyhole on the side, near the top where the head would be.

After inserting the key that had unlocked the iron door, we heard a distinct click, and the casket slowly opened before us. Upon the breach of the seal, an intense gust of wind emerged from within, puffing out the torch by the statue. At that moment, from inside the dark came a whisper——a name I dare not repeat. I firmly believed my colleagues were going to flee the cavern, but they didn't. Once we relit the torch that had gone out, we peered into the massive stone cist. The bodiless casket held a pair of rare finds, extraordinary to say the least.

First

There was a large ruby fastened to a casting made of solid gold. We immediately knew it was the missing pummel that screws into the hilt of the sword.

Second

An exceptional prize, something I never expected to find in this world, something my predecessor often talked about. Inside ten ivory black canisters were the ancient parchments few even know exist. "The Scrolls of Lucifer"

According to legend, the scrolls were written with the blood of newborn children, while their skins were used for the parchments. I attest this horror to be true. Upon our return to the village, Jonathan informed me he would be departing for New York in the morning. I understood his reasons for leaving, and wished him a safe and speedy trip home.

Feb 11th, 1943

Father McDaniel was still missing.

I spent the entire day with the three remaining archeologists deciphering the scrolls. We found it quite the challenge since they were never meant for human eyes. The ancient parchments were ripe with immorality.

Feb 12th, 1943

The hot air was becoming harder to breathe, and our water supply was running dreadfully low, not a drop to be used to cool the sweat from our faces. Fortunately, we no longer had to tolerate the foulness of that decaying calf, as the poor beast was dragged away by animals, most likely a pack of hyena's.

Feb 13th, 1943
My friend should be here soon.

Feb 14th, 1943
We are trapped inside the village!
Johnathan's head was discovered nailed to the side
of my hut by a large iron spike.
We saw dreadful looking footprints throughout the
village, and our horses have been slaughtered, a few
partially eaten.

Feb 15th, 1943
Not only was our food supply reduced to half rations,
but our water situation had become dire.

Feb 16th, 1943

THE SCROLLS ARE GONE!!!

Feb 17th, 1943
The morning greeted us with the unsettling
sound of feasting vultures. Johnathan's mutilated
body was found just outside the hut where we kept
the scrolls. Due to severe dehydration, my colleagues
were exhibiting malaria-like symptoms.

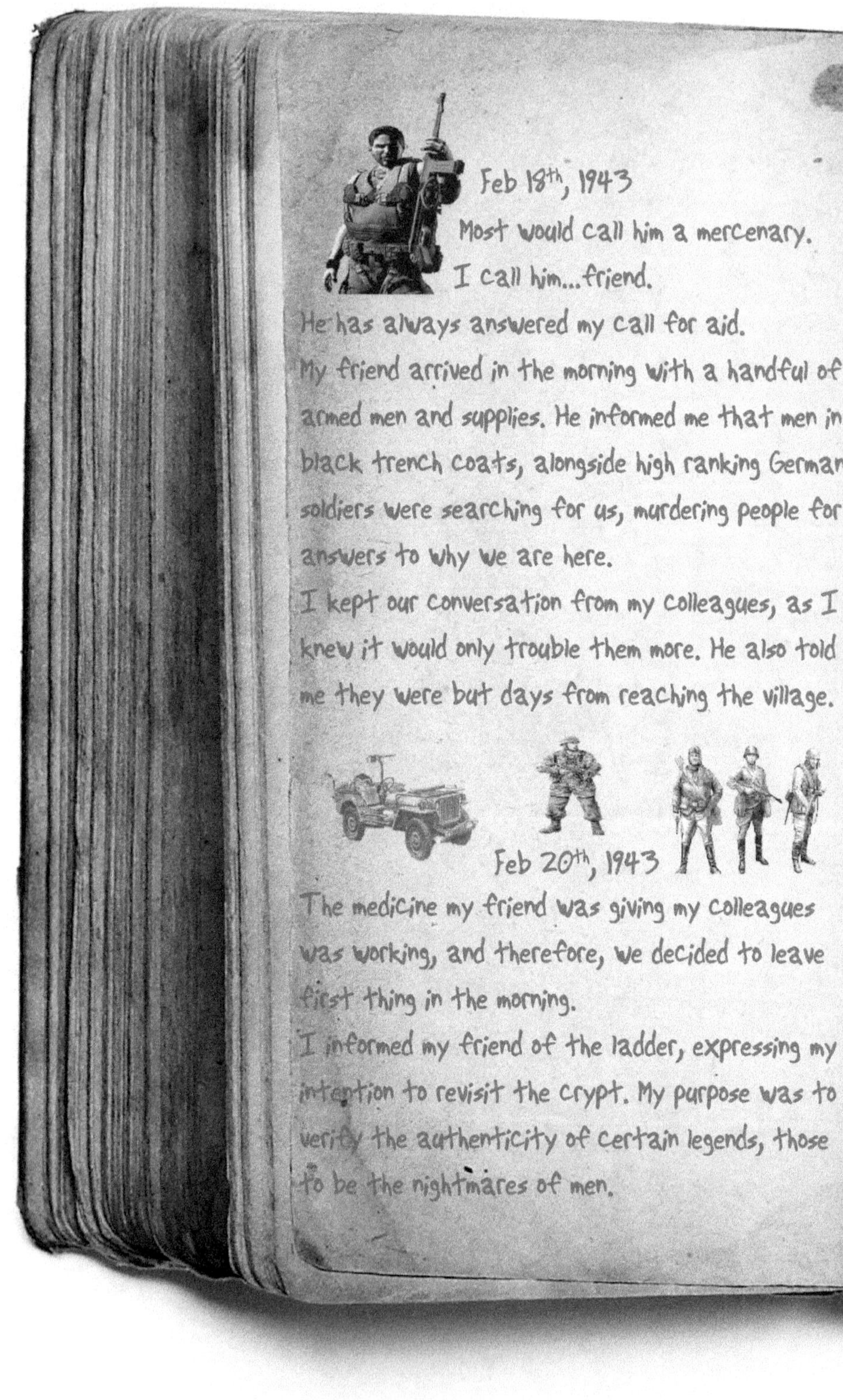

Feb 18th, 1943

Most would call him a mercenary.

I call him...friend.

He has always answered my call for aid.

My friend arrived in the morning with a handful of armed men and supplies. He informed me that men in black trench coats, alongside high ranking German soldiers were searching for us, murdering people for answers to why we are here.

I kept our conversation from my colleagues, as I knew it would only trouble them more. He also told me they were but days from reaching the village.

Feb 20th, 1943

The medicine my friend was giving my colleagues was working, and therefore, we decided to leave first thing in the morning.

I informed my friend of the ladder, expressing my intention to revisit the crypt. My purpose was to verify the authenticity of certain legends, those to be the nightmares of men.

With two of his men, my friend accompanied me back
down to the crypt, where we discovered that iron
door already opened. We had closed it when we left
the first time. Moreover, those strange footprints we
had seen inside the village were scattered about the
area, leading directly into the crypt.
After kindling the interior torches we
learned the fate of Father McDaniel.
He was nailed to an inverted cross just
above Baal's closed casket.
The iron chains supporting the cross were
spiked directly into the earthen ceiling.
Both of his ears, as well as his tongue, and all of his
fingers were severed. His legs were wrapped together
in a soiled cloth of some type, and his shoes were gone.
I wanted nothing more than to remove his body from
the cavern, and give him a proper burial, but the
cross was much too high for us to reach.
The thought of having to leave him there filled me
with sadness, knowing this unholy hollow was going to
be his final resting place.

As I expected, the scrolls were not inside the casket. Fortunately, we had taken the ruby in the gold casting with us when we left the first time. Returning to the dragon statue, I 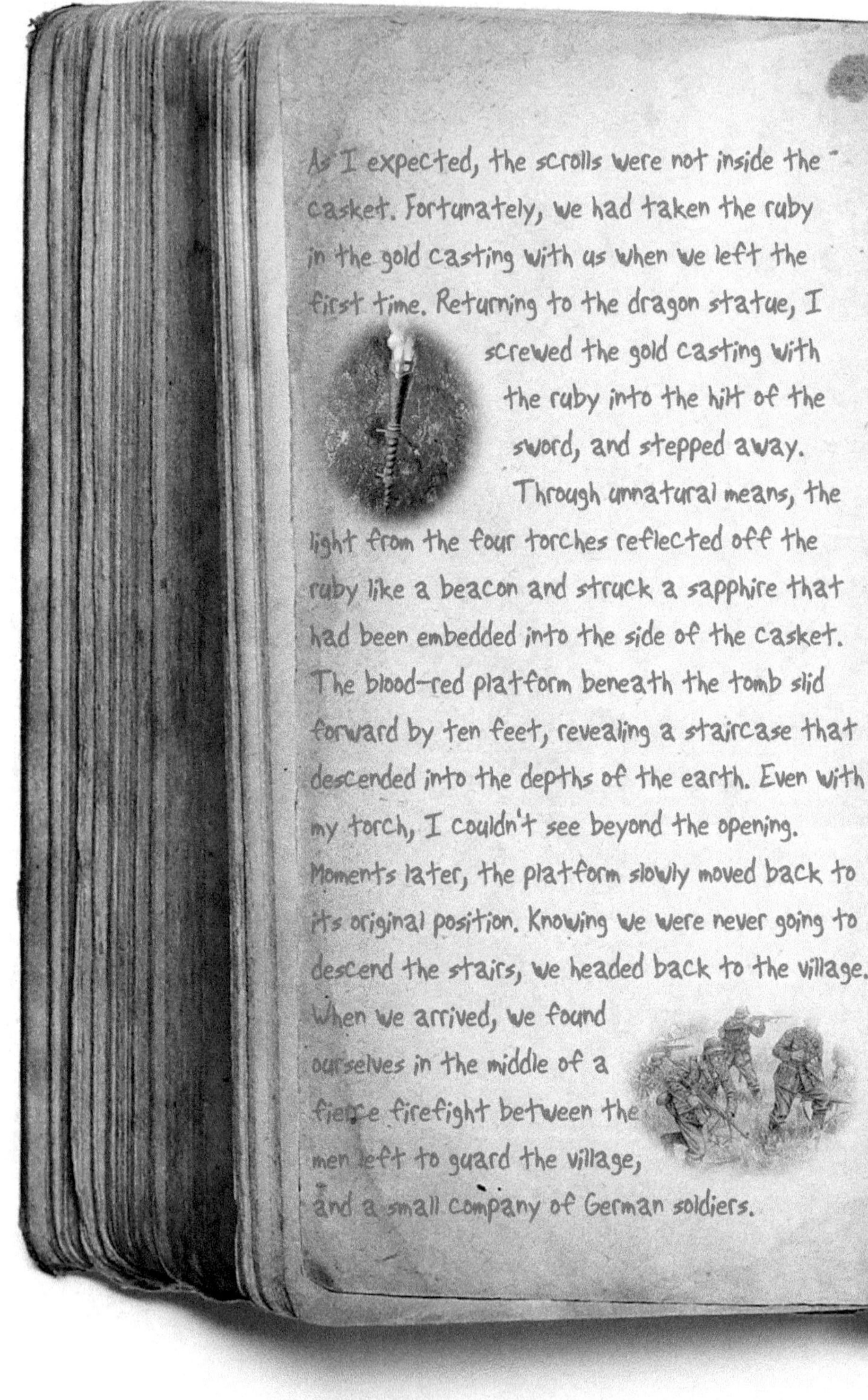 screwed the gold casting with the ruby into the hilt of the sword, and stepped away.

Through unnatural means, the light from the four torches reflected off the ruby like a beacon and struck a sapphire that had been embedded into the side of the casket. The blood-red platform beneath the tomb slid forward by ten feet, revealing a staircase that descended into the depths of the earth. Even with my torch, I couldn't see beyond the opening. Moments later, the platform slowly moved back to its original position. Knowing we were never going to descend the stairs, we headed back to the village. When we arrived, we found ourselves in the middle of a fierce firefight between the men left to guard the village, and a small company of German soldiers.

Hell is inhabited by many demons,
one of which is known to be a Cerberus.
I believe what I saw near the huts my
fellow archaeologists were staying in was
one of them. Frozen in terror, I was unable to move.
Fortunately, my friend managed to get me into one of
the jeeps they had brought, and together with five
surviving men, we escaped the massacre. With the
village overrun by soldiers, we weren't able to get to
my colleagues. As we drove away, I looked back at
those huts and witnessed the horror of my friends
being savagely torn apart by those beasts, their
blood soaking the dirt beneath their quivering feet.
Their screams were dreadful!

May 17, 1943

It has been a few months since I escaped the
village of Mequat Mariam. I returned to my home
in Israel to finish the deciphering of the scrolls.
Even though the ancient parchments were stolen
from us, I was still able to write down what I
had read word for word, thanks in large to my
acute, photographic memory.

The scrolls begin with the narrative of Samuel. Described as an angel of God, Samuel is portrayed as traversing the entirety of the known universe through what are referred to as "dimensional doorways" or phenomena's now understood as black holes. It was there inside one such doorway that he encountered an 'omnipotent being.'
In Evil's presence, Samuel perished, giving rise to the birth of Satan.

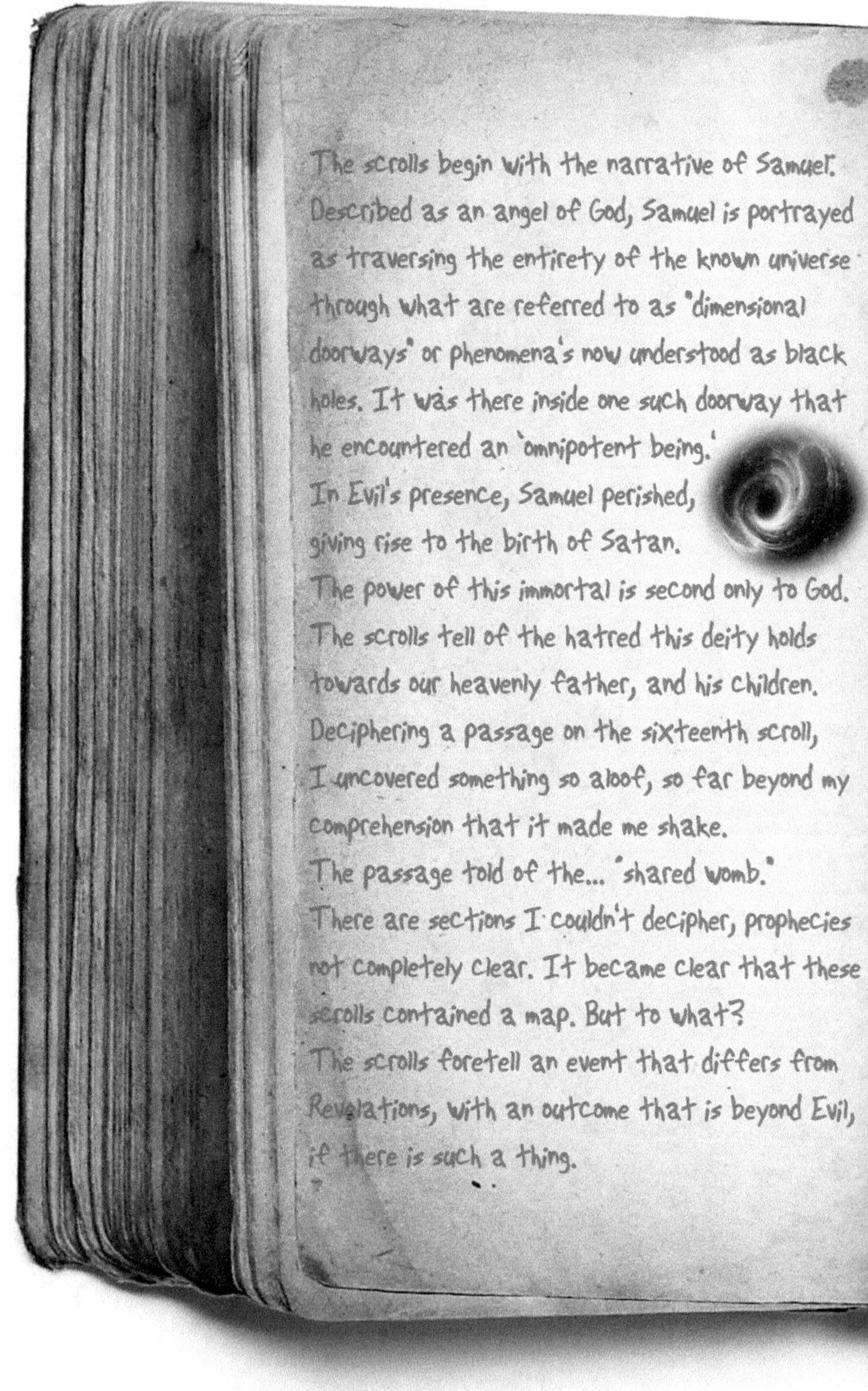

The power of this immortal is second only to God. The scrolls tell of the hatred this deity holds towards our heavenly father, and his children. Deciphering a passage on the sixteenth scroll, I uncovered something so aloof, so far beyond my comprehension that it made me shake.
The passage told of the... "shared womb."
There are sections I couldn't decipher, prophecies not completely clear. It became clear that these scrolls contained a map. But to what?
The scrolls foretell an event that differs from Revelations, with an outcome that is beyond Evil, if there is such a thing.

The ancient scrolls went on to recount Michael's tale, revealing how the angel chose to turn away from the Dark One, refusing to be reborn into evil, unlike his brother Samuel. In the eyes of this omnipotent being, Michael's treachery would not go unpunished.

A powerful archangel who had also turned to evil, was sent to kill Michael. However, on Aryan's moon, the angel of light easily defeated him. Recognizing his error of sending just one, the Dark One dispatched three more to kill Michael.

The ancient scrolls recount how Metatron came to his brothers aid, and together they slew those corrupted angels of Evil. Angered, the Dark One ordered Satan, and his entire legion of Dominions to hunt down and destroy both Michael and Metatron.

Gabriel, Rafael, Uriel, and the other archangels who had also refused the Dark One joined with Michael and Metatron in combat.

The battle was extreme...to say the least. In the end, Satan and his unholy horde suffered defeat, and was driven back into the fires of Hell. It was in the latter scrolls that I learned of the terrifying events that occur on the seventh plane of the netherworld. Blood sacrifices are not only performed here on earth, but in the realms of Hell as well, and those who dwell there are named. Heretical priests are amongst those giving homage to the Dark One.

On the last day of decoding, I discovered the existence of the 'Portal,' a mystic gateway that sends doomed souls to hell.

The parchments indicate the portal is located on the sixth plane, on an island enclosed by liquid fire. I have found it strange that some of the scroll's contents doesn't coincide with their age, as texts on the last three Antichrists look fresher, and the ink is younger, which means the scrolls are being updated, but by whom? I have provided both a brief summary and a full account of what is recorded in the scrolls. In conclusion, I believe that dark forces are on the move. God help us!

"Red Dragon"

The scrolls of Lucifer

Satan

Michael's betrayal

Hell

Blood rituals

The Antichrist's

The Abyss

"Lipton, I think we really need to read the section on the Antichrist's," Scott says, following a brief pause.

Looking at the back window, then over at the shadowy staircase, Lipton utters, **"something's wrong!"**

"Is someone coming?"

"No, that's what worries me."

"I'm not sure I follow you."

With his eerie reflective eyes still glued to the staircase, Lipton responds, **"the Blackfists should have attacked us by now. We should be dead already!"**

"What do you think they're waiting for?" Scott asks, glancing in the same direction as the dwarfish youth.

Spinning his head toward Scott, Lipton replies, **"I don't know. Find out what you need, and quickly!"**

"I'll read the shorter version." Scott begins reading the section on the Antichrist's.

The Antichrist's

According to the scrolls, there will be six Antichrists, the final being the 'Dark One' himself. He will command a legion so powerful that it will bring an end to all of GOD'S children—Everywhere!

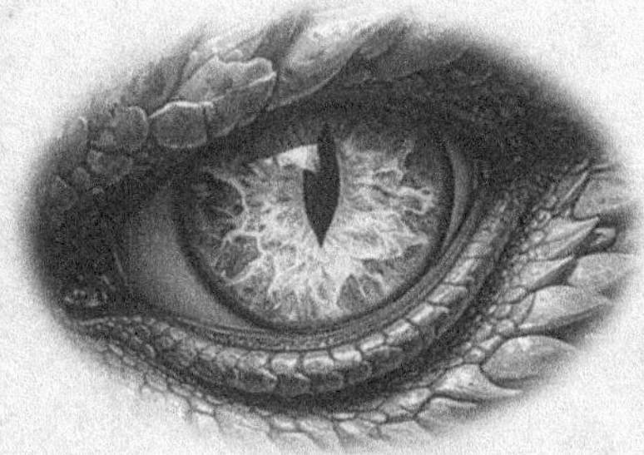

The scrolls reveal the first Antichrist was born in 666 BCE in Thrace, near the city of Byzantium. The unholy child was conceived in a cave overlooking the Black Sea, when the eclipsed moon was the color of blood. It was written that the child's Mother made a pact with Satan upon the shores of the wicked, during the days of Adam. The parchments gave a name...

"Lilith"

Adam's first companion was not Eve, but rather
a spirited young woman named Lilith, and it was
she who was initially fated by our father above
to be the mother of man. Casted out of the garden,
she came to live by the shores of the great ocean.
It was there she met her beloved, he who gave
her eternal life. A lover of Evil, Lilith became an
enemy to man, a crucial piece in the overall plot
to destroy the children of God!
The ancient scrolls recount the tale of a mighty
Archangel joining forces with Satan in his battle
against Michael. It reveals how this fallen angel
became a powerful warrior in the black legion.
It was on the twentieth scroll that we learned
the name of this angel, and it was this angel
who held the unholy seed for the first Antichrist.

"Abaddon"

Lucifer 5; 2

Abaddon and the succubus Lilith conceived the first
Antichrist in a sacred cave that has been shallowed
up by time. They performed the heretical act upon
an ancient altar surrounded by black robed beings,
those who dwell inside the darkest dimensions of Hell.
The unholy ritual involved the sacrificing of children
who were beheaded, and drained of their life's blood.
The blood was poured into clay jars that were used
to nourish the demon child. Afterward, the headless
bodies were tossed into the fires.

The scrolls reveal the mother stayed with the child
until it reached the age of six. Shortly thereafter,
she vanished in the mountains. What happened to
Lilith remains a mystery, but it's foretold that
one day she will return to our world to complete
prophecy. We learned Abaddon returned to the realms
of Hell long before the child was born. The location
of the cave was uncovered on the eleventh scroll.

Lucifer 5; 5

"Baal"

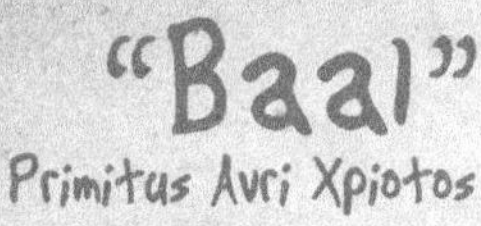

The newborn was taken to a village in the east, where he was raised by a woman as if he were her own. At the age of twelve, the boy murdered the woman and traveled north into the cold Bashkir Mountains, where he learned powerful enchantments such as foresight, hypnotism and self-healing from his true father.

In 650 BCE, at the age of fifteen, he fought alongside the Kimmerians, a ruthless tribe from the frozen lands north of the Caucasus line. Less than a year later, he vanquished their mighty chieftain in single combat.

Lucifer 5; 9

Baal was invincible on the battlefield, his combat skills unmatched. Once he became chieftain, he led the Kimmerians into battle against the other clans in the territory. He burned villages and slaughtered thousands, including women and children.

Around 640 BCE, a secretive sisterhood known as the 'holy order of Michael' brought a male child before King Dascylus, the monarch of Lydia. Upon learning this child was fathered by the angel Michael himself, the king raised the boy under the fictious name of Gyges. In time, the boy grew to manhood and became a formidable warrior.

In 615 BCE, Baal attacked the city of Sardis with an army consisting of Kimmerians, and warriors from vanquished clans. Gyges and his soldiers fought valiantly against the antichrist and his warriors. In the end, it was Baal who was the victor. He nailed Michael's son to a cross, along with thousands of his people. Following the carnage, Baal placed his army under the command of a cryptic warrior, and went north into the mountains where he wasn't seen for half a century.

Lucifer 5; 15

In 585 BCE, a Nephilim named Sêmyâza tricked Nebuchadnezzar, the king of Babylon, into waging war against the kingdom of Jerusalem. Fathered by a fallen angel, Sêmyâza discovered that Solomon's temple contained an artifact of great historical significance; a relic that could benefit the Dark One in future events.

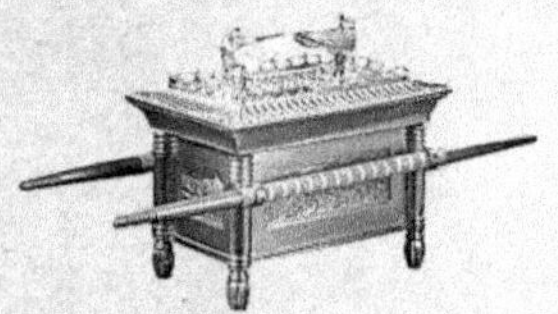

"The Ark of the Covenant"

Emerging from the icy lands of the north, Baal took command of the surviving Kimmerians, along with the entire army of the Babylonians and attacked the kingdom of Jerusalem. Days later, the temple fell, however, the Ark wasn't found. Before the attack, priestly robed figures were seen leaving the temple in the middle of the night with horse drawn carts. The scrolls suggest the sacred chest may have been taken into the wastelands where its whereabouts are still unknown today.

Lucifer 5; 25

After setting fire to the temple, Baal returned to the northern lands and vanished once more, this time for nearly three hundred years. In the meantime, the Kimmerians returned to their ancestral lands to renew their wars against their bitter enemies.

In 218 BCE, amid the Hellenistic era and the Second Punic War, Baal resurfaced, seemingly unchanged by the passage of time. Sêmyâza and his group of Nephilim's known as the "Watchers," became aware that a new champion opposing the Antichrist was expected to be born at the stronghold of David, believed to be somewhere inside Rome. History has no record of this place. The scrolls revealed the Romans were providing protection to the women of the Order of Michael, and that an instrument of death capable of killing the Antichrist was acquired by them. After gathering the Kimmerians, Baal went to Rome to slay the child as well as the women, and to find this weapon.

It was at the battle of Cannae that the stronghold of David was found, and ultimately destroyed. During the assault, the Antichrist was killed with a dagger of otherworldly origin, by a Nephilim who belonged to the group known as the "Ancients."

The scrolls indicate that prior to attacking Cannae, Baal and his Kimmerians carried out a raid on a small village, to which Baal had raped a young girl. Nine months later, she gave birth to a boy, dying during the delivery.

A small band of nomads took the newborn into the mountains, bringing them to the very cave where the first Antichrist was conceived.

Following his earthly death, Baal was burned atop a large pyre. Sometime during the night, his unscathed body was stolen and taken to a mountainous tomb inside Africa. During Baal's reign of terror, over one hundred thousand people were crucified, one third of them being women and children.

Lucifer 5; 42

Azazel

Secundus Avri Xpiotos

In 149BCE, the third and bloodiest of the Punic Wars
between Rome and Carthage began, and once again
an Antichrist was commanding the armies against the
Romans. Contrary to what was previously thought,
the second son of Michael didn't die at the stronghold
of David during the Second Punic War. Prior to the
attack on Cannae, the mother of the unborn child
was taken west to one of the Romans bastions.
Under the tutelage of a legendary gladiator, the boy
grew into a powerful warrior and leader, a real
threat to the survival of the Antichrist's.

Lucifer 5; 48

The son of Michael led the Romans to the gates of mighty Carthage, with both sides suffering heavy losses. On the steps of the palace, Azazel engaged Michael's son in a remarkable swordfight and killed him, severing his head with one swift stroke of his blade.

In 240 AD, Azazel discovered that the dagger used to kill Baal was in the possession of another Nephilim belonging to the Ancients. Rounding up the Kimmerians, and as many coldblooded warriors as he could, Azazel hunted this half-human, half-angel for two hundred years. Evading capture, this devoted Nephilim waited for the day he would use the dagger to kill the Antichrist, and end the chain of terror. Azrael commanded the most coldblooded band of cutthroats the world had ever known.

'The HUNS' 

In 442 AD, Azazel employed trickery to lure the Nephilim out of hiding. Having trapped the half-angel, half-human in a remote region of the world, he butchered him, tossing his body into a fiery pit; the Nephilim didn't have the dagger with him.

Lucifer 5; 52

After killing the Nephilim, Azazel vanished inside the frozen lands of Macedonia for nearly five centuries, slumbering in a crypt similar to Baal's. Aided by the Ancients, the Order of Michael scoured the earth for his tomb. Their efforts were unsuccessful with many going missing in the quest.

In 1060 AD, Azazel reappeared during the feudal period known as the Dark ages. Following the capture of a stronghold in Ostreich, this Antichrist unleashed a reign of terror upon the countryside, releasing the demons of hell to feed!

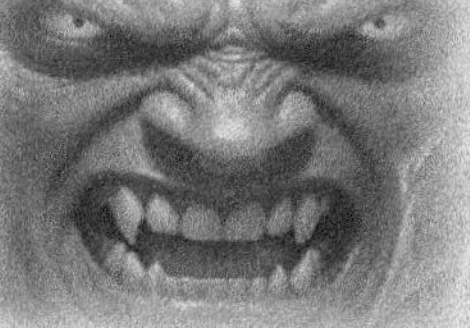

To quench his insatiable thirst for blood, Azazel roamed the shadows during the twilight hours.

Men, women, and even small children fell victim to his bloodlust. Beheaded and dismembered, these poor souls were fed to the beasts that stalked both the living, as well as the dead. Turkish mythology knows this 'creature of the night' by an entirely different name.

In 1096 AD, under the threat of infinite pain and suffering, Azazel forced the hands of kings and bishops into launching a crusade against the Seljuq Turks. Commanding a legion of ten thousand strong, Azazel seized the city of Jerusalem. Many of the captured Turks were impaled on iron poles, their blood staining the earth beneath their sandaled feet. The reason for the crusade was to find an artifact from the days of a prophet, who went into the mountains.

"The Staff of Moses"

The scrolls foretell the power of the staff could unearth another artifact, one mightier than the staff itself. However, they didn't say what or where this other artifact was, only that it could turn future events in favor of the Dark One. The staff was never found. For centuries, tales have spread about an unidentified traveler who took the staff into the desert and disappeared into the sand dunes.

Lucifer 5; 66

In 1136 AD, the Order of Michael began uniting the kingdoms against Azazel. Regrettably, the plot was foiled by the tongue of a traitorous Queen who had informed the Antichrist. The demons of Hell were set lose upon those who had joined the alliance against Azazel. An extremely powerful elixir was created by the high priestess of the Order, and given to the foot soldiers, archers, and knights who battled the beasts of the netherworld. During this time, countless castles and strongholds were torched. The mangled carcasses of the dead warriors were trampled into the dirt as if they were but mice amongst wolves.

In 1146 AD, Azazel received word that the dagger was located within Saint Catherine's Monastery at the base of Mount Sinai. To set the trap, the traitorous Queen was tricked into betraying the dagger's location. In the hands of an Ancient, the son of the angel Raphael, the dagger was in play to be used against the son of the Devil.

Lucifer 5; 68

Entering the monastery, Azazel was ambushed, and put down under a barrage of warriors. But, it wasn't the dagger that slew him. As the antichrist laid mortally wounded on the stone floor before an altar of God, the high priestess of the Order sent him to Hell by performing a celestial sacrament that had been passed down from her predecessor. The scrolls indicate that Azazel's death did not mark the end of the unholy bloodline, and that it was the deceitful Queen who had long since given birth to another male child. The boy was brought to the kingdom of Croatia where he was placed under the protection of King Demetrius Zvonimir.

Lucifer 5; 84

Mephisto

Tertius Avri Xpiotos

Masquerading as a monk under the imperial banner of Roman Catholicism, this Antichrist was free to travel the world undetected. Taught the deadly craft of Pestilence by his father, Mephisto released one of the greatest terrors the world had ever witnessed... "The Black Plague."

In 1347 AD, this devasting plague claimed millions of lives, spread through the bites of infected fleas, and the saliva of diseased rats. The purpose of this plague was to kill Michael's third son, while he was still in his mother's womb, but it did not succeed.

Lucifer 5; 87

During the 1400s, in the dark towers of Cardiff Castle located in South Wales, England, Mephisto devised another scheme to murder Michael's son. Ferdinand II of Aragon and Queen Isabella I of Castile aided Mephisto in pressuring the cardinals into forming a Holy Tribunal, which became known in history as the "Spanish Inquisition."

As Grand Inquisitor, Mephisto widened the scope of carnage by deceiving these so-called 'Men of God' into killing the innocent, rewarding the naive priests with gold. In the end, their deaths were far worse than the victims of the Inquisition. At night, brown robed figures entered the dungeons to feed on the tormented, their blood staining the walls as well as the cold, stone floors.

The scrolls disclosed an additional objective of the Inquisition, and that was Mephisto was actively pursuing information regarding the location of the five sacred scrolls of Aaron, identified in scripture as... "the Keys of Aaron."

Lucifer 5; 93

The legend goes as followed...

Five brothers who had followed Moses during the exodus from Egypt to the mountains, were called to a secret meeting with Aaron; Moses' brother, and first priest of the house of Levi. Around the same time his brother was given the Commandments, Aaron was being entrusted to safeguard an 'otherworldly' book from a wounded angel. The angel divided the book into five scrolls... or "Keys." Aaron tasked the brothers with hiding the scrolls until the 'Day of Judgement'. He gave each brother a scroll, instructing them to take it to a distant part of the world, unbeknown to the others.

With broken hearts, theses five brothers surrendered their future as brothers for the sake of keeping the scrolls from uniting. If united, a catastrophic secret would be revealed. The Torah, also known as the five books of Moses, was written centuries after the prophet died. Be it myth or truth, a codex was discovered within the pages of the books. Using the codex on the sacred scrolls would reveal the time and birthplace of the Second Coming.

Lucifer 5; 102

The Inquisition gave Mephisto the means to track
down two descendants of the five brothers.
Tortured to near death, the first descendant
revealed that the scroll his great-grandfather
guarded is hidden inside a cave in Siberia, Russia.
Using the terrifying mind-controlling
abilities he learned from his father,
Mephisto drove the second descendant
to madness. With a mere gaze from his black eyes,
he placed the man inside a never-ending nightmare.
Though drooling lips, he babbled the key-scroll's
whereabouts, revealing it's hidden in the jungles of
southern Africa, amid the remnants of a forgotten
civilization. During his flight into Africa to retrieve
the key-scroll, Mephisto met his death at the hands
of a young, Zimbabwe prince. The dagger that
killed Ba'al was used to slay the Antichrist.
As Mephisto laid dead in the sands, the prince and
his tribesmen were attacked, and torn asunder by
beasts not of this world. Ripped from the prince's
lifeless hand, the mysterious dagger was brought
into the bowels of Hell.

Lucifer 5; 127

We learned that Mephisto continued the chain of the
bloodline. On the night before his untimely death, a
young, brown-skinned woman came to him, and an
unholy mating ritual was performed.
Nine months later, the fourth Antichrist was born
into our earthly domain. With his faithful warriors,
the newly crowned brother of the prince hunted down
the woman, and slaughtered her. However, by that
time she had long since given birth. The child was
taken to Azazel's stronghold inside Ostreich, where
he was raised by a Druid until he reached manhood.
While examining one of the scrolls, we came across
a set of letters and symbols. Among these markings
is one that directly relates to the crucifixion of
Christ, though its specific meaning is still unknown.

Hitler

Quartus Avri Xpiotos

History defines him not only as a monster, but a true enemy to all of mankind. When Hitler emerged into public view, some noted traits associated with that of an Antichrist, although this connection was never conclusively proven. The reason was that there were actually... 'two of him.'

In 1941 AD, the most disturbing event in modern-day history began: the Holocaust. Unbeknown to the world, the main objective of this great Evil was not about murdering Jews, but something far more sinister, more twisted.

Lucifer 5, 166

Before Germany's invasion of Poland that sparked the outbreak of World War II, a disturbing number of Jewish males had already been removed from their homes. Placed into trains bearing the grim color of black, they were brought north to a location once thought to exist only as a frightening tale—a place where evil dwells!

The laboratories of Knochenmühle
"The bone grinder"

Troubling stories I had heard in my younger years were confirmed by the ancient scrolls. One such story was about Hitler's immoral surgeons experimenting in human modifications. Advancements in DNA splicing, and stem cell manipulation allowed these scientists to develop methods transforming humans into animals.

Imbued with power from the Dark One, these beasts drew their first breath in 1943.

These half-human, half-canine monstrosities possess remarkable strength, and amazing endurance.

According to mythology, these creatures are called, "Cerberus" and are described as having a desire for human flesh! Ominously, Adolf means..."the wolf."

Lucifer 5, 178

The scrolls revealed that Hitler's bodyguards,
deemed to be nothing more than a quirky band of
mystics called...the Thule Society, were in fact
Nephilim's charged with guarding his true identity.
It was written that the devil's fourth son played
a crucial role in advancing the chain towards its
unholy finale. In order for the fifth, and the most
powerful of all the Antichrist's to be born into our
earthly realm, a `cosmic rift` must occur.
The ancient scrolls revealed that this rift would
produce a Celestial child, a kind of buffer so to
speak, between the fourth and fifth Antichrist.
In the cave where Lilith and Abaddon conceived
the first Antichrist, Hitler and a Croatian witch
performed a similar mating ritual. At the moment
the seed was passed, a great comet ripped through
the heavens, its cosmic tail burning oh so brightly
inside the nocturnal skies.

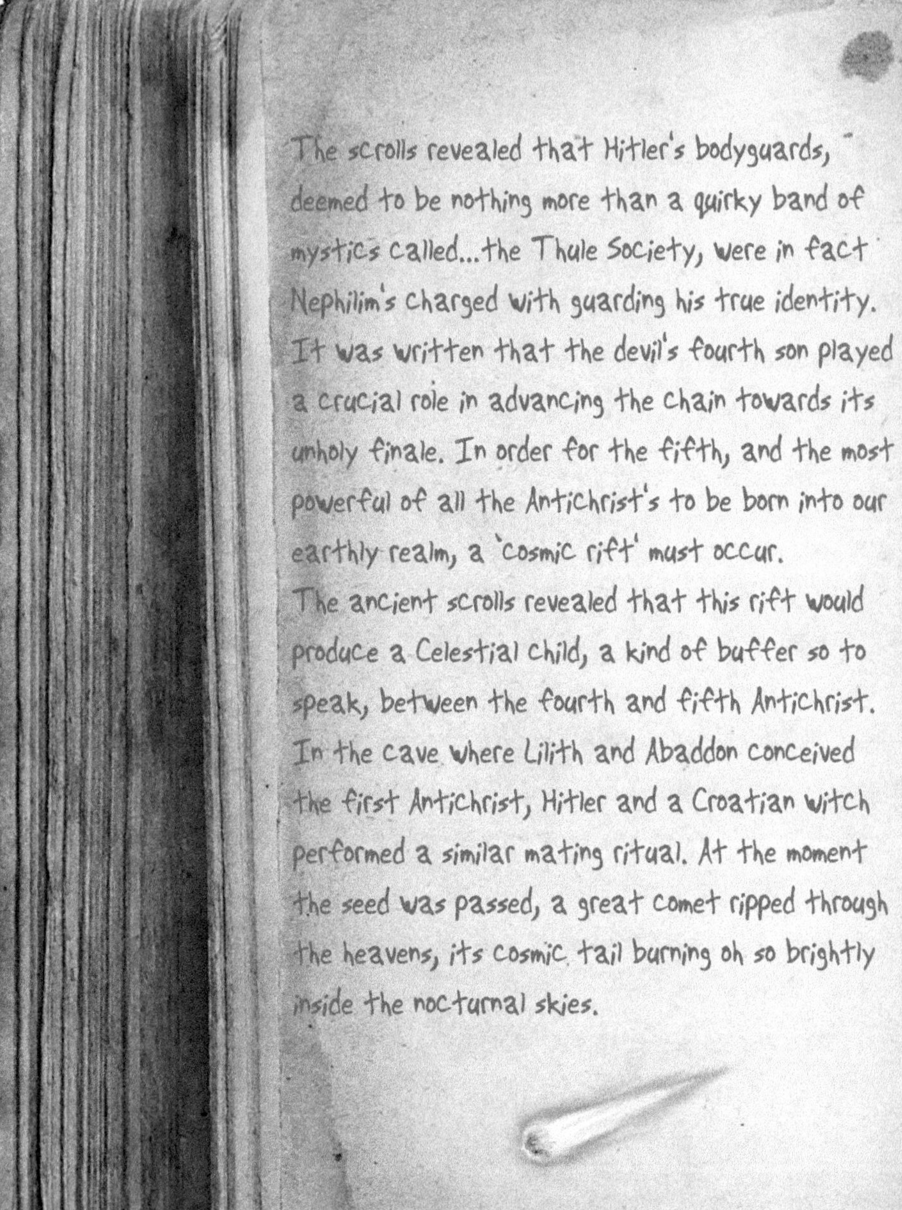

Lucifer 5; 179

Beyond monstrous! Beyond grotesque!
Dying in the delivery, the witches intestines were fed
to the newborn. As the child grew, it was nourished on
the embroys of rats. It also feasted on gastropods,
such as snails and slugs. It's been told that the mere
sight of this extraterrestrial abomination would drive
a grown man to madness. This celestial terror would
plant the seed for the birth of the fifth Antichrist.

Born in the year of the Dragon, this Antichrist will be
indestructible. Evil will flow from him like a river of
blood! The whereabouts of Hitler are not mentioned in
the scrolls, nor the fate of the hideous creature.
The Order of Michael failed to prevent the progression
of the chain, resulting in many deaths and vanishings,
including three of Michael's sons.
The identity of the fifth Antichrist is revealed in
the latter scrolls. He is truly the beast, the unholy
executioner of man!

Little horn – Rapture

Quintus Avri Xpiotos

Little was written about this Antichrist.
According to the scrolls, following a devastating
war that descends upon humanity, he will rise from
the dark waters to fulfill prophecy, which involves
a woman and a man from another time, as well as
the sacrificing of lost children.
Born with hair of red, this juggernaut of Evil will
be the purveyor of the Master himself...for upon
his seed the Dark One will enter our world, and
bring death to all of God's children, everywhere!

Lucifer 5, 204

The sound of breaking glass reverberates throughout the library, immediately followed by the sound of that steel entrance door slamming down on the floor. Just then, an evil laughter touches both Lipton and Scott's ears, convincing them to hasten over to the staircase. Looking down from the fourth floor landing, they observe a throng of young males storming into the library----via the front door, which now lies atop the cracked, marble-tile floor. The males are wearing ragged red shirts underneath crudely made leather breastplates: there's a strange symbol on their breastplates that is hard to make out.

"We're in trouble," Lipton hisses.

"Are these the Blackfists?" Scott gulps.

"No!"

"Then who are they?"

"They're *his* executioners!"

The smashing of a nearby window steals their attention from the mayhem on the main floor. Spinning around, they stare hard at the back window where the crash occurred, between eighty to ninety feet away, partially concealed in shadow. A glance over their shoulders confirms a second wave of executioners storming through that same doorless entrance. With no time to waste, Lipton hastens toward the back window with Scott close behind. Less than ten feet from the window, Lipton freezes like ice, staring intensely at a shadow to the right of it: broken glass litters the area.

328

Moments later, eyes glint from within the shadow, and before Scott's heart can falter, a lone assailant appears, clutching a dreadful looking blade in his murderous right hand. Standing just outside the shadows brim, the youth flashes a homicidal grin—his disturbing black eyes locking steadfastly onto his prey. Swift as a cobra, the young male flings his blade toward Scott's head. Predicting the move, Lipton steps forward and skillfully deflects the blade with his sword, altering its directory. With a snarl, the young man stretches his right arm over his shoulder, and grabs a pair of steel nunchakus, which seem to have been fastened to his backside with tape.

With homicidal intentions, the youth shoots forward and swings his nunchakus at Scott's head. Acting on impulse, Scott parries the attack with his bat. Gliding forward on the balls of his feet, Lipton slashes outward with his sword, cutting deep into the midsection of the youth; this prompts Scott to step forward, and whack the young male soundly on the left side of his head—sending him to the floor with blooding gushing from his chest and head. At the sound of scaling footsteps on the staircase, Lipton swipes at the remaining shards lining the insides of the windowpane with his sword. Examining the exterior fire escape through the glassless window, they both take notice how its structure is significantly compromised due to extensive rust; unfazed, they step out onto it regardless.

Thanks either to divine intervention or an extraordinary stroke of luck, they managed to make it safely down to the ground. Sprinting toward the front of the library—to the sidewalk where the English Racer was left, they stop within twenty feet of the spot, eyes brimming with anxiety.

"F--K!" Scott curses: the bike isn't there.

Upon hearing the sound of feet clattering down those iron stairs, Scott swivels towards the fire escape, spotting the spectral outlines of Rapture's executioners, all of them carrying weapons. Looking over at Lipton, who stands no farther than ten feet to his right, Scott notes how he stares at a patch of darkness draping a severely damaged, three story building on the other side of the street. Following the dwarfish youths eyes, a reflecting sheen of what can only be the handlebar of his Racer escapes the shadows; the bike is leaning against the side of the building.

From within that gloomy shroud, wearing a long, black trench coat, a young male walks out, his beastly, reflective eyes continuing to slice the same darkness. From the corner of his eye, Scott sees more executioners storming out of the entrance door of the library, running in their direction, howling like a pack of rabid wolves. While maintaining direct eye contact with Scott, the mysterious young man slowly retreats into the obscurity of those shadows, until he is no longer visible.

"Let's go!" Lipton barks.

Hightailing it over to the bicycle, Scott secures it and quickly hops aboard. And, once Lipton settles himself on the handlebars, Scott steers the Racer toward the town's exit as the intensifying howling steadily draws closer with each passing moment. Peddling as fast as his legs permit, Scott's attention is averted to the countless reflective eyes piercing the shadows on the rooftops, and windows **of the surviving downtown buildings;** they are being scrutinized by those Lipton refers to as...the Blackfists.

Misfortune happens!

Reaching the three-mile marker from the city, Scott hits a small crater in the road, sending them both airborne.

"You alright?" Lipton asks, slowly getting to his feet.

Standing up on wobbly legs, Scott responds, **"Sorry, I didn't see that hole."**

"That's all right," Lipton says, readjusting the sheath strapped to his back. **"I didn't see it either."**

Staggering back to the Racer, a faint, hideous laughter touches Scott's ears. As he turns towards the remains of downtown Buffalo, a mild breeze sweeps across his face. As he gazes at the blood-red moon looming above the city, two ominous eyes emerge; carried by the wind, a voice he fears reaches his ears.

"*I SEE YOU*"

From the Author...

It's been a pleasure spending this time with you, and I hope you enjoyed, Scrolls 1- 8.

Now remember, this is merely the first of eight in the... "Red Dragon Series". This epic journey continues with --

Tome one: The Antichrist's -- scrolls 1-8

***Tome two: The Antichrist's -- scrolls 9-16**

Tome three: Lilith -- scrolls 17-24

Tome four: Lilith -- scrolls 25-32

Tome five: Keys of Aaron -- scrolls 33-40

Tome six: Keys of Aaron -- scrolls 41-48

Tome seven: Battle in Megiddo -- scrolls 49-56

Tome eight: Battle in Megiddo -- scrolls 57-64

For the latest updates and information related to this series and other publications, please visit us at... **charleswstaunton.com**.

Thank you, and we'll see you soon.

Charles W. Staunton

I dedicate this tome to the...

"Gang of Sheffield"

Year: 1980

Place: Buffalo, NY.

As well as to the following:

Mr. Kelly Barker {Bestest Bud}

Mrs. Stephanie Barker {Close Chum}

Ms. Carol Hoffman {Dearest Friend}

Mr. Emmanuel Balligui {Comrade in-arms}

This is the account of the first born of Adam. It tells of a mythical being who travels through time, recording history, and events of man! Professor Robin, "1955"

"The Shofar of YHWH"
"Yahweh"
The ineffable name of God.

I am Yahweh your God, who brought you out of the land of Egypt, out of the house of bondage. You shall have no other gods before me. You shall not make for yourselves an idol, nor any image of anything that is in the heavens above, or that is in the earth beneath, or that is in the water under the earth: you shall not bow yourself down to them, nor serve them, for I, Yahweh your God, am a jealous God, visiting the iniquity of the fathers on the children on the third and fourth generation of those who hate me, showing loving kindness to those who love me and keep my blessed commandments – *Exodus 20:1-6*

Thus says Yahweh, he who created the heavens
and stretched them out, he who spread out the earth
and that which comes out of it, he who gives breath
to its people and spirit to those who walk in it.
"I, Yahweh, have called you in righteousness,
and will hold your hand, and will keep you, and
make you a covenant for the people, as a light for
all the nations; to open the blind eyes, and to bring
those prisoners out of the dungeon, and those who
sit in darkness out of the prison.
I am Yahweh. That is my name.
I will not give my glory to another, nor my
praise to any engraved images." – *Isaiah 42:5-8*

The Creation of Man,
by Italian artist Michelangelo.
Painted around 1508-1512
on the Sistine Chapel ceiling,

According to the scrolls of Genesis, the creation of life on earth began with God. According to written accounts, Adam, regarded as the first human ever created by God, represented the sacred covenant between God and man. Following the creation of Adam, a woman was created and given to him to keep as his wife. There is a disagreement among scholars regarding Adam's first wife; many believe that a spirited and beautiful young woman named Lilith was his first wife, with Eve coming after her. – **Book of Isaiah.**

The scrolls indicate that, at a subsequent time, Adam consumed the forbidden fruit from the tree of knowledge. As a result, he and Eve were expelled from the Garden of Eden. It is written that Lilith had already been forced out of the garden after refusing to submit to Adam, and that it was she who tricked Eve into eating the fruit before Adam.

Lilith Tempting Adam and Eve
"The Fall of Man and the
Expulsion from Paradise"
Michelangelo - Sistine Chapel,
Vatican

According to scripture, Lilith was with child, and that it was this child who would be the first born from woman. Adam refused to conceive the child as his, knowing Lilith had fornicated with the angel Samuel on the shores of the great waters. Having her own toils with Adam, Eve went to the shores to see what another woman looked like, and upon discovering they were similar, and not the demon Adam had made her out to be, she befriended Lilith.

It was written that the Seraphim angel, Metatron, sent the angel Ariel into Eden. As the angel walked the garden, Eve came to him, and informed him of the upcoming birth. Ariel approached Lilith and tried to convince her that the child would be safer with him, but Lilith refused to give up her unborn child. Upon learning about the upcoming birth, Metatron suggested that the child serve as a "instrument" for the purpose of "witnessing" to our heavenly father.

In short, the child would act as a scribe, and record the lives of man. During the night on the eve of the child's birth, Metatron entered the garden and found Lilith asleep on her bed of straw inside her hut; this powerful angel induced the delivery of the child, while keeping Lilith in a deep sleep.

With divine approval, Metatron brought the newborn to heaven, where the child was granted immortality as well as additional unique abilities. After the birth of Noah, when the child had grown to adulthood, it was sent to earth to begin recording. Metatron alone knows the child's gender. This was done to hide its identity from those who would seek to destroy them.

Ascension to heaven

Man wasn't aware of the existence of this holy scribe; but, all that changed when ancient scrolls were unearthed in the late twentieth century, near the caves where the 'Dead Sea Scrolls' were found. At first, these scrolls appeared to be nothing more than a sham.... for they didn't match the others. Upon closer inspection, they were confirmed as authentic and identified as the "Shofar of Yahweh."

Even though they were in a state of deterioration, the scrolls gave valuable insight into the life and purpose of the Shofar. It was written that besides immortality, the Shofar has the ability of unlimited travel; rainbows have been linked to the holy observer.

The original scrolls were written in an ancient Hebrew text, but have since been translated by Professor Robin in Jerusalem, Israel, 1965.

The story of the shofar of Yahweh is an addition to our incredible story. It tells the journey of this legendary figure who has left footprints throughout history. The recordings of events are through the eyes of the Shofar at the time it happens... in our story!

Below is a sample of a chronicle marker, which you should have seen on the pages.

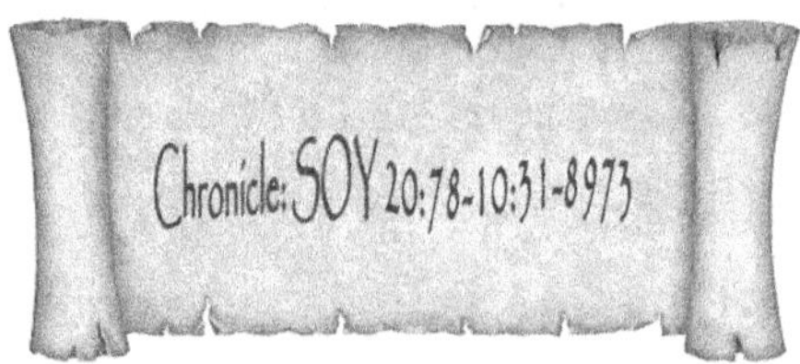

Chronicle SOY 20:78-10:31-8973
Century / year / month / Day /witness order for that month
20   78   10   31   8973

Chronicles can be freely read, and heard {audio} on our website at -- **charleswstaunton.com**

www.ingramcontent.com/pod-product-compliance
Lightning Source LLC
Chambersburg PA
CBHW070051120726
47909CB00002B/355